BACKWATER
JUSTICE

Books by Fern Michaels

Books by Fern Michaels (*cont.*)

Safe and Sound
Need to Know
Crash and Burn
Point Blank
In Plain Sight
Eyes Only
Kiss and Tell
Blindsided
Gotcha!
Home Free
Déjà Vu
Cross Roads
Game Over
Deadly Deals
Vanishing Act
Razor Sharp
Under the Radar
Final Justice
Collateral Damage
Fast Track
Hokus Pokus
Hide and Seek
Free Fall
Lethal Justice
Sweet Revenge
The Jury
Vendetta
Payback
Weekend Warriors

The Men of the Sisterhood Novels:

Hot Shot
Truth or Dare
High Stakes
Fast and Loose
Double Down

The Godmothers Series:

Far and Away
Classified
Breaking News
Deadline
Late Edition
Exclusive
The Scoop

E-Book Exclusives:

Desperate Measures
Seasons of Her Life
To Have and To Hold
Serendipity
Captive Innocence
Captive Embraces
Captive Passions
Captive Secrets
Captive Splendors
Cinders to Satin
For All Their Lives
Texas Heat
Texas Rich

Books by Fern Michaels (*cont.*)

FERN MICHAELS

BACKWATER JUSTICE

ZEBRA BOOKS
Kensington Publishing Corp.
www.kensingtonbooks.com

First Hardcover Printing: September 2024

First Paperback Printing: January 2025
ISBN: 978-1-4201-5716-1

ISBN: 978-1-4201-5718-5 (ebook)

10 9 8 7 6 5 4 3 2 1

Printed in the United States of America

MEET THE CHARACTERS OF THE SISTERHOOD

Myra Rutledge

- Heiress to a Fortune 500 candy company, who became the founder of the Sisterhood after her daughter was killed by a hit-and-run driver with diplomatic immunity. She is married to Charles Martin, a former British MI6 agent. They live on a farm in Virginia called Pinewood.

Anna Ryland De Silva

- Annie is a countess and Myra's childhood friend. She is very wealthy and owns the *Post* newspaper and a Gulfstream private jet. She lives with life partner, Fergus Duffy, former head of Scotland Yard. She is known for her white rhinestone-covered cowgirl boots and will occasionally don her tiara. She can pick almost any lock and knows a few tricks.

Charles Martin

- A former British MI6 agent who came to the US to work for Myra's candy company as head of security after his cover was blown as an agent. He is married to Myra now, but did not know that Myra's daughter, Barbara, was his biological daughter from an affair they had when they were young.

Fergus Duffy

- Charles's best mate and former head of Scotland Yard. He and Charles surreptitiously use their former colleagues for information and covert operations.

Maggie Spritzer

- Crackerjack reporter who works for Annie's newspaper, the *Post*. She is petite and has a voracious appetite.

Pinewood

- The mid-nineteenth-century farm owned by Myra Rutledge where she and Charles live. It served as a waystation for the Underground Railroad, and the tunnels are still intact today. Below the farmhouse, among the tunnels, is the center of operations for the Sisterhood. This state-of-the-art technology complex is known as the "War Room."

Isabelle Flanders

- Architect who was framed for a drunk driving accident with fatalities by a colleague who also stole her fiancé. She now has her own architectural firm. Her husband, Abner, is a computer whiz, who has taught her to be a keen hacker.

Kathryn Lucas

- Cross country driver of an 18-wheeler and former engineer. She was raped by three white-collar professionals who were part of a motorcycle group, while her debilitated husband was forced to watch. She is blunt, brash, and outspoken, and was the first member of the sisterhood to be avenged.

Yoko Akia

- Owns a flower shop and plant nursery and is a martial arts expert. Her mother was brought to the US at age fifteen by a famous movie star under false pretenses, but was forced into a life of corruption and prostitution. She died two years later.

Avery Snowden

- Private investigator who utilizes the most advanced high-tech equipment. Sasha and Eileen are his go-to people for the Sisterhood.

Alexis Thorne

- Ex-securities broker who was framed by colleagues for fraud and now works for Nikki's law firm. Nikki helped her get a new identity after her release from jail. Her Red Bag of Tricks makes her a master of disguises.

Nicole "Nikki" Quinn

- Lawyer and Myra Rutledge's adopted daughter. She was Myra's daughter, Barbara's, best friend. She is married to Jack Emery, a former prosecutor.

Pearl Barnes

- A retired Supreme Court Justice who runs an underground network to assist in resolving abusive situations. She can make people disappear. Don't ask. Don't tell.

PROLOGUE

The small Oregon town of Mountain Valley seemed like the perfect place to safely raise a family, away from the dangers of the big city. Vanessa's parents thought so, until the day their fourteen-year-old daughter didn't come home for dinner. They called her cell. Straight to voice mail. They called her friends. Nothing. No one had seen her since they'd left school. Posters and flyers were placed within a fifty-mile radius, and her photo appeared on local television every night. An attendant at the local gas station phoned the sheriff's office, claiming he'd seen a girl fitting Vanessa's description. He described her getting into a pickup truck with the S.E.I. logo, the one that represented Spangler Enterprises Inc. Everyone knew the Spanglers—the richest, most influential family for miles around.

Patriarch Milton Spangler offered a $50,000 reward, determined to quash any notion that his family might be involved. But more importantly, Milton

Spangler didn't like the idea that a young girl could go missing in such an idyllic community, one that he'd helped to build. But as search parties failed to yield any clues, and days went by without a phone call or ransom note, the rumors grew. And then another woman disappeared. Were these simply runaways? Or did the Spangler family have something to hide?

Spangler Enterprises was the biggest employer in Oregon, valued at over 600 million dollars. Not bad for a man who began working part-time in the back office when he was in high school. But it was a fatal accident that gave him the office desk that started his financial climb.

The Spangler Family was powerful but rarely flexed their influential muscle until one of the family members got into trouble with the law. Rather than invoke the ire of the patriarch of the family, local law enforcement made a pact. Anything that implicated someone in the family would be ignored, and they would turn a blind eye. In a small town like Mountain Valley, it was known as Backwater Justice.

CHAPTER ONE

Salem, Oregon
Sixty Years Ago

Fifteen-year-old Milton Spangler came home to a wailing mother, a hysterical sister, and a phone ringing off the hook. "Papa is dead!" the thirteen-year-old girl shrieked. Milton stood in the doorway with his mouth agape.

"What are you saying?" He ran over to his little sister and placed his arms on her shoulders. "What do you mean Papa is dead?" He looked at his mother, who was too bereft to speak.

"Papa! Dead!" She continued to sob as the phone went on ringing.

He gently released her and lifted the receiver. "Spangler residence. This is Mill."

"Oh, dear. I am so sorry to hear about your father." A woman's shaky voice sounded on the other end.

"Your father. There was an accident. At the mill." She was gasping between sentences.

Mill turned to his mother for a clue, but she was sobbing into an already soaked kitchen towel. "Aunt Jill? What is going on?" He tried to remain calm, but he knew he was going to hear nothing good.

It was right after World War II when Josephine met Harold Spangler at the Geiser Creek Sawmill outside of Salem, Oregon. Josephine worked in the back office, posting invoices into the company ledger. Harold worked in the mill, debarking the trees after the loggers brought them in. Two years later, they were married and had their first child. They named him Milton. They decided that since they'd met at a mill, it was an appropriate name for their son, who was affectionately called Mill. Two years later, they had their second child. A girl. They debated as to whether or not they should call her Milly, but then thought it might be too confusing. They decided on Helen, after one of the magnificent volcanoes in Oregon. Little did they know, Mount St. Helens would explode twenty-eight years later, killing fifty-seven people, making it the deadliest eruption in U.S. history.

Harold had an impeccable work ethic and never refused overtime or to cover for his coworkers. He made what some considered "decent money." Even with Josephine being a stay-at-home mom, they were able to pay for a modest three-bedroom ranch, albeit with only one bath, an automobile, utilities, and to put food on the table. Family vacations were trips to national parks, and the kids got new clothes each school year. Purchases were made out of necessity rather than luxury, they were never indulgent. Life was good. Calm.

But just after his fortieth birthday, a careless mistake took the life of Harold Spangler and changed the course of his family forever.

It had been a typical day at Geiser Creek. The flatbeds were delivering the newly felled timber to the debarking area. While Harold was waiting for the all-clear signal, one of the fasteners holding the logs on the flatbed snapped, causing the load to tumble off the truck, crushing Harold to death. Some said it was Harold's fault. Some blamed the crooked foreman, who was rumored to overlook the well-being of the employees. But it wouldn't be for another six years that the Occupational Health and Safety Administration (OSHA) was formed, establishing safety standards for workers.

The Spanglers had no life insurance to speak of. A mere $2,000 barely covered Harold's funeral expenses. The company took no responsibility, but offered a job to Mill as a consolation. Josephine vehemently protested, but Mill had no choice. The family needed to eat and pay the bills. The company compromised with Josephine and promised her that Mill would be out of harm's way. They gave him a desk job doing similar work to what his mother had done before she decided to stay at home and raise her family.

Josephine was also adamant that Mill was not going to drop out of school, and she got no argument from either Mill or Geiser Creek. They didn't want to look bad to the community and made concessions to the grieving family, proposing a late-afternoon and weekend schedule. It wasn't quite a full-time job, but it helped the family make ends meet.

With two teenagers, it was time for Josephine to get out of the house and find a job. She couldn't expect Mill to be responsible for all the household expenses. The mill offered Josephine her old job—another consolation prize—but Josephine wanted no part of Geiser Creek Mill, and she took a part-time job at a local dress shop as a seamstress during the day while Helen was at school. Thanks to Mill's keen eye for finances, he and Josephine paid their bills with a smidgen left over to put in a savings account. This routine went on for three years, until Mill finally graduated from high school, with a bright future ahead.

CHAPTER TWO

Milton Spangler

The Early Years

The majestic Cascade Mountains served as the backdrop of Milton's life, with Mount Hood and Mount Jefferson posing like two bookends in the distance. Milton had a great appreciation for the outdoors and the pristine waters of the lakes and rivers. When he was old enough, and his father wasn't working a sixty-hour week, they would spend hours fishing. The day his father taught him how to bait a hook, Milton got hooked on nature. He spent as much time as he could walking through the woods, admiring the trees. The trees brought much profit to the area. Milton once asked his father what would happen if they killed all the trees. His father explained that Oregon was the first state to enact a reforestation program, in which landowners had to leave at least two seed trees per acre, but as time went on, the building of new American homes required more trees to be planted. Mill became more curious about the process and about everything having to do with the lumbermill.

As often as possible, Milton would ride to Geiser Creek with his father to pick up his paycheck. Mill loved the smell of sawdust. He knew almost everyone's name at the mill and would wander around the lumberyard while his dad was in the office. Mill often wondered if this was a place he'd like to work, but he saw the physical toll it took on his dad. No. He'd rather smell the wood than handle it. Besides, he was a bit of a whiz when it came to math, an ability he'd inherited from his mother. Maybe he could eventually figure out how to do both. And it was his father's terrible accident that gave him the opportunity.

Before his father passed, Mill had had a good relationship with both of his parents. It wasn't *Father Knows Best* or *Leave It to Beaver*, but it was close. Good manners. Being polite. And most of all, being honest. His father taught him it was a lot easier to remember the truth than a lie. Lies required a lot of energy to keep track of. Harold Spangler was considered a fine man; gone too soon.

Growing up, Mill had a typical relationship with his younger sister, Helen. They'd fight over who spent too much time in the bathroom, or whose turn it was to fold the laundry or dry the dishes. But they were loyal to each other. No matter how much they argued, no one was going to pick on either of them, not without the other getting into it. Those occasions were rare. With their father gone, Helen looked to

Mill for advice and guidance, which he was happy to provide. He also looked after his mother. She never got over the shock of losing her husband. She was able to function, but there was an emptiness in her eyes now.

Milton had big shoes to fill. Despite his school-work, and his part-time job at Geiser Creek, he managed to help with the chores, cooking, and shopping. He wasn't going to let his family down. Even though Harold was no longer around, Mill wanted his father to be proud of him.

During his part-time stretch at Geiser Creek, Mill discovered more efficient ways to file and organize the company's accounts receivables. Of course, he always ran his ideas past the office manager, who was willing to give Mill a shot at it, especially if it meant the office manager could get away with doing less.

By the time he turned eighteen, he'd become the office manager's favorite employee, because the young man actually made his life so much easier. When Mill was about to graduate from high school, the manager offered Mill a full-time job. Mill, who wasn't about to veer off his path of further educating himself, carried out his first negotiation: he would continue to work, but his hours would be flexible so that he could take classes at the local community college, where he planned to study business admin-istration.

Helen was about to graduate from high school, and the savings he and his mother had squirreled away would help pay for her college tuition. A scholarship would cover the rest. Mill insisted she do the full four years and become a teacher. No ifs, ands, or buts, so she enrolled at Western Oregon University, a half hour's drive from home, thereby saving money on room and board. She majored in early childhood education and met a fellow student named Gary Bahr, whom she fell in love with.

Mill and his mother approved of Gary, which was saying a lot. Mill was very protective of his sister. He felt she'd never gotten over the trauma of losing her father. She was as vulnerable as her mother. But Gary was kind and thoughtful, working on a degree in special education. Mill knew it took a special person to work with special students. By the time Helen finished her internship, they were engaged. Milton was happy his sister had found someone who loved her dearly, and he proudly walked her down the aisle.

Most of the people Helen knew either worked at the mill or knew someone who worked at the mill. It was a constant reminder of what had been taken from her. It was time to move on, and she and Gary found jobs in the small town of Bandon on the Oregon coast. Josephine was troubled that her daughter was moving four hours away, but the trauma of Helen's father's death would never leave Helen until she could leave the anguish of her past behind. Within a year of their marriage, Helen and Gary had their first child. A girl. They named her Christina.

Promises were made that Mill and Josephine would visit often, but Mill became consumed with Geiser Creek Sawmill. He was determined that the mill would repay him for the loss of his father. Legitimately, of course. His goal was to eventually own the place and make it a safer environment for all who worked there. Turning a profit would be the icing on the cake.

Long before computers were the caretakers of cashflow, Mill created a calendar to keep track of payments due to the company. Anyone who was a day late got a notice. Not a nasty one, but a "friendly reminder." By the time he completed the two-year college course, he became the youngest assistant office manager in the history of the mill.

With the receivables coming in on time, the mill was turning a good profit, allowing it to expand and grow. Over the next few years, Mill proved to be a valuable asset to the company, and at the young age of twenty-five, he was asked if he wanted to become a partner in the business. The only issue was the 20,000 dollars required to buy his shares.

Having worked on the books for so long, Mill knew the company had the potential to be valued at a few million dollars. He believed if he had some influence over the company's practices, he could make that potential a reality. His family home was free and clear, so he took out a loan using the house as collateral. His mother was hesitant, but she also had faith in her son. He had certainly stepped up when his father died. Her biggest concern was that he was still single at twenty-five, and still living with his mother. But times were different back then. He wasn't a basement dweller playing video games. Most hadn't been invented yet. No, he lived at home to help support his mother, just as he had for the past ten years. But with Helen, Gary, and Christina so far away, Josephine decided it was time for her to retire from the dress shop and bring her nimble fingers across the state.

Mill lived modestly, in the same house where he'd grown up. He now had enough earnings and savings to look into real estate in Bandon and bought a fifty-acre parcel of land for 5,000 dollars. At the time, undeveloped acreage was cheap, and Mill saw it as an asset. Something for the future.

Mill insisted on helping his sister and brother-in-law finance a house on the property that could accommodate the young family and Josephine. In the beginning, it was a modest ranch with a separate room for Josephine, where she could set up her sewing machine. When Josephine moved, she made Mill promise he would meet a nice girl and settle down. He made good on half the promise.

During a political fund-raising event, he met the "nice girl" he'd promised his mother. Her name was Patricia Wakeman, daughter of a U.S. senator. Milton wasn't the most handsome man in town, but he wasn't the ugliest, either. He was average-looking but had a nice smile and was very personable. It didn't take long for Patricia to see the potential in Milton, and Milton didn't mind the idea of having a senator as his father-in-law. It was always good to have someone in the Senate who could expedite things that would ordinarily take years. It wasn't that Milton was an unscrupulous man, but he knew when an opportunity presented itself, it was worth pursuing.

Patricia had recently graduated from Towson University in Maryland. She was involved in a sorority and was invited to many on-campus and off-campus activities. She was, beyond a doubt, the daughter of a U.S. senator. Patricia was being groomed to be a socialite. She never planned on working, but having a college degree was important to her father and his reputation.

Patricia was pleasing-looking, but not stunning. She made up for her slightly above-average looks with her charm, good hair and makeup, and a high-end wardrobe. Well-dressed and well-spoken, Patricia could easily carry on an interesting conversation. She didn't seem spoiled at the time, and Milton found her likeable. He'd never had a girlfriend for whom he felt a deep sense of romantic love. His mind and heart were consumed with expansion. His passion was accomplishment. For Milton, having a partner was more important than having a lover, except for the brief affair he had just before he met Patricia. That was as close as he ever came to a relationship that tugged at his emotions. But it was ephemeral, and the geographic locations made it impossible. At least they had remained friends.

During the boom of the 1970s, profits soared, and Milton parlayed the company's assets into several divisions, buying back stock from other shareholders who were looking to retire. By his thirty-fifth birthday, Mill owned half of the lumber company. Before the next three years had passed, he would own all of it. The first thing he did was change the name from Geiser Creek Sawmill to Geiser Creek Lumber and Millwork. He felt the word *sawmill* limited the perception of the company. And he was right. When contractors sought lumber, they went to Geiser Creek, an all-service company.

Milton spent endless hours reviewing the books, expenses, and ways to be more efficient. That practice was what had gotten him to where he was. He realized renting trucks was a waste of money, so he invested in trucks and leased them to other companies during slow months. He called the new company Interstate Trucking. Not very original, but that's exactly what it was. As the business grew, he needed more space, so he invested in real estate, building two more lumber and millwork facilities between Salem and Lebanon.

Geiser Creek had become the second-largest supplier of lumber in the entire state. Two years later, it would become one of the largest in the country under the umbrella of Spangler Enterprises Inc. The conglomerate included real estate holdings, as well as a regional hotel chain designed to accommodate truckers, called the Cascade Inns. There were five of them in the Pacific Northwest, attracting many long-haulers, giving them a reasonably priced, more comfortable place to sleep, shower, and eat, than a truck stop or the back of their cab. The inns were refurbished buildings and motels that were scheduled for demolition, and Milton got a tax incentive for renovating the properties. Geiser now had three mills, and a fleet of vehicles including pickup trucks, box trucks, flatbeds, and eighteen-wheelers.

Every Friday, Mill would visit one of the facilities, rotating them every week. He'd have sandwiches delivered and sit with the men and discuss their jobs. He wasn't trying to intimidate or spy on them. He was genuinely interested in how things were going. What could be improved? What was working and what wasn't? His several hundred employees appreciated the face-to-face opportunities to talk with the "big boss." Patricia often questioned why he was spending time with the underlings. "Isn't that what you have foremen and supervisors for?"

"It's not the same. I don't ever want to be out of touch. Besides, talking with the men reminds me of when I was a kid and ran around in the sawdust."

Patricia would smirk. "Whatever you say, dear. You are the boss, after all."

As the years went by, he would have to remind himself why he'd married her. He used to like her. But now? He wondered. Had she turned into one of those entitled posers she'd loathed at one time? They say people don't change. They just become the worst or best of themselves, but the core is still there. Too bad he hadn't seen her core earlier, although he would never change anything about their son Benjamin.

Milton was on the fence when it came to his

father-in-law. That connection was a double-edged sword. But he learned to live with it and made use of his father-in-law's desire to please his daughter. Milton began to discover Patricia's true nature when she insisted they hire a nanny for Benjamin. Milton didn't think it was necessary since Patricia didn't have a job, but raising a son might infringe on her leisure time, which was most of the time. The senator made the decision for them and paid for a full-time nanny. He wanted his daughter to be available for social happenings, whether they occurred in Oregon or Washington, D.C. Milton didn't particularly like getting "handouts," but he told himself it was for Patricia. And Benjamin.

After Benajamin came along, Mill tried to balance home life with work. When he had free time, he made plans to spend it with his son. He wanted to teach Benjamin how to fish the way his father had taught him. Teach him how to ride a bike. Fly a kite. He wanted to have the same kind of relationship he'd had with his father; a relationship that was cut short. He was there when Benjamin took his first step and drove him to his first day of school. Milton worked late hours but always had breakfast with his son. Patricia rarely rose before ten o'clock, but the nanny, Alissa, made sure Benjamin was dressed and ready for school. That was when Milton developed an appreciation for the extra help around the house.

When Benjamin turned eight, Milton began to plan trips with him. One of their weekend adventures included a visit to Bend, Oregon. Surrounded by the Cascades, the town had a "high desert" climate, with three hundred days of clear sunny skies and cool nights. They visited Pilot Butte, one of the only urban volcanoes in the U.S., with panoramic views of the desert, mountains, and the city of Bend below. Milton also planned trips to Bandon to visit his sister's family and his mother. He took Benjamin to Haystack Rock, one of Oregon's most popular landmarks. Its basalt sea stack arose two-hundred-thirty-five feet from the shoreline. During low tide, it was possible to walk to the base of it. Milton remembered the day he'd brought Benjamin there for the first time. Seeing the delight on his son's face was one of the most memorable moments in his life.

There was little time for much else, although he never neglected his wife or other family obligations. Patricia enjoyed the finer things, parties, galas, and travel. Lots of it. Mill did not oppose any of it, as long as he wasn't expected to be roped into all of it. Some of it, yes. All of it, no.

Patricia

For Patricia, Milton wasn't like any other man she had met before. For one thing, he wasn't a politician. For another, he wasn't looking for favors. Maybe that was the same thing. Milton was a man with a mission that wasn't "inside the Beltway." She liked the idea that he was an ambitious young man; a man who had to earn his way, without the benefit of rich and influential parents, even though hers were exactly that. When it came to the dating pool, she had had enough of the pretentious posers in search of benefits for themselves or family members. For Patricia, Milton Spangler would be a good provider, especially if she had anything to do with it. She set her sights on him, and the two formed an alliance. It appeared they came to the same conclusion at the same time. Each of them would get what they wanted from their union. It wasn't emotionless, but they each had something to gain from it.

As a wedding gift, Senator Wakeman bought the couple a piece of property in Mountain Valley, a suburb of Salem, with the unspoken understanding that it would be a wonderful place to raise a family. Two years later, they had their first child and named him Benjamin, after her grandfather, who had left her a tidy sum. Soon after, they broke ground to build their first house. It wasn't quite a mansion yet, but was designed for future expansion. The senator saw to it.

Patricia returned frequently to Washington, D.C., to visit family and friends and enjoy social activity with high-puffery politicos. She couldn't help herself. It was in her blood. The more often she visited, the more she was disenchanted with Salem. She needed a project and decided the family should have a vacation home on the Oregon coast. Bandon was the perfect choice. It took very little coaxing for Milton to agree, since his sister, her family, and his mother were there, and there was plenty of property to build a showcase home, as big and as lavish as the Salem residence. She decided it would have five bedrooms with en suite baths to accommodate weekend guests, family or otherwise. Milton gave her full control of the project, which eventually ran over a few million dollars. She had a professional photographer submit photos to *Architectural Digest*, which ran a story about the senator's daughter and her brilliant project, even though she had a team of designers work on it.

She planned a lavish housewarming party and rented another house for the guest list overflow. Her father thought it would be a good opportunity for a mingling of political rivals. Not that the gathering would encourage getting more done in Washington, but it would make a good story about politicians playing nice in the sandbox.

The Secretary of State, several congressmen, a handful of senators, and a federal judge were on the list. It made national news: "The grand hostess at her spectacular vacation home with the sensational view." Nothing was mentioned as to who paid for the transportation, but some of Senator Wakeman's rivals muttered it was the taxpayers. And they were back to the usual news cycle of name-calling, infighting, blaming, finger-pointing, and a whole lot of nothing getting done.

A year later, Oliver was born, an unplanned surprise to the family. Patricia was thirty-four. Patricia took it as a "sign" and Oliver was a "gift." It was clear she connected with him more than she had with Benjamin. She coddled Oliver—something she'd never done with Benjamin. Milton thought she might be maturing.

With the difference in their son's ages, it was natural that Benjamin spent time with his father while he waited for his younger brother to be old enough for them to enjoy activities together. But when Benjamin turned eighteen, his younger brother was only nine. It was going to be two decades before they were on the same page. If it ever happened.

Over the years, Milton and Patricia formed a mutual understanding, and a satisfactory relationship. They rarely argued. Milton simply let Patrica do whatever she wanted.

When Milton turned sixty-five, he began to delegate some of the operations to Benjamin, who took to the work like a duck to water. He had his father's DNA and was equally sharp and insightful. Oliver was second in command and dabbled in the Cascade Inns and transportation end of the business.

With Benjamin at Milton's side, the company continued to show profits, but there were times when Benjamin questioned some of his brother's expenses. Oliver would give him a few lines of double-talk regarding negotiations, and Benjamin would look elsewhere in the company to cover the deductions.

But things began to get murky after the first fourteen-year-old went missing. Oliver denounced the reward, claiming it would focus too much attention on the family business. "We don't need people picking through our rubbish for a story." Milton wasn't as concerned. He had nothing to hide. If anything, he wanted the family name to be cleared. It troubled him that the witness recalled a pickup truck with the company logo.

Milton decided to call a family meeting. He had a number of items to discuss. Oliver was the first to arrive in his father's study, followed by Benjamin. Patricia came in to say hello, then turned and said, "I'll leave you three to talk business."

Milton picked up his half-filled glass of brandy. Oliver was having his favorite tequila. Within a half hour, Milton started to breathe heavily and complain about a pain in his chest. Moments later, he was going into convulsions. Benjamin called 911 and then loosened the collar of his father's shirt. He was about to administer CPR when EMS arrived. After all, this was the Spangler family. All hands were on deck.

As Milton lay connected to tubes and wires in a hospital bed, he had time to reflect on the seventy-five years of his life. He thought back to the trips he and Benjamin had taken and drifted off to sleep, wondering if he would make it through the night.

CHAPTER THREE
Benjamin Spangler

B enjamin was a curious child. He wanted to know how things were made. At six years old, he relished going to the lumberyards with his father, just as Milton did with his dad. Mill saw a lot of himself in his son. By the time Benjamin was twelve, he began taking scraps of two-by-fours to try making something. Anything. His first project was a stool that listed to one side. That's when he discovered the use of a level. A few misses with the hammer caused shouts and black-and-blue fingernails, but he never whined or complained.

Patricia would sigh in frustration. She didn't want her son to grow up to be a blue-collar carpenter. One afternoon while she was bemoaning her son's future, Milton interrupted her. "Jesus was a carpenter." She never uttered another word after that.

Besides woodworking, Ben had an ability to see

the big picture. He learned by studying blueprints and was able to envision projects in three dimensions. As he grew older, he considered studying architecture, but business was also one of his interests. The best school was in Austin, Texas, but Benjamin had no interest in going that far south. Another option was Miami, which was also too many miles from home. He was accepted at Washington State University in Pullman, Washington, which suited him. It had a student population of 22,000, large enough to provide diversity without his having to leave the Pacific Northwest, a place where he wanted to stay.

Nowadays, Benjamin was a family man with a wife, Danielle, and three children, Logan, Addie, and Eva. Danielle had been an account executive at an advertising agency when she was assigned the Spangler account. She was twenty-six at the time and considered one of the brightest newcomers at the advertising firm. When she first met the Spanglers, she was prepared. She gave them an overview of how her firm could expand the Spangler Enterprises brand. She showed them a sketch for a new logo that was a die-cut fir tree, overlapped by a rooftop to signify the inns, and a wheel for the trucking line with the letters S.E.I. as the hub cap with the spokes tying all three together. The icon was surrounded by the slogan "Building a World Together." Danielle also made several suggestions for increased community involvement. Milton was quite impressed, as was Benjamin. A year later, Danielle and Benjamin were married.

Shortly after the honeymoon, Milton offered Danielle the position of Director of Marketing for Spangler. With the increased visibility of S.E.I., the company had grown by leaps and bounds. Someone had to promote the company image. He wasn't a fan of poaching employees, but in this case, it was a family matter, provided Danielle wanted to continue to work. She accepted the position and held it for two years until she and Benjamin had their first child, Logan.

Now, at forty-eight, Danielle was the mother of three teenagers: nineteen-year-old Logan, seventeen-year-old Addie, and fifteen-year-old Eva.

Benjamin's kids were good students and active in sports. Logan had always been interested in computer science and was in his sophomore year at Stanford University. Addie was a high school senior and had been recently accepted at Pratt Institute in New York. Her plans were to pursue interior design. At fifteen, Eva was still on the fence between pursuing professional soccer and playing guitar.

They lived in a custom-built, four-thousand-square-foot, two-story home surrounded by nature's beauty. The main level had floor-to-ceiling windows allowing the scenery to be the focus. Beautiful French doors opened to a wraparound deck for indoor-outdoor living and entertaining, with serene views of mountains and trees. The house was not at all ostentatious but beautifully appointed with simple lines and design.

On the second floor, each of the kids had their own room, with an adjoining bath for the girls to share.

Growing up, Logan had a bathroom to himself, with a walk-in shower, which was just fine as far as the girls were concerned. They didn't want boy cooties in their double-bowl vanity. The master suite included a stone fireplace, balcony, large marble-tiled bath, and dressing area.

The lower level of the house had a guest room and home office, and an ample entertainment area with a wet bar, pool table, and large-screen TV. It opened out to a meticulously landscaped yard and patio that surrounded a pool. On the opposite side was a pool house that served as Eva's music room when she wasn't playing soccer. It was a house that was built to live in and enjoy, not a museum piece on display.

Benjamin was like his father. He had a strong work ethic and was satisfied with an unpretentious vehicle. While his brother wore Rolex watches, Benjamin wore Seiko. Not that his wasn't considered a luxury watch, but it cost ten thousand dollars less than his brother's.

Benjamin rarely, if ever, pulled the S.E.I. card to get things done. He didn't have to. People were always ready to please members of the family. The only time Benjamin or Danielle used the Spangler influence was to get donations for charity, such as the local animal rescue association, the children's hospital, and the food pantry. Each year Danielle would chair fund-raising events for all three, and she made sure her children were involved. Community service was important, particularly if you had the means to do it. No one was allowed to take anything for granted. All in all, it was a relatively normal family, albeit a powerful one.

Benjamin didn't like his brother very much. He never felt a connection with him. Granted, Benjamin was nine when Oliver was born, so by the time Oliver could play with other children, Benjamin was a teenager. Now Benjamin was forty-eight, and Oliver was thirty-nine. They were almost a generation apart. Oliver had a more entitled viewpoint, and with Patricia's doting, that wasn't about to change any time soon.

Oliver

Oliver's story was not unique. Born into a wealthy family associated with high-ranking politicians, he was afforded luxuries and special treatment at every turn. He was entitled in a way that most over-indulged children expect. Patricia had doted on him from the time he was born, making excuses for his bad behavior and often rewarding it. Her theory was that eventually, Oliver would begin to appreciate everything that was handed to him. But that wasn't the case. As he grew bigger, so did his expectations, and his expectations became more expensive. Between his senator grandfather and his pampering mother, Oliver was spoiled rotten.

When Oliver turned eighteen, his grandfather bought him a Porsche. It was a status symbol he cherished. He drove it across the country to Towson, Maryland, his mother's alma mater, where he was to begin his college education. It was the only school that accepted the less-than-average-grade student with few extracurricular activities to speak of. A huge donation from his mother's family might have played a role in his acceptance, but no one uttered a word about the endowment.

Towson had a reputation of being a "party school," and Oliver felt compelled to uphold the college's status. Before the holiday break, Oliver slammed the Porsche into a tree after slugging down a bottle of tequila. The local authorities didn't want to incur the wrath of a senior politician who believed Oliver's story: it was a prank that had gone bad; some of his buddies had slipped him a mickey and let him drive home. Oliver had the good sense to claim he couldn't remember who he was with. His grandfather was outraged and insisted on knowing who was responsible, but Oliver stuck to his story. "I don't remember, Gramps. It's all a blur." Senator Oliver Wakeman took his grandson at his word, dropped the subject, as did law enforcement.

During his freshman year, he was failing miserably and was put on probation. He had one more semester to redeem himself if he wanted to return. It was a struggle, but he managed to squeak by with a C average. A little bit of cheating helped.

As his sophomore year began, he quickly jumped back into party mode, and his grades began slipping once again. Out of fear of embarrassing the family, his mother hired a tutor to help him improve. But Oliver had a better idea. He'd pay someone to do his homework, and in the two-hundred-plus classes, he'd pay someone to take the tests for him. Unless someone was trying to get the professor's attention, the instructors were not scanning the students' faces. They were busy lecturing, writing on a whiteboard, or doing PowerPoint presentations. They were not policing the class for truancy, a fact Oliver readily noticed and appreciated.

In those large lecture halls, he always wore the same clothes and baseball cap to class. When it came time for tests, he hired a brainiac with similar build and bought him the exact same outfit. It worked for all of his final exams. His mother was proud of his B average, but Milton wasn't convinced and suggested Oliver transfer to a school closer to home. Oliver objected, as did his mother. They won the argument.

When the time came for Oliver to declare his major, he picked Communications. He was a good-looking, five-foot-eleven-inch athlete with a thick head of hair, piercing blue eyes, and a very expensive, dazzling smile. His years of playing lacrosse and skiing made him quick and agile. He had a lot of charm at the time and thought broadcasting was a good path for him. As the saying goes, "He had a face for television." His well-connected grandfather promised to lean on his media connections to help secure a position for Oliver. Oliver understood it would begin as a low-paying internship but assumed he would be fast-tracked to a well-paid, visible position.

Upon graduation, as promised, he got a job at a local television station, and his grandfather bought him a new car. This time, it was a Range Rover. The senator thought it would be a better choice than a sports car. Oliver needed to be taken seriously. Once he had his foot in the door and gained popularity, he could drive whatever he wanted. For now, Oliver had to put on a show, literally and figuratively. Perception was everything.

After a few weeks of summer vacation, Oliver began his internship at station WWDC. The job lasted for three years. He resented doing local stories about new bakery openings, or cute classroom activities. He thought it was time he should be covering major stories or sitting behind the news desk. He clashed with his boss many times, and ultimatums were finally laid out for him. "Do the assignment or get out." His grandfather got wind of his self-important behavior and encouraged him to resign. It was ironic that his grandfather had contributed to Oliver's attitude and now had to do something about it.

The senator spoke to Mill and explained that things weren't quite working out in the capital, and Oliver was going to go back to Oregon to work for the family business. Mill could easily find something for Oliver to do. Once again, the senator reminded everyone that perception was everything. As much as Oliver Wakeman loved his grandson, he didn't want the young man to sully the family reputation.

Unlike his brother Benjamin, Oliver felt no real kinship to his family or the business. He wanted to travel and see the world. But Mill wasn't going to pay for his son to gallivant without pulling his weight.

Milton was not a fan of the mollycoddling Oliver had experienced all his life. Patricia overruled her husband at every turn, but with the senator supporting him in this particular case, Mill had won a battle. Oliver moved home, where his father gave him a job as director of transportation.

Ditching the Range Rover for a new Porsche was Oliver's first order of business. He moved into a swanky apartment, where he lived for five years until his grandfather passed away. Much to the family's surprise, the senator left Oliver a sizable inheritance that he had no trouble spending.

Oliver was single and considered himself the most eligible bachelor in the county. He played the Spangler card at every opportunity. He was full of flash, and full of himself. But he had charm and money, so many people overlooked his arrogance.

He lived in a 2500-square-foot condominium with a deck and a hot tub. It was the supreme bachelor pad. His wardrobe consisted of high-end designer clothes—Italian silk shirts from Todd Snyder, tailored Ferragamo jeans, Ferragamo sneakers and shoes, and several Tom Ford suits. If it didn't have a luxury label, he didn't wear it. He had a special drawer in his walk-in closet just for his Rolex watches. He went to the most expensive barber. He even smelled expensive.

With a new sports car every two years, he was considered quite a catch. But Oliver didn't like to share, unless he was showing off in front of friends. He'd reach for the check when his pals were at The Underground, a hip speakeasy bar. He'd date a girl for a few months until she began expecting perks like Valentino handbags or vacations to Cabo. He'd have fun for a while, and then break another heart. His goal was to find someone who came from a family with more money than his. Considering the Spanglers were the wealthiest family in the area, it was an ongoing crusade. He'd take vacations to expensive resorts in search of a single, monied woman. He didn't care about her age as long as she was well-heeled. Oliver had several affairs with older women. One in particular could have set him up in a penthouse suite, but she was too demanding, and not really much fun, so he continued to play the field until another opportunity presented itself.

He never hesitated to mention that his grandfather was once a senator. Rarely, if ever, did he refer to his other grandfather, who was killed on the job. As far as Oliver was concerned, Harold Spangler was a blue-collar worker with bad luck. What he didn't seem to comprehend was that it was his grandfather's accident that had spurred his father's determination to succeed. Oliver only focused on the senator, the one who lavished him with gifts, but his inheritance was dwindling, and the indulgence train was about to come to a grinding halt. If Oliver wanted to maintain his lifestyle, he would have to devise a money-making plan that went beyond his salary. So he did.

Before the money dried up, Oliver took what he thought might be his last excessive vacation two years before. It was a trip that would change everything.

Benjamin hadn't received the same kind of bequest from his grandfather as his brother because the senator believed Benjamin had the capability to succeed on his own. When the will was read, Benjamin didn't know if he should be flattered, disappointed, or dismayed. He took it on the chin and put the token inheritance into a trust fund for his kids' college.

From an outsider's point of view, Oliver appeared to be the wealthier of the two. People surmised Benjamin lived modestly because he had a family to support. In contrast, Oliver's lifestyle was lavish. The family knew the amount of money Oliver received, and what he spent was obvious. They assumed Oliver had made investments that gave him the cash to flaunt. But Oliver wasn't that business savvy, at least not at S.E.I. His management skills were unimpressive, and Benjamin often had to cover for his brother's mistakes and faux pas. Benjamin thought it was his duty to protect the younger Spangler. Oliver expected it. Benjamin was always his fallback guy. It was surprising that Benjamin had the patience for it, but Oliver was family.

*   *   *

Oliver and Benjamin were as different as night and day. Oliver's focus was always on how much money he could put into his own pocket, not necessarily into the company or its future. He and his brother had a recurring argument about reforestation. Benjamin loved the land, the air, the lakes. He appreciated the trees. For every tree the company cut down, thirty were planted in its place, even though the law required only twenty. By Benjamin's calculation, they were increasing the new growth by fifty percent.

Oliver thought company policy was too generous. "Why do we have to do more than required?" was Oliver's battle cry.

"Because it's the right thing to do."

"But we're only required to plant twenty," Oliver would come close to whining.

"Correct. But we can do more. The company can afford it, and it's good for the planet."

That conversation would occur almost every month when the company had its budget meeting. Milton had begun adding more trees several years before, and Benjamin was not about to change his father's policy.

"But we could be making more money," Oliver would argue.

"The company is doing well," Milton would intervene. "We are up almost seventeen percent over last year, and as long as we continue to show profits like that, we shall continue what I started." Milton would repeat each and every time, "I've turned that

part of the business over to Benjamin, and he shall
continue to make those decisions. You, Oliver, are
supposed to be overseeing the transportation division and the hotels. How are you doing with that?"
Milton pulled the spreadsheets closer.

"Fine, Dad. We're doing just fine," Oliver replied
with a slight tinge of resentment, sliding his paperwork before his father. "The five hotels are showing
a small profit after the renovations."

Milton pushed his glasses farther up the bridge of
his nose. "I suppose two percent is better than none."
He slid the paper back to Oliver, but he wasn't about
to pat Oliver on the back. He knew Benjamin had
funded the renovations from the millwork part of the
business, but he didn't want to humiliate Oliver by
pointing that out.

The millwork supervisor cleared his throat. "Mr.
Spangler, will the monies from the millwork used
for the renovations impact our profit sharing?" And
there it was. On the table for all to see.

Oliver's face turned red, and he resisted the temp-
tation to tell Gerard to mind his own business. But
Gerard *was* minding his business. He was responsible for the day-to-day management of the millwork.

Milton looked up. "Gerard, as long as Spangler
Enterprises is making a profit, everyone will share
in it."

A few years prior, Milton had initiated a profit-
sharing plan for his employees. It would serve two
purposes: it would assure retention of employees,
and it would ensure solid work ethics if employees
had more to gain. It was a win-win for everyone.

Oliver was the only one who objected. *Why did they have to give away some of their profits to the workers?* Again, Milton would repeat his reasoning, and Oliver would pout. He really, *really* wanted to graduate from a Porsche to a Lamborghini. The senator had passed away seven years before, so he couldn't count on him for a new birthday present.

For Oliver, it was all about how much money wasn't going into his own pocket. Less profit for the family meant less money he could squander. What he didn't understand was the motivation profit sharing would promote in the employees, creating a more enthusiastic workforce and thereby more profit. His resentment was palpable. But until Milton fully retired, the company was run by Milton's rules. Oliver knew he would have numerous conflicts with his brother, but he'd deal with those later. For now, he had to maintain the status quo, even if it meant cooking the books from time to time. It could be years before anyone discovered the inconsistencies, if ever. He had to mind his p's and q's if he wanted that new Lamborghini he had been eyeing.

Oliver's responsibilities at the family firm were supervised by his brother. Oliver didn't care that Benjamin was technically his boss. Benjamin would always save Oliver's hide when necessary, like the time he wrecked his latest Porsche after slugging down a bottle of tequila. The police called Benjamin, who put up the bail money, and an unspoken agreement was set in motion: nothing that Oliver did would reach Milton, or the press, for that matter. Ignoring bad behavior had become an ordinary state of affairs when it came to the Spangler boy.

Benjamin never expressed resentment about the bountiful lifestyle Oliver led, or that Benjamin had been slighted by his grandfather. If anyone resented those things, it was Mill. When he didn't want to indulge Oliver, Patricia would override his decision and give their son her own money. Patricia's grandfather had also been a politician and had left her, his only grandchild, a tasty little sum. Mill never knew the exact amount and never pursued it. It was none of his business, except when it interfered with conventional parenting. Even against her husband's wishes, Patricia would bend and give Oliver what he wanted. And everything he wanted, he came to expect.

Mill started awake from a deep sleep. He was a little disoriented, but then he realized he was in the hospital and thought back to his last thoughts before drifting off. He was proud of Benjamin. He was loath to admit it, but Oliver was a huge disappointment.

Mill sighed as the heart monitor reminded him that he was still alive.

CHAPTER FOUR

Pinewood

Myra Rutledge cocked her head when she heard the landline ring in the kitchen. Very few people had that number, and whoever did usually called when there was an emergency. She quickly ran down her list of Sisters and where they were and who it could possibly be. She called out to Charles, who was making one of his gourmet dinners. "Charles, can you answer the phone, please?"

"Tried but got my hands in mitts." He was in the middle of basting his masterpiece.

"Can't you pick it up?" Myra tossed the newspaper aside and scrambled to the far end of the kitchen, whizzing past Charles in his chef's apron. The yellow phone was dangling from the receiver that was hanging on the wall. "Coming!" she shouted at the swinging telephone, taking a moment to inhale the aroma of coq au vin. "Smells delish."

She rescued the dangling object and pulled it to her ear. "Hello?"

"Myra?" A familiar but not-so-recognizable voice was on the other end.

"Speaking." She waited.

"This is Patricia Spangler."

Myra's heart dropped. This wasn't going to be good news.

"Yes, Patricia." She waited.

"Milton had a heart attack and is in the hospital."

"Oh, dear." Myra's mood dropped as she waited for Patricia's next sentence.

"He's in stable condition," Patricia said evenly.

"Oh, I am happy to hear that." Now Myra was going to start grilling her friend's wife.

"When did this happen?"

"Two days ago."

"Where was he?"

"In his study. Oliver found him first. Then Ruby, our housekeeper, ran in after she heard Mill fall."

"How long do you think he'll be in the hospital?"

"They're not sure. They're running tests."

Myra hesitated, waiting for more information.

"Myra, he asked for you."

"Oh?" Myra was still in suspense.

"Yes. He asked that I phone you and let you know."

"I appreciate it, Patricia. Is there anything I can do?"

"Not until we know more, I suppose." Patricia hesitated.

"Please keep me posted," Myra said, "and give him my best."

"I shall. Take care. Bye-bye." Patricia ended the call.

Myra held the phone in her hand for a moment before she placed it back in its cradle.

By now, Charles had his hands free and approached her. "What is it, love?"

"My friend Mill from Oregon. He had a heart attack."

"Will he be alright?"

"I'm not sure." Myra was pensive.

"When was the last time you spoke to him?" Charles asked.

"Two weeks ago, when that girl went missing."

"Right. It was on the telly."

"Yes. He offered a reward."

"Whatever came of it?" Charles asked.

"Nothing, I'm afraid." Myra had a look on her face that Charles immediately recognized.

"You want to go to Oregon." Charles stated the obvious.

She turned to him. "I do."

"Right." Charles turned the oven off. "Come." He gestured for her to sit with him at the long wooden table. He took both her hands into his. "I know when your wheels are turning, love."

"Something doesn't seem right. I realize a heart attack at seventy-five isn't unusual, but it's the missing girl part of it."

"What do you mean?"

"A girl goes missing, Mill offers a reward, the girl is never found, and Mill has a heart attack." She fidgeted with her pearls. "I know it's only been a couple of weeks since she disappeared, but there is something about this that doesn't sit right."

"You think there is some kind of connection?"

She looked up at Charles. "Just a feeling."

Charles slapped both his knees as he pushed himself away from the table. "When do we leave?"

Myra smiled. "Let me call Annie and see what she's up to."

"Splendid idea." Charles checked his chicken. "Say, you wouldn't want Fergus and me to join you, would you?"

"Let me think on that. Maybe you and I should go, and then I can fill Annie in after I've seen Mill."

Charles looked up from the beautifully browned chicken. "Or perhaps you and Annie go and report back to me and Fergus. If there's anything dodgy going on, we have everything we need here."

Myra got up from her chair and picked up the yellow phone. She actually enjoyed using the old-fashioned dial. It reminded her of a time when things were much less complicated.

Annie picked up on the first ring. "Good evening!" she said in her usual chipper voice. "What's cooking?"

"Coq au vin," Myra answered wryly, knowing Annie wanted to hear what was going on.

"Stop." Annie laughed. "Tell me. Tell me."

"You remember my friend Mill from Oregon?"

"Of course! Lovely lumberman. Why? What's up?"

"His wife called me. He's in the hospital. Heart attack."

"Oh, that can't be good." Annie's tone softened.

"She said he's in stable condition."

"Okay. That sounds better."

"But she said he asked for me." Myra narrowed her eyes; the wheels in her head were turning.

"Is that a bad thing?" Annie wasn't quite tracking what was on Myra's mind. She gulped.

"Not at face value, but why ask for me?"

"Maybe he has something he wants to share, just in case. You know. Just in case." Annie emphasized the words without going all the way. Annie anticipated the next part of the conversation. "When do you want to leave?"

Myra chuckled. "The sooner the better, I suppose."

"Tomorrow? Early afternoon? It's over a seven-hour flight, but with the time zone difference, we could be there by six if we leave here at one o'clock."

"I can be ready in an hour." Myra chuckled. She and Annie kept "go-bags" handy. There was one for every season. All they had to do was pull the bag out of the closet. "But I think I should spend the evening with Charles. He just pulled out a casserole dish of coq au vin."

"Does he know about, you-know-what?"

"No, but I think that's a good idea." Myra signaled that it was not a good time to discuss events from her past, especially her romantic past. Years ago, when Milton had flown across the country to attend her daughter Barbara's funeral, she'd been in too much shock to veer off to any other subject except the loss of her daughter. Then Myra fell into a deep depression. By the time she recovered, the thought of discussing the past never occurred to her. Why bring up something from years ago?

"Are you sure you want to do that tonight?" Annie asked.

"Possibly." Myra saw Milton at random events every few years. They remained good friends without discussing what had once been between them, knowing they both had busy lives to handle on opposite ends of the country. "But maybe not. I'll decide after dinner." She looked over at Charles as he turned the carrots that were roasting in the pan. "I'll call you later."

"O-kay!" Annie yelped. "I'll have details about tomorrow for you later this evening."

Myra hung up the phone, walked over to Charles, stood behind him, and wrapped her arms around his waist. "Smells glorious!" She took in the aroma of his culinary efforts. "I am so glad you found a hobby." That's when she decided to wait until it became totally necessary to tell Charles about her short affair with Mill. Besides, Nikki and Jack were coming over for dinner, and it was not the kind of conversation one could have in front of guests.

Myra was one of the richest women in America, only dwarfed by her best friend Annie, one of the richest women in the Western Hemisphere. Neither was pretentious, but they would occasionally indulge themselves with spa packages. They wore slip-on sneakers and jogging outfits most of the time, even though they rarely, if ever, jogged. The clothing was comfortable. When necessary, Myra would don a pair of Ann Taylor slacks, a cashmere turtleneck, and Chanel flats or Gucci loafers. And always the pearls, jogging pants or otherwise. In warmer months, it might be a long, black pencil skirt with a white blouse. Rarely was she fancy.

Annie, on the other hand, loved to wear rhinestone cowboy boots with pretty much everything from shorts to evening gowns. She would occasionally top an outfit off with her diamond tiara. Annie Ryland De Silva was, indeed, a countess. Having lived abroad, Annie was well accustomed to the movers and shakers of the world, and she knew how to navigate any kind of social gathering, whether a state dinner or a backyard barbecue. And if Fergus didn't keep an eye on her, she was apt to do a little pole dancing to entertain the rest of the party guests, ballgown and all.

Annie and Myra were childhood friends and spent their summers on neighboring farms in Virginia. Both women had enormous wealth at the ready and were not shy about spending it for a good cause, meaning animals, children, or women at risk.

After Myra's daughter was killed by a car driven by a diplomat, she spiraled into a deep depression. She spent months sitting blankly in front of the television until a story woke her from her catatonic state. A woman had lost her battle with justice, and

Myra was intent on righting the wrong. She and her adopted daughter Nikki decided it was time to take matters into their own hands and formed a bond. A bond of Sisterhood they extended to Annie and other women they recruited who thought they would never see the scales of justice balanced again.

Myra had good instincts. Was almost clairvoyant. She could sniff out a scandal, a liar, or a cheat. That night, she felt a cry for help from an old friend, three thousand miles away.

Annie phoned her pilot to instruct him to have her Gulfstream Jet ready by one o'clock the following afternoon, while Myra arranged for a car service to pick them up.

Myra set the long farm table for her dinner with Charles, Nikki, and Jack. She was buying time, and an audience would give her a bit of a respite before she confessed her past to Charles. *It has been over fifty years*, she told herself. *There is nothing for Charles to worry about* . . . but Myra felt it her duty to let him know she was going to see not just an old friend, but a former lover. She could say she was a naïve nineteen-year-old at the time, but she had never been naïve.

The dogs raised their heads at the sound of crunching gravel. They recognized the sound of Nikki and Jack's vehicle and made their way to the kitchen door to greet them. Lots of hellos, kisses, and soft *woof*s echoed through the fragrant kitchen.

As usual, Charles had prepared a delicious meal. The dogs moved back to their spot in the corner, waiting for their human family to generously share the leftovers. Charles always set aside some of the meal for the dogs. In their house, there was no such thing as "doggie bags." It was "doggie bowls." Unless Maggie was there. Maggie Spritzer worked for Annie at the newspaper and was part of the Sisterhood. She had a voracious appetite for a good story, but it was dwarfed by her appetite for food. Any kind. Anywhere. Any time.

Once everyone was seated, they said grace and began passing the platters. Myra wasn't the nervous type, but she did feel anxious; her tell was playing with her pearls.

"Mom? Everything alright?" Nikki asked while she served the roasted vegetables.

"Yes. Why?" Myra quickly moved her hand from her neck to her fork.

Nikki raised an eyebrow. Myra understood she was being obvious and knew an explanation would be necessary. "My friend Milton Spangler is in the hospital."

"In Oregon?" Nikki asked.

"Yes. Apparently, he suffered a heart attack. His wife phoned earlier and said he was asking for me." She tried to sound as if this were something that occurred often, but everyone knew it was rather unusual.

"Oh?" Nikki cocked her head. "When was the last time you spoke to him?"

"Last month, when Vanessa Rowan went missing. Annie's paper covered the disappearance. Maggie was the reporter. Milton put up a fifty-thousand-dollar reward."

"Whatever came of it?" Jack asked.

"Nothing, I'm afraid." Myra toyed with her pearls again.

"Wait. I just heard another young girl is missing. She's from the same area," Nikki said. "It was on the news earlier."

Myra took a deep breath. "I wonder if this was why Mill asked for me."

"Does he know about us?" Nikki waved her fork around the table.

"Not the extent of how we operate, but we've done favors for each other. Nothing drastic, mind you." Myra let out another deep breath. "But I know something is not right, so Annie and I are going to fly out tomorrow."

"Your mother is getting telepathic messages." Charles was half teasing.

Jack interrupted the conversation. "I know when Myra has one of those, it's time for everyone to either duck or ready themselves." That brought a nervous laugh around the table. He wasn't wrong.

"Oh Jack, how you exaggerate." Myra chuckled. "But you are probably right. I don't know how long Annie and I will be out there, so I suggest everyone put on their big-boy pants and clear their calendar."

"Meanwhile, I shall clear the table." Jack stood

and started bringing the dishes to the sink, making sure to scrape whatever was left on the plates into the already overstuffed dog bowls. Tails were hammering out a beat in anticipation.

Charles had honed his culinary skills over the years. It was a hobby he'd developed between missions, and Fergus was happy to play the role of sous chef, as well as dish and bottle washer. Charles was constantly finding new recipes he wanted to experiment with at the expense of everyone's waistline. They'd made a pact and agreed to skip dessert during the week. "It's the least I can do for my glucose and triglyceride levels."

Myra chuckled. "And that scale in the bathroom keeps lying to me." Myra was in very good shape for a sixty-something. She walked a mile or two every day, even if it was simply strolling the perimeter of the vast farm.

When the kitchen was put back in pristine condition, it was a cue for Nikki and Jack to retreat to their home. "Good luck with everything." Nikki gave her mother a kiss on the cheek. "See you when you get back."

"If not sooner." Myra gave her a wink and a look that said, *It's not just the boys who may need to put on their grown-up pants.*

Myra turned toward Charles, about to make her confession. Instead, she pivoted and said, "I think I am going to turn in. Big day tomorrow."

"No doubt." Charles smiled and followed her to

the bedroom, dogs in tow. He sat on the overstuffed chair in the corner while Myra changed into her bedclothes. He waited until she reappeared. "Before we get too cozy, there's something I think we should discuss."

Charles had an odd tone to his voice. Myra gulped, unused to being uncomfortable with him. She made her way across the room and sat on the wide arm of his chair. "What is it, Charles?"

"Love, I would not have been doing my due diligence had I taken the job of head of security for you without knowing who I would be working for."

Myra knew exactly where this was going, but it had never occurred to her that her husband would have done a thorough background check. She was stunned, annoyed, surprised, embarrassed, and not necessarily in that order. Before she had a chance to speak, he continued. "If you recall, I was MI6. Instincts and years of experience told me to always be aware of who you are dealing with." He let it sink in. "You can't blame a man. After all, Myra Rutledge was perhaps the most intriguing woman I'd ever met." He put his arm around her waist and pulled her onto his lap.

"Aren't you the charmer?" Myra said wryly.

"That, too, is part of my job description."

CHAPTER FIVE

Salem

The next morning, the Spangler family arrived at the hospital, with the exception of Christina, who was on assignment with Doctors Without Borders on the other side of the world. Helen promised she would keep her daughter informed of Milton's health. At that moment, he was in stable condition but still in the cardiac unit. They hoped he could be moved to a private suite, but it might be days before that happened.

The unit allowed only one visitor at a time, so Helen went inside. Patricia, Benjamin, Gary, and Oliver waited in the small room outside the patients' ward. Patricia had a blank look on her face, Benjamin's expression was one of deep concern, and Oliver appeared bored. He was checking his newest wrist acquisition, a Breitling, when his phone vibrated in his Luca Faloni navy blazer pocket. He frowned when he saw the caller ID. It was Dickie Morton. Oliver stepped far enough away to have a conversation.

"What's up?" he huffed into the phone.

"We got a problem."

"No doubt." A problem would be the only reason for a call from Dickie while Milton was in the hospital. "What kind of problem?"

"One of the packages is missing."

"Which one?" Oliver asked.

"The first one."

"You can't be serious." Oliver's voice got louder.

"Like a heart attack. Oops, sorry," Dickie replied. "When Dirk went out for his cigarette break, he noticed the glass on the pavement."

Oliver looked around to see if anyone was listening or watching his facial expressions. He stepped farther down the hall. "You get your men on the stick. Pronto." Oliver punched the red button with so much force, the phone flew out of his hand. An orderly was heading his way and was about to pick it up when Oliver grabbed it. "Thanks. I got it."

"You alright, man?" the orderly asked.

Oliver pulled himself together. "Yeah. Thanks. Dad's in the cardiac unit." He jerked his head toward the big wood-and-glass swinging doors. That was a good enough excuse for his agitated behavior.

The night before, during the commotion of Milton's rush to the hospital, news had broken of another missing person. This time, the woman had disappeared from one of their inns. The one in Eugene. Oliver had listened to the news as he followed the ambulance. His heart rate was up; his hands and face broke out in sweat. His new side hustle could be in serious jeopardy.

Oliver had thought he had all his bases covered. Hush money to the local highway patrol, and a nice payout to the night transportation supervisor. The small hotel staff also got a kick-back. No one would ever think of going against the Spangler family, especially if they were employed by the company. Someone hadn't done their job that morning. A new young female housekeeper at one of the inns was in search of extra cleaning products and accidentally found her way into the powder mill behind the laundry room. Two men wearing white jumpsuits, with head coverings, face-piece respirators, and disposable shoe coverings, were standing over a long stainless-steel table. At first glance, she thought they might be doing a deep cleaning of the storage room, but then she saw a machine pouring out white powder into small plastic bags. They immediately apprehended her and called Dickie. Dickie had handled that situation, but now he had a new one to deal with. The first missing girl was now really missing.

Oliver returned to the waiting area, where the rest of the family was either pacing or sitting. Benjamin gave him a sideways glance as if to ask what the call was about. Oliver blew him off with a quick shake of his head and a shrug, indicating it was nothing.

But it wasn't really nothing. It was a major problem. His side hustle was turning huge profits, and now he was faced with a dangerous situation. Two, actually. He had to rethink his strategy.

Benjamin sensed there was something wrong. His brother was too fidgety. But now wasn't the time to grill him. Their father had suffered a major heart attack, and his needs were the first priority. He noticed the cardiologist walking toward them. His expression didn't seem to be strained. That was a good sign. "Hello, Dr. Kramer. Any word on my father's prognosis?"

"He's doing quite well. We should be able to move him to a private room tomorrow, provided all his vitals are stable."

"That's excellent news." Benjamin said with a sigh of relief.

"Something is very puzzling, however."

Benjamin gave him a curious look.

"His heart muscle is strong. His EKG is close to normal."

"What does that mean?" Benjamin asked.

"I'm not sure. I realize that's not very comforting to hear from a doctor, but there is no significant heart damage. You must have gotten him here in record time."

"EMS was at our door within minutes. Their auxiliary station is only a mile from the house."

"That turned out to be a good thing for your father."

"Yes, but what did you mean by *puzzling*?" Benjamin asked.

"We're going to run some tests. Could he have ingested something that brought on the cardiac arrest?"

Benjamin balked. "Ingested something? Like what?"

"We'll run a series of blood and urine tests. If everything looks normal, then I'd like to put him on a heart monitor once he leaves the hospital."

Benjamin looked perplexed. "So you're not sure what caused this?"

"Could have been a number of things. The good news is he's out of danger for now."

"How soon can we move him to a private room?"

"To be on the safe side, I'd recommend keeping him in the cardiac care unit for another night. If his chart looks good tomorrow morning, we'll move him to where he can be more comfortable. But we cannot allow more than two visitors at the same time. It's imperative we keep his stress level down."

Benjamin held out his hand. "Thank you, doctor. Much appreciated."

"And thank you for keeping your mother calm. She was rather hysterical when she first came in."

Benjamin stifled a chuckle. His mother was often on the verge of hysterics, especially when she didn't think she was getting her way. Benjamin thought back to when his mother was easygoing. Kind. It had been years.

Benjamin and Dr. Kramer approached the rest of the family, where the doctor explained about the tests and another night in the unit, and that Milton could have a private suite the next day, providing everything looked good.

Everyone in the family looked relieved. Everyone but Oliver, who was still reeling from his phone call. He feigned a smile. His father was going to be okay, but Oliver had more important things to deal with. He kissed his mother on the cheek. "I have to get to the office. We have a trucking situation that needs to be handled."

Benjamin interrupted. "Do you want me to go with you?"

Oliver smirked. "I think I can handle this myself."

"Of course you can," Patricia chimed in.

CHAPTER SIX

The Side Hustle

Oliver smiled politely at the nurses rushing past. *Or was he the one rushing?* When he got into his car, he looked in both directions to see if anyone was watching. Not that they could hear him unless he started screaming at Dickie, which was a very good possibility. He needed answers on both issues. And he needed them fast.

"How did it happen? When? And what's the situation?" He rapid-fired questions.

"Seems like she was able to fit through the transom window in the basement. She was a little bit of a thing, ya know."

The small top-hinge awning window was designed to open out, which was why there were bars installed inside. It was to ensure that no one tried to pull the bars off with a hitch on a truck. Oliver wanted to know how a petite teenager could have dismantled them and escaped. Someone had some explaining to do. "We had safeguards in place, did we not?" Oliver's breath became short. "Isn't that what I paid for?"

"Yes, boss. But it looks like the bolts didn't hold."

Oliver thought he was going to be the next one in the cardiac unit. He shut his eyes in disbelief. Oliver had two moods: pompous and sullen. At that moment, he was about to experience a new one: rage. When he felt the flash of heat rush from his neck to his face, he tried to calm himself down. He spoke slowly. Steadily. "I want you to do three things, Dickie boy. Number one: you find that girl; number two: I want to see the person who installed the bars; and number three, I want my money back." He took another breath and pumped up the volume, chopping out the words: "Do. You. Under. Stand. Me?"

"Gotcha, boss." Dickie waited for the next round of verbal assaults.

"Good. Now get it done. You feeling me?" Oliver huffed.

"Big time." Dickey knew he was in a very bad predicament. If they couldn't find the girl, and she made it out of the woods somehow, they would all be in for some serious business. Something the Spangler family might not be able to wriggle their way out of. "She can't last too long out there. And it's miles from any road, so she'll either get lost and never be found, or we'll catch up with her."

* * *

Oliver had known he was going to have a major problem when Dickie's cousin Bart picked up a hitchhiker outside the gas station in Salem. Bart was on his way to make a quick delivery when he saw a pretty young thing with her thumb out, seeking a ride. Unfortunately for Bart, he had his delivery package in the front seat. When he tried to move it so the girl could sit, the tape got caught on the seat belt clip and ripped it open, spilling the contents onto the floor. The girl freaked out and tried to jump out of the truck, but Bart clocked her and knocked her unconscious. When Bart called Dickie, Dickie told him to take her to one of the motels. "The one that backs up against all them woods. Put her in that basement space we made for the new guys from Mexico."

They held her there for two weeks. No one knew what to do with her. They were drug smugglers. Not murderers. Oliver hadn't addressed the issue, either, hoping it would resolve itself somehow. Maybe he would have one of his men bring her to his contact in Mexico. Ernesto would know what to do. Human trafficking was one option.

His head began to hurt from banging into dead ends. Bringing counterfeit fentanyl from Mexico to Alaska was very lucrative. Three truckers and the company fleet made the operation seamless. Until now.

"You've gotta find that kid, do you hear me?" Oliver was more perturbed than ever before. Everything had lined up perfectly. Until now.

"Got it, boss." Dickie was worried. There was

something in Oliver's voice that he hadn't heard before. A menacing tone. He didn't know what Oliver was capable of, but no matter, Oliver would always come out on the clean side of things. Dickie knew he had to watch his step and get the job done. Even if he had to do the worst. There couldn't be a trail that led to any of them, especially Oliver. He was the only one who could get them out of a jam.

"What about the other one?" Oliver was referring to the housekeeper.

"She's on her way to the place near the border. Blaine. Near Vancouver. Canada."

"Are you sure about that?" Oliver mocked.

"Yep. Got her wrapped up like a nice little bundle in the back trailer, with several pallets of plywood between her and the lift gate. She ain't goin' anywhere."

"Let me know when she arrives at the inn, and put her someplace where she can't escape."

Some of the money that went into the renovations for the inns included a small area on the lower level behind the laundry facilities. This was where Oliver planned to make his fortune. These private areas were accessed by steel doors with digital locks, and a sliding door to obscure the metal one from the rest of the laundry facility. All three had a separate small studio space where the men could sleep and shower. The adjacent area was where they would manufacture the pills or powder. Those doors were also secured by a metal door with a digital lock.

The first one in Salem was up and running, including the pill compression machine. The teenager had been held in the basement living area up until this fiasco. The Eugene inn had just started manufacturing powder when the young employee stumbled upon it. The Blaine location was almost ready, but now they would have to halt its progress and stash the housekeeper there until they could figure out what to do next.

The first order of business was to find the teenager. Oliver shook his head. It was a dumpster fire in a train wreck.

The first blunder was a result of Bart's overactive testosterone. The second one was a result of someone leaving the secret door exposed. He still didn't know who was responsible for that particular gaffe. Things were slipping out of his control.

It never occurred to Oliver that the problems were a result of his bad choices in personnel. He knew Ernesto didn't send rocket scientists up north, but this? How could anyone be so stupid as to leave that door exposed? He'd had a sliding panel installed to conceal the private door. The panel was built to blend in with the wall. Once inside the secret room, people were supposed to slide it in place and shut the door. It wasn't astrophysics. *What idiot did this?*

Oliver had thought bringing in two of his men to oversee production was a good idea. They worked for the company. He could keep an eye on them. Obviously, they weren't paying much attention, and now he had two problems on his hands. Problems he had not foreseen. But then again, planning was never one of Oliver's strong suits. He had big ideas, but not necessarily the skills to put them in motion. Maybe he watched too many crime-family dramas and imagined himself as the Pacific Northwest version of Tony Soprano, even if he wasn't Italian. The setup was inspirational: a boss, two lieutenants, and their team.

The past year of raking in the money had lured him into thinking he was a lot smarter than he really was. He didn't think about the pitfalls of trusting people who could barely string two sentences together—and English was their first and only language. They would certainly be loyal, but they could say and do stupid things. Like Bart. He wondered: *What would Tony do?* Probably the same thing as Michael Corleone.

While murder wasn't really Oliver's thing, he didn't mind supplying lethal drugs to unsuspecting customers. Sure, it resulted in fatal doses, but it was their choice to do it, not his. He felt no sense of culpability whatsoever. But now he was in way over his head with no one to save his sorry behind. Benjamin had always been there to dig him out or bail him out, whatever the problem might be. But this. This was a problem he couldn't turn over to big brother. Benjamin was even-tempered, but Oliver knew something like this could push his brother to commit a felony against him. Even homicide. He couldn't solicit help from his law enforcement cronies, either. They could look the other way when it came to falsifying documents, speeding, or taking illegal detours. Kidnapping would be out of the question. Drug distribution? Also very much out of the question. The feds and Canadians were coming down hard on the opium superhighway that ran from Mexico to Canada and Alaska. But the Spangler family had a reputation for running a clean business. At least on the surface. Oliver's accomplices on the side of the law were very few. They liked the non-taxable income they were getting every month, but this transgression was beyond Deputy Sheriff Nelson's loyalty. He'd turn state's evidence in a heartbeat. Speaking of heartbeats, Oliver's was about to speed up.

He started the engine of the Porsche 911 Carrera. Granted, it wasn't the most expensive of the line, but it had that Porsche crest emblem on the hood, and Carrera spelled in cursive writing across the back. If he could pull himself out of this new glitch, he would be riding in a Lamborghini a year from now.

He reached into the glove compartment and pulled out the one-gram brown bottle with the tiny spoon attached to the screw top. Cocaine. Also known as Blow, Nose Candy, Pearl, Toot. For him, the high it gave was the better option. Oliver could not imagine why someone would want to feel the opposite: listless, stupefied. He also couldn't wrap his head around doing "speed balls," mixing cocaine and heroin. *What was the point?* He shook his head. That was what killed John Belushi. He made another scan of the parking lot. No one was around. He dipped the spoon into the white powder and snorted up one nostril, then applied another spoonful up the other.

He zipped through the parking lot as if he were in a Formula One race. His mood was elevated finally to the pace of his heart: racing. That's what he liked.

CHAPTER SEVEN

Pinewood

Myra was up early. The dogs were her alarm clock. They had to go out and have breakfast. She occasionally thought about installing a doggie door, but instinct told her it would make the house vulnerable, even with five barking dogs and a security system that would make Fort Knox blush. It was no coincidence that Charles had engaged the same company to outfit the house and property.

After the time the Sisters were placed under house arrest, Charles convinced Myra they should have better surveillance than the local authorities could provide. Over the years, Charles and Fergus kept up with the latest reconnaissance equipment. Their technology rivaled that of many counter-intelligence agencies, and their access to personal information was capable of diving to the depths of the dark web. Between Fergus's stint at Scotland Yard, and Charles's at MI6, they were a formidable pair. With Myra's calculating thought process and Annie's guile, they, too, formed an indomitable duo. Their level of expertise at covert operations only sharpened as the years went on. While no one had any idea where this trip to Oregon would end, Myra was certain there was something afoot in the foothills of the Cascades.

Annie roared into the rear driveway of the farmhouse with Fergus in tow. She was a maniac driver, even in a golf cart. Fergus smoothed his hair, then pulled Annie's luggage off the back. Annie held the door to the kitchen. "We're here!" she proclaimed above the yapping of the dogs.

Charles suppressed a smirk. No matter how many times Fergus traveled with Annie behind the wheel, he always looked as if he'd just cheated death. His eyes bulged, his breath was short, and his face red.

Myra wiggled her way through the throng of dogs and gave Annie a big hug. "Good morning! Everything all set?"

"Of course." The jet was ready to take off, and Annie had made reservations at The Grand Hotel. "Our suite has two beds, a living room, dining area, desk; it includes breakfast, has a view, and it's soundproof. And it's just a couple of blocks from the hospital."

"That will surely come in handy," Myra responded.

"Plus, they have champagne service." Annie giggled.

"I wouldn't expect anything less." Myra chuckled.

Charles and Fergus rolled their eyes as if to say, *Here we go again.* The men brought the luggage to the waiting town car. Lots of hugs and kisses from both humans and dogs, and the gals were on their way.

Myra and Annie arrived at the airport and boarded the private jet. Myra phoned Patricia and left a voice mail message saying she and Annie would be arriving around dinnertime. They planned to check in to the hotel and then head to the hospital if that was acceptable to Patricia. Patricia replied several minutes later via text.

Yes. That's fine. Mill moving to private room.

Myra read the message out loud. "That's a relief. I'll be honest. I have no idea why he asked for me."

Annie raised an eyebrow as she fastened her seat belt. "First love?"

"Don't be ridiculous." Myra gave Annie's rhinestone boots a friendly tap.

"Not you, silly. Him!" Annie laughed.

"Even more ridiculous." Myra leaned back into the plush seat, folded her hands, and closed her eyes.

"You're still nervous about flying?" Annie asked, as she watched Myra fidget with her pearls.

"Always," Myra replied, and took a very deep breath. "I used to love it, but there've been too many incidents lately."

"At least we don't have to deal with belligerent, rowdy drunks!" Annie chuckled.

"Well, there's that." Myra opened one eye. "I know Phillip is a fine, experienced pilot. It's the airborne equipment, and the people who are handling it, that I worry about."

"Maybe a mimosa would help?" Annie grinned.

"Sure. Why not?" Myra wasn't a big drinker, but an occasional champagne or wine with dinner wasn't out of the ordinary.

Annie pushed the call button. A voice responded. "Yes, Ms. De Silva?"

"When we've reached cruising altitude, could you please bring me and Mrs. Rutledge two mimosas?"

"Yes, ma'am. Should be within the next ten minutes."

"Excellent." Annie sat back and watched the ground slip farther away.

Annie wasn't fancy, but she enjoyed some of the finer things. A good massage and facial, a pristine beach, fine wine, and fast cars. The faster the better.

As if Myra were reading her mind, she asked, "Have you ever considered becoming a race car driver?"

"I think you've asked me that almost every time you let me drive."

"Well, then?"

"No, but if there's time, I'd like to check out one of the speedways."

"Of course you would. You've done it before, haven't you?"

"Only once, believe it or not. I promised Fergus I wouldn't do anything dangerous on this trip." She chuckled. "Besides what we normally do."

Myra laughed. "We sure have gotten ourselves in a few pickles, haven't we?"

"So many, I'm surprised we're not brined by now!" Annie hooted.

The mimosa did the trick, and Myra dozed off. Annie pulled out her phone and confirmed their car and hotel reservations. Then she did a little digging into the Spangler family. She took a few notes to send to Fergus and Charles, and sent a message to Maggie, her crackerjack reporter: **Do a follow up on the missing girl. You will have to come out here.**

Maggie replied within seconds: **Will do. LMK. I'm packed and ready.** Maggie knew when Annie and Myra traveled, it usually meant they were looking into something unseemly, so she was at the ready.

The flight took less than four hours while they enjoyed their aerial view of the Rocky Mountains and the Great Salt Lake. As they made their way above the Cascades, lenticular clouds hovered over the magnificent Mount Rainier, signaling a change in weather. The scenery was breathtaking. They were admiring the view when the jet was slightly jostled by an updraft from the mountains. Myra jumped, gasped, and grabbed her pearls. "Easy on those, girlfriend." Annie leaned over and patted Myra's knee. "We're almost there." Then the jet banked southward to Salem, and they could see Mount Hood in the distance. It was a smooth three-point landing. Myra thought she had been holding her breath for the last fifteen minutes and let out a huge whoosh of air.

"Atta girl." Annie grinned. "I did a little more digging into the Spangler family while you were napping, and I told Maggie to do a follow-up. We may want her to fly out here."

"Good idea. I can only imagine that Mill wants to talk to me about something serious."

Annie winked and started to sing "When a Man Loves a Woman."

"Listen, you. Two things. First, you can't carry a tune in a bucket. Second, you've gotta stop that non-sense."

Annie stuck out her tongue and made a raspberry sound. Myra laughed. "You still can't carry a tune."

"Ah, but Milton?" She raised her eyebrows up and down.

"Would you please stop that?" Myra's eyes grew wide.

"Oh, alright." Annie paused. "For now."

Myra rolled her eyes and shook her head. "Remind me. Why are we friends?"

"Because you love me. And I love you." Annie smiled.

"True, but sometimes you can be so annoying." Myra grinned.

"Another thing to love about me. My crass sense of humor."

"You said it; I didn't." Myra folded her arms and gave Annie a phony look of annoyance.

CHAPTER EIGHT

Vanessa

Two Weeks Ago

The Rowan family had felt compelled to leave Portland. The crime rate was rising, and many streets were lined with the tents of homeless people. The illegal drug situation was at an all-time high, and had almost cost the life of Bobby Rowan, their eighteen-year-old son. They sent him to a ninety-day rehab center in Arizona, and upon his return, the Rowans decided it was time to find a safer place for their two children, Vanessa and Bobby.

Vanessa was a feisty fourteen-year-old. Emotional and stubborn. She resented moving away from her friends, but her mother reminded her that they were only an hour away, and her friends were invited to visit Mountain Valley. She suggested a sleepover but with negative results. She even offered to drive the friends back and forth. Nope. Vanessa thought Mountain Valley was boring, and her friends would hate it. She wanted to go back and visit them in Portland. "Not happening" was the repeated response.

Like many teenagers, Vanessa had a chip on her shoulder, and thought her parents were out of touch with reality. "You still have your social media," her mother reminded her.

"Big deal. I want to be with my friends." She'd pout or yell, depending on her mood.

Mrs. Rowan was trying desperately to connect with her daughter and made efforts to keep up with the technology and the lingo. "Don't you have a lot of friends on TikTok or Insta, or whatever you kids are using? Oh, what about FaceTime?" It wasn't working.

"Mom, puh-lease! You really think I have two thousand friends? I mean, for real?" She'd grimace. "Like, no."

"I guess I don't understand the point, then." Julie Rowan found all of it unsettling. Technology surely made the world better. It also brought out the worst in people. She sighed. Raising a teenager today was like dealing with a tidal wave: it was coming at you, and the only thing you could do was ride it out and try not to go under. She knew arguing with her daughter was a no-win situation. And it seemed as if every conversation was an argument lately.

Vanessa was having a difficult time making real friends at her new school. Teenagers could be mean, but so could she. The guidance counselor spoke to

Vanessa several times. She spoke to the Rowans
several times. Everyone surmised it was her brother's
addiction, rehab, and moving that had thrown Vanessa off her game. Before all that happened, Vanessa
was a good student, was on the gymnastics team,
and had a decent circle of friends. She felt she was
being punished for her brother's bad behavior. "It's
not fair!" She'd scream from inside her locked bedroom and then crank up her music so loud, the doors
would vibrate. There was no use in asking her to
turn it down. She'd just make it louder. The next day,
she would be almost civil, as civil as one resentful
teenager could possibly be.

Her parents were kind and thoughtful. Good people. Where had they gone wrong with Bobby? What
had they done to drive him to drugs? They certainly
didn't want Vanessa to take the same path. Bobby
had one more month in rehab before he could return
home. Perhaps that would bring more equilibrium to
the household. Vanessa had respected her brother
until he went down the rabbit hole. She couldn't figure it out, either. The family hoped Bobby would return like his old-young self. The good news/bad
news was that the overdose episode had scared the
daylights out of him. He actually asked to go to a facility, and for as long as it took. The Rowans had a
positive attitude about the problem. Now if they
could only get past Vanessa's mood swings. But as
long as there were raging teenage hormones, it wasn't
going to be easy.

                        *   *   *

Vanessa was on her way home from school when she got a text from one of her friends in Portland:

Partizzle. 2nite. [meaning: Party tonight.]

Vanessa's mood was elevated.

WTPA? [meaning: Where The Party At?]

Response:

Bakers Shubs [meaning: Baker's House Party.]

Vanessa knew her parents would never allow her to go, so she took matters into her own hands. She made her way over to OR-99ES/Portland Road NE, where she would try to hitch a ride. If she was lucky, she'd be there in less than two hours.

A green pickup truck was exiting a gas station as she passed by. She stuck out her thumb, and the driver pulled over. A chubby face grinned through the open window. "Where you headed?" Vanessa recognized the S.E.I. logo and figured it was safe to climb in. As she scrambled into the passenger seat, the chubby guy grabbed a small parcel the size of a shoebox. The tape on the box caught on the seat belt buckle and ripped part of the top open. Dozens of glassine packages containing white pills spilled over her jeans and onto the floor mat. Before she could utter a word, the driver clocked her on the side of the head, knocking her out.

Bart had reacted reflexively. If you don't want somebody in your business, you send them to la-la land. He reached over her crumpled body, pulled the passenger door shut, and took off like a bat outta hell. He didn't know what he was going to do with her once she regained consciousness. Maybe shove one of the pills down her throat? Make it two. Take no chances.

He drove another mile and pulled onto a dirt road. He opened a bottle of water, ripped open one of the small bags, tilted her head back, shoved two pills into her mouth, and poured water down her throat. She gagged, spewing out water and wet pills. He made a second attempt. This time, he stuck his fingers into her mouth to hold down her tongue. He pushed the pills as far back as he could, poured water into her mouth, closed her jaw, and waited for her to swallow. A loud gulp confirmed mission accomplished. *That should take care of her for a good while.* Exactly how long that good while would be, Bart had no idea, but he figured it had to be at least an hour. If not, he'd repeat the process.

He watched his passenger for any signs of movement. None, but she was still breathing. He looked to see if any other vehicles were around. Nope. He got out of the truck and went to the bed, where he got some rope and duct tape. He hated to do it, but he had to be sure he had her under control before he called Dickie. And boy, was Dickie gonna be mad.

Mad was an understatement. Dickie was livid. Bart gave him the shortest version of what had transpired. "I picked up a hitchhiker, and the pill packets spilled all over the cab."

Dickie screamed every expletive in his personal

lexicon, words even Bart didn't understand. *Russian, maybe?* Bart didn't try to mount a defense. He simply listened to the diatribe until Dickie calmed down, which seemed to take forever.

"I want you to listen to me. You take her to the Inn in Salem. Put her in the storage room in the basement. The one with the bars on the window. And get someone to keep an eye on her. Ya hear me?"

"You bet, boss." Bart checked the fuel indicator. "What about the pills?"

"Put them back in the box, you idiot."

"I mean, should I deliver them?"

"With a bound and gagged teenager in your truck?" Dickie's volume was rising again. "You've got to get rid of her first."

"Got it, boss." Bart was happy the call had ended, even though Dickie had hung up before Bart finished his sentence. He grabbed a trash bag from the back and scooped up the pills, picking the small glycine bags from between the girl's legs. He actually felt creepy about doing it.

Once he was sure he'd accounted for all of the white tablets, minus the two half-melted ones and the two down her throat, he peeled off the dirt road and got on the interstate, keeping a constant eye on his new package.

Bart maintained the speed limit and followed all the laws of driving, using his blinker when changing lanes and constantly checking his rearview mirror. Beads of sweat were running down his face. His palms were clammy. He thought maybe some of that dope had gotten into his system from handling the pills. He strained his brain for the word: *trans-derema? Transdermo?* Whatever it was, he thought it might be affecting him. He cranked up the air conditioner and took a swig of the remaining water from the bottle. He looked over again. She was out cold.

An hour later, salty sweat continued to run from his forehead into his eyes. He kept wiping his face with the back of his sleeve. He needed some relief and reached over the seat with one arm to grab another bottle of water from the back of the cab. He used his back teeth to open it and then poured some on his head. Several drops splashed on the girl. She let out a soft moan and bobbed her head. Bart was about to have a freakout, but she settled down in a few seconds. He couldn't remember the last time he was this rattled. Hardly anything rattled Bart. That's why Dickie had him on his crew. But this? This was a unique kind of trouble. He might have a checkered past, but it had never included assault—or kidnapping, for that matter. Yep. Jacking a car was one thing, but jacking a teenager? Something entirely different. He could go to jail for life.

CHAPTER NINE

Salem

Myra and Annie dropped their luggage at the hotel and walked to the hospital, where they met up with Patricia and Benjamin. She looked haggard; he looked concerned. Myra sensed Benjamin was withholding something, but she'd get to that later. First things first—say hello to the patient. Patricia and Benjamin waited outside while Myra and Annie approached Mill's bed.

Milton Spangler was attached to several ports of dripping liquid, a heart monitor, and oxygen. Except for the slight color in his face, he looked like a corpse. Myra tried to hide her shock. Annie, on the other hand, leaned in and said in a loud whisper, "Milton Spangler. What on earth are you doing here?" He smiled. A good sign. He motioned for Myra and Annie to sit, but neither obliged.

Myra took his hand. "Mill. How are you feeling?"

His voice was raspy, but he managed to speak. "Better, but I feel like a pincushion. People keep jabbing, stabbing, and poking me."

Annie jerked her finger in the direction of the heart monitor. "Looks pretty steady." Then she smiled.

Milton motioned for Myra to get closer. "Something isn't right, Myra. The doctors said there was no damage and kept asking if I'd ingested something."

"What on earth could it have been?" Myra squinted at him.

"They don't know. That's why they're doing all that blood work. It's a wonder I have any left."

Annie leaned in. "Do they have any idea what caused the heart attack?"

Milton shook his head. "No. And I didn't eat or drink anything out of the ordinary."

Annie and Myra's cynical minds went to the same place. *Poison?* But who would do that? And why?

Mill slowly and quietly explained that he'd been about to have a meeting with Oliver and Benjamin when he collapsed. He had just taken a few sips of his brandy. Myra and Annie shot glances at each other. *But who? Patricia? Doubtful. Oliver? Maybe. Benjamin? Never. Or could it be someone else?*

Annie's first reaction was to get her hands on the glass Milton had been using, but it was most likely in the dishwasher if not back in the cabinet. Couldn't hurt to ask. But who? Benjamin. She'd have to trust him, and vice versa. Annie looked at Myra. "I'll be right back."

Annie went into the hallway, where Benjamin and Patricia were seated. "Patricia, why don't you go visit Milton and Myra." Patricia was zombie-like as she stood and moved slowly into Milton's room. As soon as she was out of earshot, Annie motioned for Benjamin to walk with her.

"What's up, Countess?" Benjamin was attempting to be cheerful.

"This may sound out of the ordinary, but is there any way that the glass your father was using might still be in his study?"

Benjamin gave her an odd look. "It's possible. I don't know if the staff cleaned the room or not."

"Is there any way you can find out?"

"Sure. But?" He stopped, remembering something the cardiologist had said. Then he nodded. He understood where Annie was going with this. He pulled his phone from his pocket and called the housekeeper. "Ruby? Did you clean up Dad's study the other night?"

Ruby hesitated. "Uh, not yet. I'm sorry. With everything happening the way it did . . ."

Benjamin interrupted her. "No problem, Ruby. It's okay. Please do not touch anything in the room, and lock the door until I get there."

Ruby answered immediately. "Of course, Benjamin. I'll do it right now."

Benjamin looked at Annie. "Want to go for a ride?"

"What kind of car do you have?" Annie grinned.

"A Lexus SUV."

"Bummer," Annie teased. "I was hoping for something sportier."

Benjamin laughed for the first time in two days. "I'll let them know we'll be back in a half hour."

Annie pulled on his arm. "No. Wait. We need a cover story."

"A what?" Benjamin smirked.

"Shush. I'll handle this." Annie stuck her head inside the doorway. "Benjamin and I have to run an errand. We'll be back shortly. You guys visit." Before anyone could say anything, Annie was scampering down the hall with Ben in tow.

When they got into the elevator, Benjamin looked at her. "What is going on?"

"We need to get our hands on that glass."

Benjamin nodded. Why hadn't he thought of that? Maybe it was because the idea of someone wanting to poison his father was the furthest thing from his mind. When the cardiologist had told him something didn't add up, he'd thought maybe his father had eaten or drunk something that had brought on the heart attack. Food poisoning, maybe.

It was a short drive to the Spangler mansion. When they arrived, there were several barking dogs inside. A woman opened the door. "Hi, Ruby. This is Annie De Silva. A friend of Pop's."

Annie hurriedly said, "Nice to meet you, Ruby," and followed Benjamin to the locked study, with Ruby following quickly behind her. She handed

Benjamin the key. Her hands were trembling. She was still shaky from the events two nights before.

"Thanks. You're a peach." He smiled at her.

Annie and Benjamin looked around the room. A Baccarat crystal tumbler lay on the rug next to one of the upholstered leather barrel chairs. It must have slipped out of Milton's hand, and no one took notice of it during the commotion. Annie turned to Benjamin. "Do you have a clean handkerchief?"

He reached into his jacket pocket and handed one to her. Annie gingerly picked up the glass at the bottom. There was little liquid left. Most had spilled. She looked at Benjamin, then at the spot on the rug. He let out a deep sigh. "Mother is going to kill me." He then proceeded to open his Swiss Army knife and make a four-by-four-inch cut in the rug.

"It's tiny enough," Annie said, as she pushed the barrel chair over a couple of inches to cover the hole. "See? All better."

Benjamin smirked. "You are as funny as Dad said."

Annie took a bow. "I met him on a few occasions. Lovely man. And we are going to get to the bottom of this." She wrapped the four-inch square piece of hand-knotted Serapi wool in her scarf. "No reason to upset Ruby." She winked. Now they had to find a lab that could test both for toxic substances. And fingerprints. Time to alert Charles and Fergus, but not until she had a little more privacy. She didn't know how far this would go and didn't want to entangle Benjamin at that particular moment.

"Listen. I know all of this seems a little bizarre,

but you're going to have to trust me. Okay?" Annie
looked into Benjamin's eyes.

"I have no idea what you're talking about, do I?"
It was a half-question.

"Correct. Leave this part of the mystery to me.
And Myra."

"Are you junior detectives?" Benjamin asked wryly.

"No. Not junior." Another wink, and she placed
the items in her tote bag. "Come on. They'll be wondering what we're up to."

"Yeah. So am I." Benjamin grinned. He was fine
with his father's friends playing out an Agatha
Christie story. He had a business to run and a duty to
look after the rest of the family. When they got back
into his car, he turned to Annie. "I'm glad you and
Myra are here. You add a bit of chaos, and it's good
to have some distractions, especially for Dad."

"We are happy to help in any way we can." Annie
smiled back as she clicked her seat belt. *Myra was
right. Something is definitely off.* Not that she had
any proof. Just a gut feeling. Same as Myra.

Annie's phone vibrated in her pocket. It was Maggie, confirming her flight time for the next morning.
Annie didn't want to talk in front of Benjamin, so she
sent her a text.

9:00AM wheels up. Talk later.

The first thing she was going to have Maggie do
was to go back and interview everyone again about
the disappearance of Vanessa Rowan. Tell them she
was doing a follow-up story on runaway teens. There
were plenty of them, so it wasn't a far-fetched idea.
The plan was for Maggie to speak to the Rowans

first and let them know she was looking into the situation further, and this wasn't merely a puff piece. She would also caution the Rowans not to discuss the case with anyone. If somebody asked why a reporter was coming around, the Rowans would give them Maggie's phone number, and they could ask her themselves. No reason for the Rowans to be go-betweens. They had enough to deal with.

When Benjamin and Annie returned to the hospital, Oliver was standing in the hallway, talking to his Aunt Helen. "Annie! How nice to see you!" Oliver was effusive. No surprise there. And Annie was going to use it.

"Oliver! Great to see you, too! You're looking dapper." Annie eyed his custom-fitted jeans and blazer, pinstriped shirt, the iconic sideways T on his Tom Ford belt, the Ferragamo driving shoes. She mentioned them right at the start. "I suppose you have a car to match?" She chuckled and nodded toward his feet.

Oliver snorted. "A Porsche 911 if that counts." He knew it did. At least for some people.

"Indeed it does. Maybe you can take me for a spin while I'm here."

"It would be my pleasure," Oliver gushed. A nurse shushed them. "Oops. Sorry." He flashed the woman one of his winning smiles. She blushed.

Myra came out of Milton's room. "We're going to let him get some rest."

"Good idea," Annie replied. She knew Myra was

chomping at the bit to find out where she and Benjamin had run off to. "We should probably head back to the hotel and get some dinner."

"I can have Ruby fix something," Patricia offered.

"Thank you, but it's been a long day for us," Myra replied. "We're still on East Coast time."

Patricia smiled. "Yes. Of course."

Oliver placed his arm around her shoulders. "I suppose we can all use a little rest."

Helen went into Milton's room to say a quick good night. Benjamin took his turn after Helen returned to the hallway. Milton looked up at his son and winked. "Everything is going to be alright, son."

"I am sure it will be. You rest up. We want you out of here." He leaned over the lines of fluid and kissed his father on the top of his head. "Stay out of trouble."

Milton wiggled his eyebrows. That's when Benjamin was sure his father was doing much better.

As the group rode down the elevator, they made plans for the following day. Annie was going to corner Oliver and get that ride he'd promised. A thrill ride in a sports car wasn't anything unusual for Annie. She wanted to flatter him into letting his guard down. Find out what skeletons he might have in his closet. He was just a little too slick for her liking.

Everyone agreed to meet at Patricia's for breakfast, and then they would split up visitation hours and whatever else needed to be taken care of.

Annie and Myra were barely out of the building when Myra grabbed Annie's bicep. "Spill it, girl."

Annie laughed out loud. "Spill it. And he did. And here we are!" She looked to see if anyone was watching, then held up the piece of rug by one of its corners. "And there's this." She gently removed the glass from her tote.

"You are so brilliant," Myra said, in awe.

"I know." Annie hooted as they gave each other a high five. She carefully placed the items back in her bag; they linked arms and made their way back to the hotel. "We're going to have to find a lab that can run tests on these."

Myra was already dialing Charles's number.

"Hello, love." It never failed. His British accent made Myra swoon, even after all these years.

"Charles, dear. We need you to find us a lab. We have reason to believe someone may have tried to poison Milton."

"Say what?" Charles's voice got louder.

"I told you something was fishy. Mill was drinking brandy or something just before he collapsed. He told me the doctors can't find the cause of the heart attack."

"And naturally, you and Annie think something is amiss?"

"Of course we do, Charles!" Myra was emphatic.

"I know, love. Just a bant. Tell me what you're looking for."

"That's just it. We don't know. I guess we should start with the usual suspects: arsenic, digitalis, washer fluid."

"I'll check with Fergus. I am sure we can find a place that can handle such a thing. It may take several days."

"Well, we'll just have to extend our stay until we get some results."

"Right-o," Charles replied.

"Let me speak to him, please," Annie told Myra. "Charles, I've asked Maggie to fly in tomorrow. She's going to do a follow-up story about the missing girl."

"Brilliant. We'll get cracking on our end."

"Thanks, dear," Myra said. "We'll chat in a bit."

"Tootles." Charles signed off.

When they arrived at their suite, Myra switched on the TV, and Annie ordered food to be delivered. There was a story on the news about the most recently missing girl with her photo. She waved at Annie. "Maggie needs to add this one to her list."

Annie nodded, and Myra took copious notes from what the news commentator had to say:

"Lorraine, Lori George was last seen going to work at the Cascade Inn outside Eugene. She had punched her timecard, showing she arrived at six-thirty in the morning. One of her coworkers said they saw her in the locker room when she changed into her uniform, but she has not been seen since. Lori is twenty years old. Dark complexion, shoulder-length black hair. Her personal belongings were left on the premises. If anyone has any information, please call this special hotline number: 1-800-FIND-HER."

A photo of a young woman who appeared to have American Indian heritage appeared on the screen above the number.

Annie finished placing their food order and walked over to where Myra was sitting. "Maggie is going to have her hands full. Should we call for some backup?"

Myra blinked several times. "Cascade Inn. That's one of Milton's places. There are several of them between Eugene and Vancouver, Canada. It's for truckers who want to take a break from the road for a good night's sleep in a real bed."

Annie twisted her mouth. "Coincidence?"

Myra raised an eyebrow. "I don't think so."

"Kathryn!" They both said her name at the same time.

"Let me see where she is." Myra punched Kathryn's speed-dial number and the speaker button.

A sleepy voice answered. "Hey, Myra. What's up?"

"I guess *you* are. Now, anyway." Myra chuckled. "We need you in Oregon."

"When?" a groggy Kathryn asked.

"Like now," Annie said.

"Oh, hey, Annie." They could hear Kathryn rustling. "I'm in Boston. I don't think I could get there in less than two days."

"Can you leave your rig there?" Annie asked.

"I think so." Kathryn yawned.

"Good. Maggie is coming out tomorrow morning. I'll book a flight for you, unless you can get to McLean by nine."

"Not by truck." Kathryn yawned again.

"Okay. I'll book a flight for you and text you the information."

"Not too early, please." Kathryn was not one for whining, but it was late, and she had been on the road for ten hours. It was more like pleading.

"I'll aim for noon," Annie said.

"Great. See you tomorrow." Kathryn had to move her rig to a long-term lot, then get herself to the airport. It might be a little tricky, since she was in the middle of nowhere, but they'd gotten through much worse.

Annie immediately called her concierge service and made a reservation for Kathryn on the noon flight from Boston to Portland and arranged for a car rental. If all went according to plan, Kathryn would be in Salem by dinnertime.

Myra and Annie sat at the table and began to put a strategy together. Myra would tell Milton to give Kathryn a job in his transportation department. She could be on the swing shift making a run if there was an issue with one of the other long-haulers, or if a short run was needed. She'd be on call.

Next was Maggie. Someone needed to be her wing person. Probably Izzie. Fergus and Charles would find a lab and then run background checks on the closest players in the company. Management, foremen, supervisors. Once they narrowed down the field, they'd need one of Avery Snowden's people to do surveillance. Either Sasha or Eileen. Maybe both. It would depend on what Fergus and Charles came up with.

"What about Izzie?" Myra asked. "We're going to need someone on the inside at the Cascade Inn where the other girl worked. Do you think Izzie would want to play housekeeper?"

"Let's ask her." Annie picked up her phone and called Izzie, putting her on speakerphone. A groggy voice came on the line.

"Annie. Everything alright?" Izzie cleared her throat.

"Yes, but we need some backup."

"What's going on?" Izzie was completely awake at that point.

"How would you like to be a chambermaid for a week or so?"

"A what?" Izzie was rubbing her eyes and her head.

Myra explained about Milton's heart attack, the first missing girl, and now the second.

"She went missing from work. She clocked in at the Cascade Inn in Eugene but seems to have vanished. Kathryn will be going to work in the transportation department; Maggie is going to retrace her previous interviews. We need someone to get inside the inn. See how that girl could have disappeared."

"Aha. Sure. I just got the Certificate of Occupancy for my latest job, so I'm free for a while. When do you want me to come out there?"

"Maggie is taking my jet tomorrow morning at nine. Can you make it?"

"Yes. Where is Kathryn?"

"She's in Boston, but I made a reservation for her to fly directly from there. Otherwise, it was going to get too complicated."

"Got it." Izzie sat up and tried to shove her Burmese dog, Rufus, out of the way. "Come on, pal. Move over."

"Are you harassing Abner again?" Annie chuckled.

"No. Abner is on an assignment. Rufus is taking up the entire bed."

"That's his job," Myra joked, knowing full well about dogs in the bed.

"I'll let Maggie know you'll be traveling with her, and then we'll rent a car for you. You'll need it to drive to Eugene."

"What about an interview for the job? Do I just show up?"

"We'll handle everything from here. Once you all arrive, we'll have a meeting in our room. Charles and Fergus are working on a few things already."

Izzie let out a chuckle. "You've been gone for what, twenty-four hours, and you're already in the thick of something. Why am I not surprised?"

"Exactly!" Annie said. "See you tomorrow. Safe travels."

It was the beginning of the Sisterhood's next mission. Even though they had very little information, they would unearth whatever shenanigans were happening in the Pacific Northwest.

CHAPTER TEN

Maggie Spritzer
And So It Begins

Maggie had been working for Annie for several years. She was one of Annie's top journalists. She was also a compulsive nail-biter when she wasn't looking for something to munch on. Petite, with red curly hair, she often had smudges of orange dust on her fingers and her cheeks from digging into the bottom of a bag of cheese puffs. She blamed her penchant for junk food on the thousands of hours she spent on stakeouts, always being the first to break a story. Being Annie's right-hand, Maggie was involved in most of the missions, and this one was no different.

When Vanessa Rowan went missing, and Myra's friend put up a reward, Annie sent Maggie to Salem to cover the story. In the beginning, the gas station attendant said he saw someone matching Vanessa's description getting into a pickup truck owned by the Spangler family. But when Maggie interviewed him, he was rather vague. He recalled someone in a green truck filling the tank with gas, and someone, maybe a girl, on the road. Maggie had plenty of experience with witnesses who recant or "don't remember." The attendant said he was busy that day, and maybe he got confused.

Several days later, Vanessa's parents received a text from Vanessa saying:

Sorry. I'm okay. On a journey. Love you. V.

After receiving the message, her parents notified the authorities. The local police thought there was no reason to continue the search, and they called it off. News coverage of the missing teen halted. But for the Rowans, it wasn't over. As far as they were concerned, their fourteen-year-old daughter was still missing. The idea that the tracking device had been turned off was a big red flag. Vanessa wasn't supposed to know her parents had installed it, but obviously, somebody knew. Whoever had done it didn't want anyone to know of the girl's whereabouts.

Julie Rowan had reached out to Vanessa's friends in Portland, but none of them had responded. When Maggie arrived the first time to cover the story, she drove to Portland to confront Vanessa's friends. Finally, one of the girls confessed that they had told Vanessa about a party, but she never showed up. They didn't want to get themselves or Vanessa in trouble. Maggie could have a hair-trigger temper at times, and almost blew a gasket when she discovered the friends were withholding vital information. Now she was glad to be back looking into the situation. This time, she was more than determined to uncover every clue and missing piece of the puzzle.

The plan was for Maggie to meet Annie's pilot and board the jet first thing the next morning. It would give the flight crew enough time to sleep and refuel. Annie sent Maggie a follow-up text:

There will be plenty of food on the plane.

Kathryn Lucas

Kathryn Lucas began her career as a cross-country long-hauler when her trucker husband Alan was diagnosed with MS and Parkinson's. He loved the road, and Kathryn wasn't going to let him spend the rest of whatever time he had left sitting in a wheelchair on the porch. Kathryn was determined to give Alan what he loved: the open road, with Kathryn driving the eighteen-wheeler.

One fateful evening when they were at a truck stop, three white-collar-professional men approached them. The men were part of a motorcycle group, and the macho high they got from riding their hogs gave them much too much bravado. They saw a vulnerable couple and took advantage of the situation in the most sickening way. The men raped Kathryn while her disabled husband was forced to watch. Alan died shortly after the horrific incident, and the men were never brought to justice. That was, until Kathryn met the Sisters, who had their own approach when it came to accountability. She was avenged, but also alone. She decided to continue as a cross-country trucker. It made her feel close to the man she'd loved. She was brash, blunt, and outspoken, but she would always have your back.

Isabelle Flanders

Isabelle "Izzie" Flanders knew all too well about injustice. Her successful architectural career had been destroyed by a colleague who framed her for drunk driving. Not only did she lose her license, but also her fiancé. Myra heard of her plight, and the women of the Sisterhood found the means to exonerate her. She now owned her own architectural firm and was married to a computer whiz named Abner who was teaching her lots of technology tricks that she'd been able to put to good use in the past. Now she would try her skills at housekeeping, which would make Abner laugh out loud. It was the one thing she really hated. But she'd do anything Annie or Myra would ask; anything *any* of her Sisters would ask.

There were two young women who were believed to be in peril. It was time to join forces again.

CHAPTER ELEVEN

Vanessa
The Escape

Vanessa wasn't sure how many days she had been locked in what appeared to be a basement in a commercial building. There was a small awning window near the ceiling. It had bars on the inside to allow the window to open a few inches, but she noticed the crank was missing. She thought she heard trucks pass by from time to time. Otherwise, it was quiet.

The room looked as if it had been set up for someone to crash for the night. It had two cots, an upholstered armchair, and a small table with a lamp. A microwave sat on a narrow shelf on the opposite wall next to a closet-sized toilet area with an accordion door. There was a step-in shower with a plastic curtain, a wall-hung sink, and a bare lightbulb over the spot where a mirror should have been. Privacy and luxury were not on the menu. Stairs led to a locked and bolted door. Once a day, someone would unlock it, open it quickly, and leave a tray of food for her. The timing of the food delivery was also difficult to track.

By the second day, she realized she was being held captive. But why? Was it the pills she'd seen tumble out of the box? Why would anyone care? She rubbed the side of her face. It felt swollen. She figured she probably had a bruise, as well. But there were no mirrors. No way to tell. Her wrists were still raw from the rope, and her lips still had some of the glue from the tape. During the last food drop, she ran up the stairs and started yelling. "Somebody please! Tell me what is going on!" But she got no answer. Her backpack was gone, and of course, her phone. All she had were the clothes she had been wearing.

By the second, or perhaps the third day, the armpits of her shirt were beginning to stink. And her underwear? She didn't want to think about it. After her sandwich was delivered, she took a quick shower. At least her body was clean. Her hair was a different story. She used the strong-smelling soap that got most of the oil out of her hair, but she didn't have a comb, and it dried in clumps around her head. She wanted to wash her clothes in the sink but feared being found naked would only add to her misery. Someone might think it was an invitation to rape. *Rape*. At least she hadn't been through that torture. Yet. In fact, the only harm done her was the initial punch in the face. *But why?*

The light from the window was her only point of

reference as to how many days she had been there. She surmised it was maybe a week. There was absolutely nothing for her to do except sleep, think, and eat the sandwiches she received every day.

It was early in the morning when she decided to pull the small table against the wall and try to see what was on the other side of the window. She moved it very quietly and hoisted herself up so that her eyes were above the window frame. And the bars. She could see a parking lot that butted against a dense wooded area. As she stood on her tiptoes, she saw heavy boots walking in her direction. She ducked and almost lost her balance, but her expertise on the balance beam from gymnastics saved her from falling off the table. The person kept walking and tossed a cigarette butt onto the pavement. She noticed several of them. Maybe this was where he took his break.

When he was long past the window, she returned the table to its original place, just in case someone appeared. The next morning, she did the same thing, trying to formulate some kind of pattern, a schedule besides the appearance of a tray of ham and cheese.

She willed herself to wake up at the same time, even though she had no idea what time that was. She'd go by the amount of light coming through the window. She listened for sounds. Nothing. She quietly moved the table to the window again. She saw the boots and the cigarette butts. She did this for several days before she realized it was a pattern. The Boots Man's pattern. He was the only one. There were no others loitering in the parking lot at night.

She checked. The lampposts lit the corners, and shadows were cast outside her window. It was eerily quiet.

As she began to step off the table, she grabbed one of the bars on the window. It was loose. She tugged on it. It wasn't her imagination. Little crumbles of concrete dribbled from the holes where the fasteners attached to the wall. She gave it another tug. More crumbles. But it was still intact. She needed something to wrench the fasteners away from the concrete. The lamp. It was one of those high-intensity lamps. If she could pull off the top, she might be able to use the lip to wedge it between the screws. But then she'd have no light at night except for the bare bulb over the sink. She decided to wait until the next morning, after her food drop and after Boots went off his break. Her mind was racing. She was formulating a plan. If she got caught, they would probably kill her. But if she stayed, she might be killed anyway. It was worth the effort.

That evening, she couldn't sleep. She was anticipating her escape. Once her food was delivered in the morning, she pulled the lamp apart. After Boots's cigarette, she moved the table and began to work on the bars. It took some time, but she was able to pull one side of the bars away from the window. It still wasn't enough to get through. She kept working on it until her muscles were beginning to burn. She had to take a rest, and it was getting dark. She would resume her project the next morning when she was fortified. *Ham and cheese. Couldn't they change it up a bit?*

The adrenaline she had been experiencing was spent. She was exhausted and fell into a deep sleep. The next morning, she jumped at the sound of a door slamming. Breakfast. Thankfully, no one came down the stairs. She waited for Boots to pass by, then continued chipping away at the bars. They were coming loose. She tugged. And again. With her last effort, they gave way, catapulting her off the table and onto the floor. She was stunned but unharmed. She waited and listened. Nothing. It occurred to her the room was soundproof. *But why?* That was one question she really didn't care about. It was the only thing in her favor at the moment.

Her next challenge was to open the window, but the crank had been removed. She was going to have to break it. That would have to wait until nightfall, when the building was empty or close to empty. She studied the twenty-four-by-thirty-inch glass. She looked around the room again. Could she break one of the legs off the table? But then what would she stand on? She looked over at the glaring bulb hanging over the sink. *Maybe the toilet seat?* She hurried over, got on the floor, and unfastened the screws. She'd try using the lid first. If that didn't work, she'd try using the seat.

After darkness fell, Vanessa moved the table to the wall, hopped up, and began to bang the lid against the glass. Over and over again. Her arms were getting tired. She raised the lid over her head one more time and thrust it at the glass. Little cracks began to run through the window. She jumped down and got the pillow off the cot, then returned to her perch.

She placed the pillow against the glass and gave it her last, best shove. Shards spilled in both directions. She stopped. Listened. Nothing. She took the pillowcase off the pillow and placed it over the jagged bottom edge of the frame. It wouldn't completely prevent her from getting cut, but it would help. She hoisted herself up and pulled herself through the window until her body lay flat on the asphalt. She looked around. No one. She scrambled toward the woods with blood running down her arms and her face, with branches lashing at her wounds as she ran for her life into the dark.

She finally stopped when she was deep into the woods. She listened. No one had followed her. She was exhausted. She leaned against a large western red cedar and slid to the ground. It was dark as pitch. She'd have to wait until dawn to get her bearings and hope she wouldn't encounter any creatures of the night, animal or human. The sound of a cracked branch stirred her awake. She was almost face-to-face with a deer. They looked at each other curiously; then the deer turned and continued on its journey.

CHAPTER TWELVE

The Next Day

A sliver of light shined through the canopy of trees, signaling it was a new day. Vanessa had no idea where she was, but she could now figure out the four cardinal directions. The question was, which one should she take? North? South? East? West? She listened for any sounds of human activity. Again, nothing. She was weary. Mentally and physically. Even if she knew where she was going, would she be able to make it out of these woods?

A barking dog in the distance got her attention. Again, she wondered if it was a good thing or a bad one. She would have to take her chances for the second time in two days. She had gotten this far. She had to carry on.

Vanessa moved slowly in the direction of the sound. Everything hurt. Her face. Her hands. Her legs. She was limping. Her bloodstained clothes stuck to her skin. She thought she might collapse when she heard a voice: "Hardy! Here boy!" Then the woman whistled and called again. "Hardy!"

Vanessa leaned against a tree with one arm and cried out. "Help! Somebody help me! Please!" In a few short seconds, a German shepherd was in front of her. He eyed her with interest. She looked at the dog. "Hello, Hardy. My name is Vanessa. Can you and your owner please help me?" The dog let out a loud bark, but it wasn't a threatening bark.

"Hardy! Where in the Sam-hill are you?" The woman's voice was almost pleasant.

The dog barked again. Vanessa could hear the crunching of leaves under someone's feet. She could see a person approaching wearing a red-and-black-checked flannel shirt. Vanessa thought about waving, but she feared a sudden move might startle the dog. Instead, she let out a limp cry. "Over here."

A woman with a walking stick moved quickly toward her. She gasped when she saw the shredded and stained young girl. "Oh, my Lord! Dear, are you alright? Silly question. Of course, you're not alright." She kneeled down in front of Vanessa. "What on earth happened? Can you stand up?"

Vanessa nodded. "I . . . I think so." The woman placed Vanessa's arm around her shoulders and helped her up.

"How did you get here?" the woman asked.

"I really don't know." Vanessa wasn't lying, but she wasn't sure how much she should or could reveal.

"Come along with me. My house isn't far."

The two gingerly and slowly made their way the quarter mile to the woman's farmhouse, with Hardy following behind. The woman yelled through the screen door. "Fred! Come out here. Give me a hand!" A man in his mid-forties appeared and opened the door as the woman helped Vanessa up the porch steps.

"Come. Sit here." The woman helped Vanessa into a comfortable chair while Fred went into the kitchen and returned with a few wet towels and a glass of water.

The woman began to wipe some of the blood off Vanessa's face and hands. "Dear, we need to get you to a hospital."

"No. No," Vanessa protested. "I need to talk to my mother."

"Of course you do, but you need medical help. The hospital will have to call your folks, but we can get you there pronto." The woman seemed very kind. "What's your name, dear?"

Vanessa wasn't sure what she should say. What if these people were with the ones who'd abducted her? She made something up. She'd deal with the truth at the hospital. "Biddie."

"Okay, now, Biddie. Tell me, how on earth did you get this way?"

Vanessa strained her brain to come up with a story. "I was hiking with some friends, and I got lost."

"Didn't you have a phone? Surely all people your age have phones."

Vanessa thought again. "We decided we would unplug for the afternoon."

"Why didn't they come looking for you?"

Vanessa let out a little chuckle. "I don't know, but they're gonna hear it from me when I see them." She was beginning to get comfortable with her story.

"By the way, I'm Gloria. This is my hubby, Fred. You've already met Hardy."

"Thank you, Gloria. Thank you, Fred. And thank you, Hardy. I could have been lost forever." Vanessa sat up straight. "Could I please use your bathroom?"

"Of course, dear. Straight down the hall. Fred will get the truck ready."

Vanessa was shocked at her reflection in the mirror. She was almost unrecognizable. The ham and cheese sandwiches might have contained a lot of fat and carbs, but she had definitely lost weight. She looked scrawny. And dirty. She'd tried to wash her hair during her captivity, but cheap soap and no conditioner gave her head a matted look. She was surely a hot mess. She splashed more water on her face and dried it with toilet paper. She didn't want to get any more blood on these nice people's towels.

When she returned to the living room, Gloria was waiting with Hardy. "Come on, dear. Let's get you fixed up." The passenger door of the vehicle was open. Vanessa stepped in and buckled up. She had a flashback of her last encounter in a stranger's vehicle. She started to tremble. Fred patted her arm gently. "You're gonna be alright."

Fred tried a little small talk. "You from around here?" Vanessa answered with monosyllabic words.

"No."

"Visiting friends?"

"Yes."

Fred decided some music might be helpful and turned on the radio. "Got any favorites?"

"Not really."

"Okay. How about some oldies?"

For Fred, *oldies* meant songs like "The Tide Is High" by Blondie and "Tainted Love" by Soft Cell. Vanessa wasn't particularly a fan of either, but it was better than trying to have a conversation with someone she really didn't want to talk to.

When they arrived at the hospital emergency entrance, Fred got out and began to walk over to the passenger door. Vanessa noticed a sticker on the driver's side window. Even though it was facing out, she could see the large S.E.I. letters. She panicked. Before Fred could reach the door handle, Vanessa flung the door open, hitting Fred in the face.

"What the—?" Fred was stunned.

Vanessa shot out of the truck like a bullet, ran into the emergency room, and hid behind a curtain. A nurse ran after her as Fred stomped into the area. Vanessa put her fingers to her lips, begging the nurse not to say anything. By the looks of her, Vanessa could have been the victim of assault. In many ways, she was. The nurse mouthed the words "Stay here" and went out to the waiting area, where Fred stood, flummoxed.

"Where'd she go?"

"Who?" the nurse asked.

"The girl. Biddie."

"Biddie who?" the nurse asked.

The man shrugged.

"Are you a relative?"

"No. My wife found her in the woods."

The nurse thought that was a very unlikely story. "And what is your name, sir?"

"Fred. Fred Sorenson."

"Okay, Mr. Sorenson. If we find this girl, Biddie, we will give you a call. In the meantime, why don't you fill out the form at the nurse's station?"

"Say what?" Fred was totally confused at this point. He was simply trying to do a good deed.

"Fill out the form, please. If Biddie shows up and needs medical attention, we will know the person to contact."

Fred was already stunned and annoyed. He turned and left without filling out anything.

The nurse went back to the cubby where the girl waited. "Now please tell me who you are and what happened."

Vanessa still wasn't sure whom to trust. She'd been abducted by someone in an S.E.I. truck and then rescued by a family with a similar truck. Was this some kind of nightmare? She had to get to a phone. Call her mom.

"I'll be right back." The nurse went back to the desk to get some forms for Vanessa to fill out.

Vanessa was breathing heavily when she heard a man's loud voice in the reception area. "Howdy. We're here to see Mr. Milton Spangler." Vanessa's heart started to race. She peered around the curtain and saw two men. She recognized one of them. The man who'd punched her in the face.

She looked for a means to escape. Anything to get far away from them. She ran toward the nearest exit and began to climb the stairs. Once again, she had no idea where she was headed, but she kept on going.

When she reached the third floor, she slowly opened the door. A woman wearing rhinestone cowboy boots was standing outside one of the patients' rooms. The woman looked in Vanessa's direction and raised an eyebrow. Then she gave Vanessa a look that indicated the woman might recognize her. The problem was determining whether or not the rhinestone cowgirl was friend or foe. Vanessa ducked back into the stairwell and peered through the thick, wired glass window in the steel door. She watched as the woman came toward her. She turned and began to run farther up the stairs. Her legs ached. Her head hurt.

Annie had been standing outside Milton's room talking fast cars with Oliver when they were interrupted by two of his employees. At the same time, she noticed a raggedy-looking girl peeking her head out from the exit to the stairs. Annie moved swiftly to the stairwell and yanked open the door. In spite of the lacerations, there was something familiar about the girl's face. She heard footsteps a flight above. Annie gave a loud whisper. "Vanessa? Is that you? My name is Annie. I can help you."

The stairwell was quiet except for a slight whimper. Annie made her way up the next flight of stairs. Slumped in a corner was a disheveled, ragged young teenager. Her face and hands were covered with cuts and scratches. Her clothes were bloodstained, and her greasy hair lay flat against her skull. Tears were running down her cheeks.

Annie crouched down and put her arms around the sobbing girl. She took Vanessa's face into her hands. "It's going to be alright." The girl leaned into Annie and continued to cry.

Annie rocked her back and forth until the youth regained some equanimity. "Come on. Let's get you fixed up." Annie helped the girl from the floor and slowly walked her down a flight of stairs. As Annie opened the door, two men were standing outside Milton's room. The girl gasped and tried to pull away from Annie. The two moved quickly back into the stairwell. Annie hugged her. "It's okay, sweetie. Tell me. What did you see?"

The girl was trembling. "That man." She was breathing heavily.

"What man?"

"The man who took me." She looked at Annie with pleading eyes. "Please don't let him take me again."

"Oh, that is definitely not going to happen." Annie peered through the glass. "Which one?"

"The . . . the chubby one." Vanessa inched her way back into a corner.

Annie's wheels were turning as she recalled some of the information that was initially brought forth when Vanessa disappeared: something about a green pickup truck with the S.E.I. logo. The two men outside in the hallway were visiting Milton. When Maggie had interviewed the gas station attendant, he'd recanted his story. *Was he paid to do it?* Annie was going to get to the bottom of this, but the girl needed to see a doctor first.

Annie put both hands on Vanessa's shoulders. "I want you to listen to me carefully. Are you able to climb down a flight of stairs?"

"I—I think so." Vanessa stuttered.

"Good. Go down the stairs, and I will meet you outside the stairwell." She looked deep into Vanessa's eyes. "Okay?"

"Okay," Vanessa replied meekly.

"Good girl. See you in a jiff." Annie watched the girl move slowly to the next level; then she looked through the glass. The men must have gone into Milton's room. Annie went to check, but they were gone. Myra was the only one in the room with Milton.

"Hey, sorry. Oliver and I were chatting about cars, and then I got a call."

"Everything alright?" Myra eyed her carefully.

"Yes, but where did my racing pal go?" she asked.

"Oliver had to take care of some business," Milton said hoarsely.

I bet he does, Annie thought to herself. "I have to run an errand. I promised Maggie a bunch of snacks."

"Maggie?" Milton furrowed his brow.

"Maggie Spritzer. She's my best journalist. She was inspired by the story of Vanessa Rowan. Too many teenage runaways. She's doing a follow-up and expanding the subject."

"Good idea. I'm still befuddled about all that," Milton said softly.

"Hopefully, the girl will turn up. Many of them do," Myra said.

You have no idea how right you are, Annie thought again.

"Do you want me to go with you?" Myra asked.

Annie knew she was going to need help. What kind of help was still unknown, but help she would surely need.

"I'll go to the hotel and get the car so you can visit with Mill for a few more minutes." Annie made a slight gesture toward the pocket where she kept her phone. Myra gave her a look saying she understood. Annie was going to call her or text her shortly.

"Bye, Milton. We'll see you later." Annie kissed the back of his hand.

"Yes, you will." He smiled. He was feeling much better with all the positive energy around him.

Annie moved quickly when she spotted an empty gurney. She commandeered it as if it were something she did every day. No one questioned the woman in the white cashmere jacket. Had they been looking closely, they would have noticed the luxe fabric, plus those wild boots. But everyone was in a hurry at the hospital, including Annie.

She pushed the stretcher down the hall, in the opposite direction from Milton's room. There was a large elevator a few feet away. Someone was coming toward her with a patient attached to an I.V. Annie stepped out of the way and let them take the first car. She hoped the girl hadn't fled the scene. When the next elevator car arrived, she made sure she was the first to get in, and quickly punched the button to close the door. Then she pushed the button for the second floor. When the doors opened, she wheeled the gurney as quickly as she could without arousing suspicion. She checked in all directions and then pushed it against the wall. She opened the stairwell door, hoping the girl would be there. Annie let out a huge sigh of relief when she saw Vanessa huddled in the corner.

"You doing okay?" she asked the girl.

Vanessa nodded.

"Good." Annie peeked through the glass. Several people were milling about. "This is going to require some super-fast action. I am going to go back into the hallway. When I knock on the door, you slip out and then climb under the sheet." She watched Vanessa blink a few times. "Are you up for this?"

Vanessa nodded and repeated, "Knock. Out. Sheet."

"Good girl." She looked at Vanessa again for confirmation. Vanessa nodded.

Annie checked the hallway again. Everyone was rushing to their own emergencies. Her caper should escape everyone's notice. Should they succeed. She took a deep breath. "Okay. Here we go."

Annie quickly opened the door and slid along the wall. No one was watching. She knocked. The door opened and closed like lightning. Before Annie could even blink, there was a big white lump on the gurney. Annie had no idea where she was going to take the girl, but it had to be far away from the two men.

About half an hour earlier, Myra had been sitting with Milton while Oliver and Annie were chatting in the hallway about fast cars. An aide came in and said there were two more gentlemen here to see Mr. Spangler. "Mr. Dickie and Bart."

Oliver excused himself from Annie and approached the men halfway down the hall. He was beginning to have an anxiety attack. And he hadn't had any blow that day. Yet. He realized he had been going through a lot more than usual over the past month or so. Yep, he was blowing his money. Then it occurred to him, maybe that's why they call it "blow." *Huh.* Dickie and Bart came rambling in his direction. Oliver's collar began to get hot. He was beginning to sweat. Was he sure he hadn't had a hit of cocaine yet? "You boys got any news for me?"

Dickie scratched his head. "No sign of the package."

"And tell me again, how did this happen?"

Dickie shot Bart a look. "You tell 'im."

"Like I said, I picked up a hitchhiker, the box ripped open." He looked down at the floor. This was not easy. How do you explain a major disaster to your boss? A disaster that could send all of them to jail.

Oliver was getting impatient. "And then what happened, Bart?" An attendant gave him an annoyed look, obviously about to ask them to be quiet.

Oliver motioned for the three of them to step farther away.

"Then I kinda panicked, I guess."

"You guess," Oliver repeated sarcastically.

"I guess my instincts kicked in, and I punched her."

"Cut to the chase, Bart."

"Chase? There was no chase."

Oliver shut his eyes and bit the inside of his upper lip. He spoke slowly. "Get to the point, Bart. How did she get away?"

"She musta pulled the bars out of the wall, broke the window, and crawled out."

"Listen, Captain Obvious, I know she pulled the bars and broke the window. I want to know how she was able to pull the bars away from the wall."

Bart looked sheepish. "When we were working on it, I knew you was in a hurry. We ran out of the right kind of compound and used some spackle to hold it for the time being."

"Spackle. You used spackle."

"Yes, sir." Bart had thought it was a good idea at the time. "It was only supposed to be there until we could get back and finish it proper. But then this happened with the girl."

"And it hadn't occurred to you that she might be able to pull the bars out?"

"No, sir. She was a scrawny thing. Besides, I

guess I was kinda distracted about the whole thing, you know, getting her situated."

"I am certain that is not the end of the story." Oliver shot him a dagger-sharp look.

"Right. So, she musta been standing on the table."

"And it was with sheer force she was able to pull the bars away from the wall?"

"Well, no. She musta broke the lamp and used part of it to jiggle it. We found a piece of it on the floor next to the table."

"The table that was below the window."

"Right."

"Obviously, you hadn't thought about the many ways she could get out?"

"Like I said, she was a bit of a thing."

"A very clever one." Oliver was clenching his teeth at that point. "Find her." He spun on the heels of his Ferragamos and marched back into his father's private suite.

"Can we at least say hello?" Dickie called from the hallway.

This time, the orderly asked him to, "Please keep your voice down."

"Come on, Bart. We have a hunting trip to go on."

Milton was sitting up in bed. Most of the color had returned to his cheeks. "Everything alright, son?"

Myra took her cue and moved to the alcove sitting area of the room.

"Yeah. Just a situation with one of the drivers."

"Oh, that reminds me. I have a new employee lined up for you."

Oliver looked perplexed. "A new employee? For what?"

"Well, you're always saying how you seem to be short on drivers every so often. I thought having someone on swing shift would be a good solution. She can have a flexible schedule and be on-call."

Oliver still hadn't absorbed the word *she*. He blinked. "She? You hired a she?"

"Come on, lad. Don't be so chauvinistic. Plenty of women are long-haulers. I'm really surprised at you."

"You're right, Dad. I guess this just came as a surprise. I mean, you hiring someone without talking to me about it."

"I still own the company, son. I had a day or so to do a lot of thinking. We are a profitable enterprise. There is no reason why you should have to worry about having a route covered. You have a lot of things to manage. We lose business when we can't find a driver. We can afford another hire."

Oliver changed his tune. "I appreciate you thinking about my workload. And you're right. Adding staff can only add to our productivity."

"Now that's what I'm talking about." Milton smiled as Myra looked on.

"Listen, Pop. I've got a few things I need to get to. I'll stop by later." He leaned over and gave his father a kiss on the head.

When Oliver left the room, Myra resumed her

position in the chair next to Milton's bed. "That was very good timing, Mill."

"Thank you, Myra." He reached over with an IV-free hand.

"I wonder where Annie went?" Myra said. "I'll be right back." When Myra got up, her phone vibrated. She looked at the signs that said NO CELL PHONE USE. She texted Annie.

Where R U?

In the basement.

Where???

Basement.

You okay?

Yes. Got Vanessa.

What???

Take elevator to basement. Go 2 laundry room.

Myra looked down at her phone. She could not imagine what Annie was talking about. "Mill, Annie has the car downstairs. I'll be back later today."

"No worries. I'm not going anywhere." He let out a little chuckle. "Myra?"

"Yes, Mill?"

"I'm really glad you're here."

"Me, too. Don't go away." She moved quickly to the elevator and took it to the lower level. The room was massive, with dozens of washing machines lined along one wall. White curtains separated different folding areas. Myra looked around. She didn't want to call out anybody's name. She knew she wasn't supposed to be there and surely didn't want to draw attention to herself. As she looked around, she caught a quick glimmer of light out of the corner of her eye. *Ha. I'll never mock those boots again.* Myra scurried to the curtain that shielded Annie and Vanessa from the rest of the room.

"Myra, meet our new friend, Vanessa. Vanessa, meet my bestie and partner, Myra."

Vanessa gave Myra a weak smile. "Nice to meet you, I think."

"We need to get her to a doctor, but there were some men on the floor that she wanted to avoid."

"On Milton's floor?" Myra sounded surprised.

"Yes, long story. Vanessa has been filling me in. So, how do we get a physician to take care of this little mess without parental consent?"

"Her parents. They need to know she's okay," Myra said.

"Well, she doesn't look all that okay to me."

"Oh, you know what I mean." Myra gave a *tsk-tsk*.

"How about this? We call her parents and have them call their PCP, and they can all meet us here?"

"Or maybe we can bring her to his office?" Myra offered.

Vanessa watched the two of them as if she were at a tennis match. "Excuse me. But can we please call my parents?" she said softly.

"Absolutely." Annie whipped out her phone. It had rhinestones to match her boots.

"Ah, you brought the fancy one," Myra teased.

"I am a fashion icon." Annie perched her phone in the palm of one hand. "Phone number, honey."

Vanessa thought hard. "I usually just tell my phone to call Mom. Or call Dad."

The two women looked at each other and shook their heads. "Kids."

"My dad's office. Google 'Rowan Plumbing Supplies'."

Annie typed quickly. The contact information appeared almost instantly. Technology certainly had its good points. She hit the round circle with the phone icon that said CALL.

After two rings, a pleasant man's voice answered. "Rowan Plumbing Supplies."

"May I speak with Mr. Rowan?" Annie asked.

"Speaking. How can I help you?"

Annie handed the phone to Vanessa. "Daddy? Daddy!"

"Nessie, honey, is that really you?" The man was gasping.

"Yes, Daddy. It's me." Tears were running down her face.

"Where are you?"

"In the hospital."

"Oh my Lord. Where?"

"Well, I'm not exactly in as in 'in' the hospital. I'm in the building."

Annie motioned for Vanessa to give her the phone. "Daddy, there is a lady here who wants to speak to you."

"Hello, Mr. Rowan. My name is Annie De Silva. It's a very long story, but we found Vanessa in the stairwell of the hospital. She's been through quite a traumatic experience and needs some medical attention. Her injuries aren't life-threatening, but she's pretty banged up."

"What do you want me to do? Where should I go?"

"Can you phone your primary care physician and ask him if we can all meet at his office, including your wife?"

"Of course. Of course. Let me put you on hold while I try to get him on the other line."

Annie smiled and nodded at Myra and Vanessa. It seemed like an eternity before Mark Rowan returned to the line. "He can see us as soon as you can get her there."

"What is the address?" Annie repeated what he was saying as Myra put it into her phone's GPS.

Myra looked up. "Should take us about twenty minutes."

Annie recited the information. "Mr. Rowan, please do not tell anyone about this. Just tell your wife you need her to meet you at the doctor's office. You needed stitches or something. We don't want anyone to overhear that we have her. We'll see you shortly." She handed the phone back to Vanessa.

"I love you, Daddy."

"I love you, too."

The next challenge was to get Vanessa out of the hospital without anyone recognizing her.

"What about our bags?" Myra said to Annie. "Your tote, my purse?"

"You go upstairs and get them." Annie turned to look at Vanessa. "I have to get the car. Do you think you can walk a few blocks? Or do you want to wait on a side street?"

"I'll wait wherever you tell me." Vanessa finally believed she was being rescued.

Annie looked at Vanessa. "Come on. There's probably something you can put on over your clothes." They began to search the massive laundry room, walking along row after row of curtained areas. They finally came across sets of scrubs hanging on a rack. Annie grabbed a size small and tossed it at Vanessa. "This should fit."

Vanessa quickly obliged. Annie thought about Vanessa's hair. She took one of the shirts off a hanger and put it on Vanessa's head with the bottom around the edge of her face and hairline. She took the sleeves, tied them together, and wrapped them around the top of Vanessa's head. Odd-looking headgear, but not surprising for Oregon.

Annie took Vanessa's hand, and they followed the exit signs. When they reached the service dock, Annie stopped. "You wait right here. I'll be back in a jiffy." Minutes later, Annie was peeling around the corner and pulling up before Vanessa. "Get in the back. Stay down. We've gotta get Myra. She's at the main entrance." Vanessa piled in and followed Annie's instructions. Annie whipped around the block and came to a screeching halt in front of Myra.

"Where is she?" Myra's voice was edgy.

Annie jerked her thumb toward the back seat.

"Excellent!"

Vanessa was baffled. *Who are these two middle-aged maniacs?* She was sure of two things: she was going to see her parents very soon, and she would never, ever eat a ham and cheese sandwich again.

CHAPTER THIRTEEN

How It Started

Cabo San Lucas
Two Years Before

Oliver was treating himself to a week at Pueblo Bonito Sunset Beach Resort, located at the western tip of Baja in Cabo San Lucas, on fifty acres of private beach. Situated within Quivira Los Cabos, it overlooked the Pacific Ocean on a secluded private coastal bluff. He booked a suite. He liked the idea of having exclusive access to the Jack Nicklaus Signature golf course at Quivira Golf Club. That would surely be something to brag about.

Oliver had been burning through his inheritance quickly and figured this might be the last lavish vacation he could take for a while unless he could devise another means of increasing his income. He was already working on manipulating the invoices for the tree restorations. He had a deal with one of the accounts receivable personnel at the supplier. The invoices would say "fifty," but he actually received thirty. S.E.I. paid the supplier for fifty, then the supplier would split the difference with Oliver. A little extra cash in each of their pockets. How the guy at the supplier finagled the extra cash from the invoice was none of Oliver's concern. He never complained, so it must not have been a problem. If you're smart enough, embezzlement is one way to increase your income. This scheme of Oliver's was giving him a few extra thousand dollars every month. Enough to cover his new cocaine use. He refused to call it a "habit." He viewed it as a "recreational sport." Plus, if he was with other people, he'd gladly share if they felt so inclined. Real addicts don't share. At least that was what he told himself.

One late afternoon, after a round of golf, Oliver pulled up a seat at a patio bar. The view was breathtaking. A man around Oliver's age sat a few stools away. He was even more richly dressed than Oliver. The man wore white linen pants, with an untucked silk tropical print shirt, silver-tone Saint Laurent boat shoes, a huge gold coin pinky ring on his left hand, and a watch with a diamond-encrusted bezel. It was the Iced-Out Rolex, arm bling to the stars. Oliver figured it cost just under 20,000 dollars. Not overly ostentatious, but a little too much sparkle for his taste. He preferred his Rolex Submariner, or his Breitling Top Time B01. Both cost about the same as the other gentleman's shiny wristwear. The man turned and nodded at Oliver. Oliver noticed the man was also wearing a heavy-link gold chain around his neck, a gold and diamond ID bracelet, plus another gold ring. The second ring was a David Yurman Memento Mori Skull Ring with black pavé diamonds. Oliver nodded in return while he calculated the amount of gold the man carried. Probably could buy that Lamborghini he had been eyeing. But it was the skull ring that caught his attention. It could represent a number of things. *Interesting.* He watched the gold-clad man ask the bartender to buy him a drink. "Tears of Llorona Extra Anejo," Oliver told the bartender.

"I see you have good taste." The man in gold smiled.

"Thank you." Oliver held up his glass to toast the man. "Oliver. Oliver Spangler."

The man nodded. "Ernesto Calavera."

Oliver remembered his short stint studying Spanish. *Calavera* meant skull. He was intrigued; got up from his seat and approached the man. "Mind if I join you?"

"Please. Sit down." Ernesto had a refined Spanish accent. "Did I see you playing golf this afternoon?" he asked.

Oliver chuckled. "Guilty. But I doubt anyone would call that playing. I was fumbling."

"We all have our own talents." The man took a swig of the liquid in his glass. It was a similar amber color as Oliver's.

"What are you drinking, Ernesto?"

"Marques de Casa Noble Anejo."

"Also a man of good taste." Oliver lifted his glass.

"We enjoy fine things." Ernesto swept his arm around, indicating the view.

"Indeed," Oliver answered. "You here alone?"

"Yes. I come here to get away from the busy life. And you?"

"Same thing." It occurred to Oliver that the man might be hitting on him, or perhaps the man thought Oliver was flirting. "Lots of beautiful women here." He figured that would notify Ernesto of his preference for females.

"Ah. Yes. But alas, most are here with their very rich boyfriends."

Oliver chuckled, held his shot glass up, and nodded to the bartender. "We'll have another round." He turned to Ernesto. "This one is on me."

The two men chatted for about an hour. Nothing of major importance. A little politics, a little celebrity nonsense. Then the conversation turned to what the men did professionally.

"Spangler Enterprises." Oliver was on his fourth shot of tequila. "Up in the Pacific Northwest. Oregon, actually."

"Ah. I see your trucks. Lumber?"

"Yep." Oliver was wondering if he should order another round. "And you?"

"Import and export," Ernesto replied.

Oliver was now leaning with his elbow on the bar, his head resting on his fist. "Maybe we can do some business together. What do you import and export?"

Ernesto looked around the bar area. No one was paying attention. "I do custom jobs."

Oliver was intrigued. "Oh, do tell."

Ernesto signaled for the check. "Come. Let's take a walk."

Oliver hoped he wasn't being set up to get mugged. He had a very nice buzz on. He got up from his stool and followed Ernesto to a secluded area. A large boulder blocked them from the hotel patio. Ernesto pulled out a familiar brown bottle. "Care to join me?"

Oliver thought he'd died and gone to heaven. The scenery was spectacular, his head was floating, and now he was going to be exceptionally high. "Don't mind if I do."

Ernesto stared at the seascape. "I wonder if you could do me a favor." He realized he was taking a big chance, but that's where big rewards come from.

"I can try." Oliver was squinting at the sun.

"I have a package I need delivered to a friend in Vancouver, Canada." His eyes were as dark as coal, burning into Oliver's head.

"How big?"

The man turned away. "Maybe the size of a Louis Vuitton Rolling Trunk. Fifteen by twenty-two inches. It could easily be stored in one of your trucks behind the driver."

Oliver thought he was catching on. "And you don't want to send this via regular shipping?"

"That is correct, my friend." Ernesto faced him again. "I will make it worth your while. Say five thousand U.S. dollars. Cash?"

"Am I not supposed to know what is in the case?"

"You are a very smart fellow." Ernesto placed his hand on Oliver's shoulder.

"Explain the logistics. How do we get the case to my truck? And then where does it go?"

"You have deliveries to Mexico, correct?"

"Absolutely."

"The truck must return, no?"

"Of course."

"Do they bring products back to your Pacific Northwest?"

"We try not to have our guys dead-head it. Waste of fuel, so we work with some of the local produce companies and bring their goods up north."

"Excellent. In which cities do your trucks stop?"

"It all depends. There is a lot of new construction in Querétaro, and of course Mexico City."

"Ah. Perfect. So if someone should meet one of your trucks, say off I-25, they would be able to deliver it to you?"

"That's entirely possible. But then what do I do with it?"

"You arrange for another truck to bring it to Canada."

"It sounds a bit risky." Oliver continued to squint. He wasn't sure if it was the sun, or if his brain was trying to wrap itself around what Ernesto was proposing.

"Life is risky, my friend." Ernesto took another hit from the brown bottle and handed it to Oliver.

"True." Oliver thought for a moment. "Would this be a one-time thing?"

"It doesn't have to be." Ernesto turned toward the sunset again.

"How many trips do you envision?"

"Perhaps one per week."

Oliver was struggling with the math in his fuzzy head. "I'll have to give a vig to the drivers."

"Of course. Is it possible to have the same drivers? We do not want too many people in our business. That is, if you want to do business with me."

"Sounds intriguing." Oliver was sobering up with the idea of making so much money. "We'd have to take measures to mitigate the hazards. Can you increase the fee?"

"I would have to increase the size of the package. Can you fit something eighteen by twenty-six?"

"Should be no problem."

"*Bueno*. Then you shall get seventy-five hundred dollars for every delivery. One per week. You will receive your money when the trunk arrives in Canada."

"How about the border? I have a trucker's inn just outside Blaine, Washington. That could be a drop-off point."

"Even better." Ernesto smiled. He knew he had found the right person. He had an ongoing relationship with several of the hotel personnel here. They had alerted him that a single, rich American male was staying at the resort, and his family business was transportation.

"I shall call you in the morning. We will have breakfast and discuss the details. For now, I must leave. I have a dinner engagement." He held out his hand to Oliver. "I look forward to a long business relationship with you."

"Same here." Oliver shook his hand vigorously. This was the miracle he had been hoping for. Thirty-thousand extra smackeroos each month. He'd have to pick two drivers he could trust implicitly. He figured a weekly bonus of a grand would surely buy their loyalty. Then he rethought the math. Maybe that was too much. Five hundred? That was two thousand a month. Surely enough to buy a good amount of allegiance.

For two years, Oliver raked in over a quarter of a million dollars. But problems started to develop. Opioid-related deaths were on the rise. It had become an epidemic among people between the ages of twenty-five and fifty-four, with non-pharmaceutical fentanyl contributing to seventy-nine percent of the overdoses. There were lawsuits against drug manufacturers for creating the addiction, but illegal drugs had also flooded the market, from China to Mexico to Canada, and the U.S., with Canada having a seventeen-percent increase in illegal use. The DEA was cracking down on the opium superhighways in conjunction with Canada's special task force.

Ernesto had been arrested several times, but because of his own backwater arrangements, he skated. After his third encounter with law enforcement, he knew he was coming perilously close to losing his freedom, especially if he was caught in the U.S. He decided it was time to retire and move to

Cuba. He wasn't about to start looking for his replacement. Getting out of the business and out of
the country was his priority.

Ernesto was moving out of the picture, and Oliver
could not afford to take his chances with someone
else. The drug cartels were ferocious and territorial.
They would think nothing of shooting a driver in the
head, then dismembering them for the rest of the
narcoterrorists and narcoterrorist wannabes to see.
The business had become too dangerous, and Oliver
liked his face. He didn't want to end up mutilated
and dumped in a ditch. The idea made him shudder.
Even though he wasn't the one transporting the
goods, he was the capo-di-capo. He was just another
moving target.

Ernesto's departure could ruin all of Oliver's
plans, so they made an arrangement. Ernesto introduced Oliver to a handful of people he trusted, and
Ernesto would serve as an adviser from his new location for a small fee. Ernesto's men needed to get
out of Mexico, and Oliver arranged for them to
travel to Oregon. The plan was to give them room
and board, and a counterfeit green card so they
could move about in the community without draw-
ing attention to themselves. The green cards were
only supposed to be shown in case of an emergency.
Oliver paid the men cash, and they lived in the base-
ments of the Cascade Inns. In exchange, they brought
pill- and powder-making skills and the knowledge
of how to manufacture counterfeit fentanyl, fifty

times more potent than heroin and one hundred times more potent than morphine. They brought the recipe, and it wasn't difficult for Oliver to procure the ingredients.

But now there was a problem. Two, actually. Someone had stumbled into the first lab, and someone had gotten a look at the goods.

CHAPTER FOURTEEN

Later That Day

Fergus and Charles had their phone on speaker. Annie and Myra were also on speaker, and Annie was talking a mile a minute.

"Slow down, love," Fergus said calmly. "Start from the beginning."

Annie proceeded to explain that she had literally found the missing teen huddled in a stairwell. Apparently, she'd managed to escape from where she was being held. They were at the physician's office, waiting for Vanessa's parents to arrive.

"I say, it didn't take long for you to find yourselves in the weeds, eh?" Charles chuckled.

"Charles, this is not funny." Myra leaned into the phone.

"Sorry. Go on, then."

"We only have bits and pieces of the story. The

poor girl is exhausted, and we figured it would be better if she told all of us the story at the same time."

"Have you notified the police?" Charles asked.

Myra and Annie looked toward Vanessa, who shook her head vigorously. "Not yet, Charles. There is reason to believe there are some shady things going on here, and we don't know who is on which side of the fence. We should have more details shortly. Meanwhile . . ." Annie disconnected the speaker, picked up the phone, and moved to the bathroom. She didn't want Vanessa to hear the rest of the conversation. Not that Vanessa would know what Annie was proposing, but the less Vanessa knew, the better, for her own safety and peace of mind.

When Annie felt she couldn't be heard by the others, she continued the conversation. "Charles, Fergus, I need you to do some background checks on Milton's boys, Benjamin and Oliver, but it's Oliver I'm mostly focused on. Also, check on Patricia, Milton's wife. There's something going on there, too. Not sure what it is, but she is hiding something. Then there's Dickie Morton, and a fellow named Bart. I didn't get his last name, but I'm sure you can find out easily enough."

"Right-o," Fergus said. "We'll get on it. Do we need to contact anyone else?"

"We're thinking maybe have Sasha and Eileen come out here to tail whoever comes up looking suspicious."

"Aye. Dodgy, bounders, and buggers," Charles added.

"Yep. Now get busy. We have an injured girl to

tend to." Annie ended the call and returned to the examining room. Myra and a nurse were helping Vanessa peel off her clothes; then the nurse began to give Vanessa a sponge bath to clean the wounds.

"You're a bit of a mess, eh?" The nurse had a noticeable Canadian accent. She smiled at Vanessa. "You're gonna be right as rain. Some of this is gonna sting, and you might need a little stitchin' up, but we won't be able to tell until we get all this blood off ya." She tossed the soiled sponges into a biohazard bin. "But we have to wait for yer mum and dad before we can do anything else. They gave us permission over the phone to clean you up, so that's what I'm doin'."

Vanessa squeezed Myra's hand as the nurse continued to wipe her lacerations with antiseptic. There were long scratches on her skin as well as deeper pierce marks. Vanessa squeaked and flinched at every stroke of the cotton balls. It was an excruciating twenty minutes for the girl, but she was beginning to feel better and cleaner in the paper gown she was wearing. She ran her fingers through the glob of hair on her head. She looked up at Annie. "Rat's nest?"

"Nah. Maybe a mouse." Annie smiled. She was confident Vanessa would be alright, at least physically.

There was a soft rap on the door. Myra went over and answered it. Before she could step out of the way, a woman and a man pushed past her. "Vanessa!

Honey! Oh, my! Geez! Are you alright?" It was hard to tell who was saying what at the moment. The nurse tried to hold them back.

"Ah, Mr. and Mrs. Rowan? Can you just let me finish up here? We don't want any of these cuts to get infected."

"Oh, of course!" Julie Rowan tucked herself against her husband's chest.

Someone tapped on the door. It was Dr. Foster. "How is everybody doing in here? Vanessa, you're looking a little better than you did when you first got here."

"I'm feeling better too, thanks." Vanessa managed a weak smile.

"Nurse Crowley took care of all your cuts, did she?"

"Yep."

"Just take a look at this one, doc." Nurse Crowley moved part of the paper robe aside. There was a significant gash running from Vanessa's knee to her ankle. He scrutinized the wound. "No stitches, but you're going to have to keep it clean and bandaged."

"I'll make sure of it, doctor," Julie replied.

"Good. I'll let Nurse Crowley finish, and then you can be on your way."

Mark Rowan had tears in his eyes. In fact, everyone did. The nurse finished cleaning, dressing, and bandaging the wounds. "Okay, you can hug now! But be careful."

The three Rowans were clasped together, rocking back and forth. After several minutes, Mark and Julie stepped back. Julie wiped her nose. "How did you find her?" she asked the two women who were watching the family reunion.

"Maybe we should let Vanessa start," Annie suggested. "By the way, I am Annie De Silva, and this is my friend Myra Rutledge."

"Oh, so sorry!" Mark blurted, introducing himself and his wife. "That was pretty rude of us. Thank you. Thank you." Julie nodded in agreement.

Annie looked at Vanessa. "You up for it, sweetie?" Vanessa bobbed her head and gulped. "I was on my way home from school when Morgan sent a text about a party. I was really, really mad at you guys, and I knew you wouldn't let me go."

Julie was about to say something, but Myra gently placed her hand on Julie's arm, as if to say, *Let her tell the story*.

"Anyway, I'm really, really sorry." She started to sniffle. Annie handed her a box of tissues. "I figured I'd hitch a ride to Portland."

Again, Julie was about to interrupt with a parental warning, but Myra put a stop to it once more.

"A green pickup truck stopped. It had the S.E.I. logo, so I figured it was safe. It's the Spanglers, you know." She took a breath and a drink of water from a plastic cup. "When I got in, there was a box on the seat. The guy tried to move it out of the way, and the tape or something got caught on the seat belt buckle clasp. A bunch of bags with white pills spilled out." She paused.

"Then what happened?" Mark asked.

"Then I guess he punched me in the face or something, because when I woke up, I was in a basement somewhere. My wrists hurt, and my face was stinging."

"Probably from the tape they had over your mouth."

"I guess so." She shrugged. "There weren't any mirrors."

Annie pulled up a stool. "Can you describe the place?"

"Shouldn't we call the police?" Mark interrupted.

"Mr. Rowan, we don't know how or who may be involved in this situation right now," Myra explained. "It would be advisable for everyone to keep this among the five of us, until we can do some further assessment."

"Oh, are you private investigators?" Mark asked.

"Federal marshals?" Julie's turn.

"No, neither," Myra answered. "What I can tell you is that we have a network of individuals who can explore the situation."

"A private company?" Mark kept pushing.

"Mr. Rowan, it would be best if you would only concern yourself with your daughter's well-being right now. She has been through a very traumatic experience. We also don't want anyone to know Vanessa has been found."

"Why not?" Mark asked with a furrowed brow.

"As I mentioned, we don't know how far-reaching the wrongdoing goes, and we do not want to alert anyone who may have had a hand in this. If I recall, the search was cancelled when you got a bogus text from Vanessa."

"That's right, Mark," Julie agreed.

"So, let's keep all of you out of the public eye for a bit," Myra suggested.

Annie snapped her fingers. "I have an idea." She turned to the parents. "Can the two of you take a few days off from work?"

They looked at each other and shrugged. "I suppose so. Why?"

"How would you like to go to Lake Tahoe for a couple of days?"

"We can't afford a trip like that."

"You don't have to. Myra and I will take care of all the details."

"I don't understand," Julie said.

"In addition to our network, we have resources that can provide safe and discreet travel and accommodations."

The Rowans had no idea who they were dealing with, and the expressions on their faces showed tremendous confusion.

"I know it may be difficult, but you're going to have to trust us."

Mark and Julie had bewildered looks until Vanessa spoke up. "Mom, Dad, these ladies helped me. I wouldn't be here now if it weren't for them." She let out a huge sigh. "I don't know where I'd be, actually. I mean for real. If that guy at the hospital saw me, I could be back in that dungeon, or worse." Her eyes were pleading.

"I guess we're going to have to go along with Vanessa," Mark said. Julie agreed. "So what should we do next?"

"The two of you go back to your house and pack

a bag for each of you. Say three or four days' worth of clothes. Bring some shampoo and a blow-dryer so Vanessa doesn't look like grunge gone overboard. Also, a baseball cap and sunglasses for her. Bring everything back here. Once we get Vanessa sorted, someone will drive you to the airport."

"What about tickets?" Mark asked.

"You'll be on my private jet, which is about to land any minute now." She checked her watch. "My pilot will bring you to Tahoe, where a car will meet you at the airport. A person will have a sign that says 'Lady's Friends'."

Myra jumped in. "My dog. We don't want your names to be bandied about anywhere."

Vanessa giggled. "I like dogs."

Annie continued with the instructions. "The driver will take you to a privately owned lodge. We don't want you to stay at a hotel. Vanessa could be recognized. The kitchen will be stocked with food and beverages. There are fresh linens on the beds and in the bathrooms. There's Wi-Fi and several televisions, also a bookcase filled with a large selection of reading material. There's a laundry room behind the kitchen. If you need anything, there is a name and number next to a landline in the kitchen. Please, whatever you do, do not go off the property. As I said, we can't risk someone identifying you." Annie observed the baffled expressions on their faces. "Any questions?" There were none. "Okay, then. All good?"

"Very good," Mark said, and shook Annie's hand and then Myra's.

"Be back in a flash." Julie smiled at her daughter and gave her a gentle hug.

Once they were gone, Vanessa looked up at Myra and Annie. "Who are you guys?"

Myra and Annie hooted. "Just a couple of gals, visiting a friend in Oregon."

Within the hour, the Rowans returned with a couple of weekender bags, shampoo, and blow-dryer. Mark waited outside while Julie tended to her daughter. Julie helped her off the table and walked her over to the sink, where she proceeded to wash Vanessa's hair, being mindful not to get soap near the bandages. "I remember when you used to love having me do this."

"Me too, Mom." Vanessa had never imagined she would be this happy to be around her parents.

Annie called a car service to bring the Rowans to the airport. "We'll be in touch. We're going to need more information, but it's better if you skedaddle for now." She looked at Julie. "Let me put my number in your phone and vice versa. I want you to contact me if anything, and I do mean anything, comes up that doesn't seem right." Annie and Myra looked everyone in the eye.

"Got it?" Myra asked.

"Got it!" Vanessa said.

Myra and Annie held up their hands for a group high five. They walked the family to the car. "Try to relax and enjoy each other."

Vanessa wrapped her arms around Annie. "Thanks for saving me." Then she turned to Myra and gave her a big hug.

"You guys rule!"

The family settled into the back seat while the driver stowed their luggage in the trunk. Everyone waved as they pulled away.

Annie's phone vibrated. Maggie had sent Annie a text:

On our way to hotel. See you in a bit.

Annie sent a text to the pilot: **Reserved rooms for you and the crew at the Marriott Grand. Fifteen minutes from airport. Enjoy & relax. Don't want you going over your limit.**

Shortly thereafter, she got a reply: **Thanks, boss. Will do.**

"Whew. We really have a lot of people to keep track of, don't we?" Annie let out a big gush of air.

"And we're just getting started." Myra put her arm around her friend.

CHAPTER FIFTEEN
Lorraine (Lori) George

Lori George was a descendant of the Kalapuya tribe. The Kalapuyans were an Indigenous group whose traditional homelands were in the Elk Creek and Willamette watersheds of Western Oregon. They were hunters and gatherers between the Cascades and coastal regions. The Kalapuyans did not belong to a single homogeneous tribal association, but rather to multiple autonomous divisions speaking three closely related languages. The tribe made use of obsidian, a natural resource from the volcanic rock of the Cascades, turning the rock into spearheads, arrowheads, and other projectile shapes. Today, there were approximately 4,000 Kalapuyan descendants enrolled in the Confederated Tribe of the Grand Ronde Community of Oregon, about an hour southwest of Eugene.

* * *

Lori's grandfather was more adventurous than his contemporaries. He wanted his family to be integrated into the rest of society and went to work at a local sawmill. It was eventually taken over by the Spangler family and renamed Geiser Creek Lumber and Millwork. Her grandfather was determined that his children and their children would have a good education and stressed the importance of knowledge. He would remind them, "Knowledge is Power." Lori's father went on to become a professor of Native American Studies at Portland State University. Lori was enrolled at Lane Community College with an interest in the hospitality business. Her goal was to continue her education and work toward a bachelor's degree.

Because of her grandfather's long-standing employment with Geiser Creek and S.E.I., Lori got a part-time job working at one of the Cascade Inns. Her advisor thought it would be beneficial for her student record, and it was conveniently located, just a few miles from the school. She managed to schedule her work and studies without too much conflict.

It was her first week on her own at the Cascade Inn outside Eugene. She had just finished her two-week training program and was anxious to get started. She went to the locker room, changed into her uniform, and punched in. There was a bulletin board with everyone's assignments.

Lori George
Room trolley—for first floor
Guest towels

Sheets
Cleaning towels and paper towels
Disinfectant spray cleaner

Lori knew the job wasn't very glamorous, but this was one of the best ways to learn about hospitality: from the ground floor up.

The laundry room was well-stocked with fresh linens, but as she looked around, she didn't see any cleaning products. *Probably stored somewhere else.* The first door she tried had the maintenance supplies for the heavy-duty cleaning. The next one was an electrical closet. She went back to the laundry room and spotted a door in the back. "Huh." She didn't recall seeing it there before. She shrugged and walked toward it. When she got to the door, she noticed there was a touch pad combination lock. *Odd for cleaning products.* Maybe it was where they kept the security monitors? The door was slightly ajar. *Odd for something that needs to be locked up.* But then again, some products are corrosive. Perhaps someone opened the door so she could get what she needed. She pushed it open wide, never expecting to see what was in front of her.

The sight took several moments to register, long enough for one of the men to grab her arms, spin her around, and band her arms together with the coated rope they used to tie the bundles. One of them stuffed a pair of latex gloves in her mouth; then they covered her head with a cloth. *A sheet, perhaps?* She was trying not to panic. Breathing was difficult with the gloves in her mouth and the sheet over her head. She knew it was futile to fight them. She inhaled slowly through her nose. Someone picked her up. She thought they put her on one of the service carts. Another sheet. She could tell they were wheeling her somewhere. Then she was in the back of a vehicle. After what she thought might be about twenty minutes, the vehicle stopped. She could hear voices, but not what they were saying. Then she heard a loud engine start. Like a big truck. She heard the sounds of metal. Maybe a lock. Then the sound of a sliding door. Someone picked her up and handed her to someone else. The sound of beeping began. Like the sound when a truck is backing up. The person who was holding her stepped onto something metal. They began to move. The motion felt like an elevator, but then it stopped short. She could smell the familiar scent of fresh-cut lumber through the sheet. It was almost like the mill where her grandfather used to work. The man kept moving. She counted his steps. Maybe ten or twelve feet. He set her down on a metal floor. A truck bed? He reached under the sheet and pulled the gloves out of her mouth. "Do not say a word. Do not scream." Lori was not about to test those menacing words. Then she heard footsteps retreating. More beeping, and then the sound of a rolling lift gate, and a bolt. About a minute or so later, the driver engaged the truck, and it began to move. She closed her eyes and prayed: for someone to save her, or to be able to escape. But Lori was a bright, realistic young woman. She knew the odds were not in favor of either. At least not for the moment. She fell into a deep sleep, imagining her ancestors watching over her.

Lori woke with a pain in her neck. She tried to get into a more comfortable position when the truck came to a stop. Several minutes later, she heard men's voices again. And again, she could not make out what they were saying. She heard the sound of the lift gate rolling open. The same man who'd put her into the truck picked her up again. She could tell by his size and his smell. For a moment, she was glad to have a sheet over her head.

He carried her over his shoulder like a firefighter. She could hear doors opening and closing. He finally set her down on something that felt like a wooden chair. She felt his face come closer. "Okay, listen here, little lady. I am going to loosen the ropes around your hands and feet. It'll take you a little time to wiggle out of them. You can take the thing off your head when your hands are free. I'll be gone by then. But I warn you. Don't try anything funny if you want to live to see another sunrise. Now nod your head if you understand."

Lori nodded slowly. The man tugged on the knots. Lori could feel the tension release around her wrists. "You're gonna have to work on them ankles yourself." Within moments, the man left the room. She could hear several locks shutting her in.

Growing up, she and her grandfather used to go camping and fishing. He taught her many types of knots. She felt around with her fingers to see if she could recognize this one. It was a classic constrictor knot, the type that gets tighter when you pull, but the man had loosened it. She went slowly, methodically, until she was able to disentangle herself. She pulled the sheet off her head. She was in a totally enclosed room. The walls looked like they were made of some kind of plastic. Something you could vacuum or wipe down easily. She guessed the space was the size of a two-car garage. It had a long metal table and the chair she was sitting on. It reminded her of the interrogation rooms on *Law & Order*. Then it hit her. It looked like the secret room she'd stumbled upon, except without the men in white and the white bricks they were feeding into some kind of slicing machine. She hadn't had time to absorb her surroundings before she was whisked away. The only other thing she spotted was a door with a combination digital lock.

Lori tried to figure out how long it took to get to wherever she was, but she had dozed off. She didn't know if it was day or night. And worst of all, she didn't know if someone was going to kill her. She shuddered when she heard the click of the lock on the door. A man appeared wearing a ski mask. He looked like an executioner. Lori was horrified. She closed her eyes and started to pray.

The man spoke. "You must tell me who you are working for."

Lori stuttered. "I . . . I work for Cascade Inns."

"That's what your uniform might say, but who else are you working for?"

"No . . . no one."

"Don't lie, little lady. We want to know who you're working for and what you were looking for."

Lori shook her head. "Honestly. I work for Cascade Inns. I was looking for cleaning products."

"How did you find the door?"

"The door?" she asked.

"Don't play cute. The door. D-O-O-R. Door."

"It was open."

"I doubt that."

"How else would I have gotten in?"

"That's what we want to know."

"I swear, it was slightly open."

"Well, missy, that's just not possible."

Lori strained her brain, trying to remember every little detail. Maybe then he'd believe her. "It looked like another door panel was slid open. Like a closet door. Then there was the door with the lock, but it was open. Open a few inches."

"And why did you go inside?"

"I told you. I was looking for cleaning products." She fished in her pocket and pulled out her assignment sheet. It was as crumpled as she was. She held it out.

He snatched it from her hand. "Lori George. So that's the name you're using."

"That *is* my name. Lorraine George. People call me Lori."

"How long you been working at the Cascade?"

"This was my first week. I was in training for two weeks." Her voice was even. She knew she had to convince this man that she wasn't anything other than a college student, working part-time at an inn so she could put it on her résumé when she finished school.

"You always break into locked doors?" he asked.

"It wasn't locked, I swear!"

"But it had a lock on it, didn't it?"

"Well, yes."

"And you thought it was okay to just mosey into the room?"

"Please, mister. *Please* believe me. I figured they kept it locked because of the caustic cleaning solutions, and that somebody opened it so we could get what we needed for our shift."

The man wasn't convinced, although it was a rather convincing story. But if she was working for a competitor, then she was a pro at her con game. "You sit tight. Don't go anywhere." He grunted a snarky laugh and left the room. The sound of the lock engaging was deafening. Or so it seemed.

Several minutes later, another man entered the room. This one was wearing a screaming skeleton mask. He grilled her just as the previous man had. As menacing as he looked, she still had nothing more to tell him and repeated her story. He got up, left, and locked the door. She feared what was going to happen next.

CHAPTER SIXTEEN

Back At The Grand Hotel

Myra and Annie went back to the hotel to meet up with Maggie and Izzie. It was a couple of hours before Kathryn would arrive. Annie ordered lunch. A lot of it. She didn't want to hear Maggie whining. Annie had no idea where that girl put all the food she ate. She was barely a hundred and ten pounds, and much of that was her curly red hair.

Sometime after one o'clock, the two women arrived. The bellman brought Maggie and Izzie's luggage to their room while Maggie and Izzie went to Annie and Myra's. Lots of hugs, high fives, and fist bumps—otherwise, it just wouldn't be "a proper greeting," as Charles would say.

Maggie flopped herself down on the sofa and grabbed a handful of grapes that were sitting on the coffee table. She held a bunch out in front of her. "See? Healthier."

"For now," Izzie teased.

"Oh, shut it."

"You should have seen her on the plane," Izzie mocked. "Annie, you'd better tell the flight crew they're going to have to stock up on snacks."

Maggie rolled her eyes. "And beverages. Geez. I've been here for what, like four minutes, and it's dogpile on Maggie."

Everyone laughed. It was an ongoing joke. You'd think they'd get tired of teasing her, but it was just too easy.

"As long as you wash your hands first." Annie shot her a look.

"Oops." Maggie dashed toward the bathroom. "I used to be so vigilant during the pandemic, but everyone seems to have slacked off, including me. Be right back." She brought the grapes with her.

Several minutes later, the phone rang, informing Annie that their lunch was being delivered. Myra opened the door. "Oh, my. Is all of that for us?" She stared at the tray piled with boxed lunches.

Annie cleared her throat and jerked her finger toward the bathroom.

"I heard that!" Maggie called from inside.

"I didn't say a word," Annie chided.

As soon as Maggie returned to the seating area, Annie and Myra fired up their laptops. Myra spoke. "Girls, you may want to log in, as well. We can catch Kathryn up when she gets here."

Maggie and Izzie followed suit and pulled their laptops out from their tote bags.

Everyone logged in to the VPN, and within a few

seconds, all of them were connected to Charles and Fergus via a secure chatroom. They exchanged greetings; then Annie ran the meeting.

"This morning we located Vanessa Rowan, the missing fourteen-year-old. She's doing okay."

Gasps of excitement filled the cyber airwaves. "Where? How?" Maggie's journalist instincts kicked in.

Annie explained how she'd discovered Vanessa in the hospital stairwell. The girl had managed to escape the night before and was found by a woman in the woods. The woman brought Vanessa to her house, where she and her husband decided to take her to the hospital. But Vanessa noticed the truck had an S.E.I. logo, the same logo she'd seen when she was abducted. She panicked and ran off through the hospital. "I spotted her as she was about to exit onto the floor where Milton's room was, but she bolted back into the stairwell. I was able to convince her that I was there to help. Myra and I smuggled her out of the hospital, phoned her parents and her PCP. She explained that she was hitchhiking and got into a pickup truck. There was a box on the seat, but it caught on something and the top ripped off, exposing bags of white pills. The man punched her in the face, and when she regained consciousness, she was being held in a basement room." Annie went on to finish Vanessa's story of her escape, explaining that she and her family have been reunited and are en route to Lake Tahoe.

"So she ran from the couple because she saw the logo." Maggie was taking copious notes.

"Yes, she didn't know if she could trust them."

"But they brought her to the hospital," Izzie mused.

"Keep in mind she had been terribly traumatized. I probably would have done the same thing," Maggie added.

"True."

"Has anyone notified the police that she's been found?" Izzie asked.

"Not yet. We think there is more to unveil, and if the Spanglers are involved, they may have their tentacles everywhere," Myra replied.

Charles chimed in. "Fergus is running some background on the sons. So far, Benjamin has come up clean as a whistle, but Oliver seems to have been able to get his hands on a lot of cash over the past two years. We don't believe it's due to genius investing, as there is no paper trail. Just lots of receipts for high-end goods."

"Not surprising," Annie said.

"We're also taking a look at the company's transactions. There are some questionable purchases that do not appear to be in accordance with their business enterprises," Fergus added.

"What do you mean?" Myra asked.

"There's an invoice for four-piperidone hydrochloride," Fergus replied.

"What is that exactly?" Myra asked.

"It's a chemical used in the synthetic manufacturing of opioids. Fentanyl, to be exact."

"The pills," Myra and Annie said in unison.

"So, what's next?" Izzie asked.

Annie began to tick off the next few steps:

"Myra is going to ask Milton to offer you a job as the regional facilities director for the Cascade Inns. That will give you the opportunity to scope them out. Download the blueprints and surreptitiously check them against the physical buildings."

"What about Oliver? Isn't he in charge of them?" Maggie asked.

"We're going to use the same story we came up with for Kathryn," Myra added. "Since Milton is recuperating, he wants his sons to have some backup. Enter Kathryn in transportation, and Izzie at the Cascade Inns."

Annie continued. "Maggie, you're going to re-interview everyone. You're doing a follow-up story about runaways. That will fit in with the latest disappearance of Lori George."

"Does Milton know about it?" Izzie asked.

"I'm not sure. The news broke the night he was taken to the hospital, and he didn't mention it this morning. We left around noon, but that's a good point," Myra said. "We'll take a quick ride over to the hospital and let him know about the news. Or maybe that's not a good idea. It may upset him."

"Yes, but he has to be part of the ruse. He has to tell his sons he wants additional staffing until he's up and about. It's the only way Izzie can be introduced into the scheme."

"Do you think he'll go for it?" Charles asked.

"He doesn't have a choice. He knows something isn't right, and I know he wants answers," Myra said.

"He may not like what we find out," Izzie added.

"It's better that he knows the truth than have things blow up in his face," Myra pointed out.

"And he knows about us?" Maggie pointed to everyone.

"More or less," Myra replied. "Surely not everything, but he trusts me enough."

"He specifically asked for Myra. He had his wife call her." Charles had a mischievous look in his eyes.

Myra pushed her face closer to the camera on her laptop. "You put a lid on it, mister."

"Lid on what?" Maggie asked.

"None of your business." Myra and Annie, again, in unison.

"Oooh." Maggie pursed her lips.

Annie shot her a look that emphasized *drop it*. She quickly changed the subject. "What about a lab? We have to find out if there was anything in his drink."

"Right," Charles said. "We're waiting for a callback from a place just north of Salem. Should be shortly."

"Do you want Avery to send his people?" Fergus asked.

Everyone glanced around the room. Fergus continued. "Probably a good idea. We're still digging into the financials. Oliver has been spending a lot of money on renovations for the Cascade Inns. We're checking invoices for anything dodgy."

"What about employees? Those two in the hallway this morning that got run off by Oliver—Dickie and Bart. Need to get a handle on them," Annie added.

"Sasha and Eileen?"

"Probably a good bet," Charles said. "Put one of them on that Dickie fellow, and the other on Bart. Any man who would hit a young girl needs some follow-up."

"We'll get there, Charles." Myra raised her eyebrows. "But what about Oliver? Someone needs to track him."

Annie waved her hand. "He likes fast cars. *I* like fast cars. I'll ask him to take me to the speedway and try to get a peek at his daily routine. Maybe we'll go test-drive a few Maseratis or Ferraris. He'll love it. I'll be his best chum."

"Brilliant!" Fergus chimed in. "Let someone else wet his pants while you drive." Everyone broke out laughing. Most of them never wanted to be in a car when Annie was behind the wheel. Not that she was careless. She simply liked to put the pedal to the metal and zoom off. Even her golf cart was built with a fast engine for her trips back and forth to Myra and Charles's house.

Annie checked the time. "We should go back to the hospital and get Milton up to speed."

"See? That word again." Fergus chuckled.

"Maggie, Izzie, you guys hang out here. Go to the spa while you have the chance. Tomorrow we're going to hit the ground running," Annie said. "By the way, the Spanglers will refer to you as 'Isabelle,' and Kathryn, you're going to be 'Kat.'"

"That's leaves me," Myra said. "How should I play it?"

"Spend some time with Benjamin and Danielle,

especially Danielle. Nothing like getting insight from an in-law. Get her take on the family," Maggie suggested.

"Excellent idea. Maybe I'll suggest we have lunch while Benjamin is at the office." Myra nodded.

"What time is Kathryn arriving?" Charles asked.

"Around five," Annie answered.

"Right. Go on, then. We'll catch up, say, nine o'clock? That will give us time to check in with Avery," Charles said.

"Midnight, your time, correct?" Myra wanted to confirm.

"Correct, my dear. I'll stay up late for you any night." Charles gave her a wicked grin.

"Oh, Charles, you're going to make me blush." Myra giggled.

"Alrighty. Go on then." Charles signed off.

Fergus followed with "Mind as you go."

"Alright. Let's head over to the hospital. We'll be back in an hour or so," Annie said.

"Just in time for a massage," Izzie added.

"I'm doing a facial," Maggie said. "My face keeps breaking out. I thought this would end after my teens."

"It will end when you give up junk food." Annie smirked.

"Yeah. Yeah." Maggie huffed.

"See you in a few," Annie said as she grabbed her tote. Myra followed.

*   *   *

When they arrived at the hospital, Patricia was on her way out. "I need to pick up a few things for Milton. They are going to keep him for two more days, and then he can go home. But he cannot go back to work. Not even part-time." Patricia sighed. "Lately, he's been rather antsy. I don't think he'll be able to follow his doctor's instructions."

Perfect timing, Myra thought. "Perhaps he can take on some temporary help."

"Yes, he mentioned something about a woman who was going to be an on-call driver. I'm not sure what that means, but if it helps Oliver, then it should be fine."

Myra noticed she made no remark about Benjamin.

"You can hide his phone." Annie smiled.

Patricia still had that same vacuous expression on her face that she'd worn for almost two days. She turned and walked away without saying goodbye.

"I wonder what's going on with her besides Milton's health scare? She should be happy he'll be going home," Annie whispered to Myra.

"I was thinking the same thing." Myra stroked her pearls.

The two women entered the private suite, where Milton was sitting up in his bed. "Hello, ladies." He smiled. "Is it still alright to call you 'ladies'?"

Myra and Annie gave each other a quizzical look. "Yes, it's fine."

"Well, you never know these days. People are very touchy. You can't even tell a woman she looks pretty without getting yourself into trouble," Milton replied.

"You can tell us we're pretty any time. In fact, you can call us gals, too!" Annie laughed.

"Or girls." Myra grinned.

Myra turned and closed the door. Milton tilted his head. "What are the two of you up to?"

"You need to call a meeting with Benjamin and Oliver."

"I tried that two nights ago, and look where it got me." He lifted the arm that was attached to an I.V. drip.

"Exactly," Annie said. "You had a reason to meet with them, correct?"

Myra placed her hand on Annie's forearm. "Be careful. We don't want him to get riled up." She looked at his heart monitor. It was steady.

Milton took a big inhale and let it out slowly. "If you must know, there have been some strange purchases lately. Our business manager brought it to my attention. They were charged to the Cascade Inn account. It had something to do with the renovations. I wanted to see if Oliver or Benjamin were aware of them."

"Did Oliver know that's what you were going to discuss?"

"I told the boys I wanted to go over the costs for the renovations, but I didn't mention the specific charges."

Annie thought about the brandy tumbler. Charles and Fergus had to find a lab quickly before anything that could be of use degraded.

"Milton, did you see the news last night?"

"No. Why?"

"A young woman from Eugene is missing," Annie said cautiously.

"A woman? Another one?" He struggled to re-arrange his position.

"Yes, unfortunately." Myra was fussing with her pearls again.

"Wait a minute." Milton winced. "Oliver told me one of our employees walked off the job. In Eugene."

"Not exactly, Milton." Myra was going at a care-ful pace. "It was a young woman. Lori George. She punched in, but no one saw her."

Milton furrowed his brow. "What do you mean no one saw her? Oliver told me she punched her timecard and then walked out."

"Not according to her parents." Myra waited for a reaction.

"So the woman showed up at the inn in Eugene, but then left without telling anyone?" Milton was having difficulty reconciling what his son had told him with what Myra was telling him. "But Oliver said . . ."

"Maybe he didn't want to upset you," Myra added.

"This is terrible news. Two missing girls that are associated with our company." He shook his head. "Are you sure?"

"We saw her parents on TV last night. You know the police won't let you file a missing persons report until the person has been gone for over twenty-four hours. So her parents took to social media, and the local television station picked up the story. Her parents insisted Lori would never vanish into thin air. She's of Kalapuya heritage. They think it could be a cultural incident. They may call in the Bureau of Indian Affairs."

"Oh, dear. We can't let that happen." Milton's monitor bleeped.

"What if you have Benjamin meet with her family and let them know you are doing everything in your power to help find her?"

"A lot of good it did when I announced the reward for the Rowan girl." He sighed heavily.

Annie looked at Myra. Maybe it was time to tell Milton that the girl had been found and was being kept in a safe place. Annie shook her head slightly. The fewer people who knew, the better. "Maggie is going to do a follow-up story. Vanessa had friends in Portland. Maybe she's staying with one of them on the Q.T."

"That would be a good resolution to this situation," Milton replied. "I don't know how her parents are coping."

"Let's keep thinking good thoughts," Myra said softly.

"So now what is it exactly you need me to do?" Milton snapped to attention.

"In addition to Kat Lamont in transportation, you are going to hire Isabelle Fleming to be your regional properties manager. Their last names have been slightly altered. We don't want anyone to try to do a search on either of them," Annie explained. "You know how people can be when someone new comes on the scene. They get paranoid that their jobs might be in jeopardy. We're simply being cautious."

Milton nodded. "You gals sure know how to plan some kind of operation."

If he only knew. Myra and Annie had the same thought at the same time.

"We want you to call a meeting with Benjamin and Oliver and tell them your latest request. We'll bring Izzie here tomorrow so you can meet with her first, then introduce her to Benjamin and Oliver. Meanwhile, Annie and I will disappear, because we don't want your sons to think we're running things."

"Alright. My life is in your hands." Milton smiled.

"Uh, that would be a big *no*. Your life is in your doctor's hands. We'll take care of business."

"I knew there was a reason I asked Patricia to call you." Milton smiled at Myra.

"And I thought it was because you missed me," Myra teased.

"Always."

"We'll see you in the morning. Say, ten o'clock?" Myra asked.

"You're the boss. Bosses." Milton saluted; the I.V. tube slapped against the bed.

Myra and Annie returned to the hotel. Maggie and Izzie were still at the spa. Annie decided to order dinner for everyone. Kathryn would be arriving shortly, and it would give them a chance to catch up inside their soundproof room.

Annie called Bentley's, the famed restaurant at the hotel. She ordered steaks for everyone, baked potatoes, creamed spinach, and a couple of wedge salads. "Yes, the works for the baked potatoes." She knew it would put Maggie over the moon. She opted to skip dessert. For everyone. Maggie didn't need another pimple, and no one needed the sugar. Too bad if somebody made a fuss. There were still a few grapes on the table.

Izzie and Maggie returned to the room wearing plush spa robes and slippers. "You didn't really walk through the lobby looking like that, did you?" Myra asked.

"Ha. What if we did?" Maggie joked.

"I wouldn't be the least bit surprised." Annie snickered. "Are you going to change into something else?"

"Oh, no! This is too comfortable." Maggie rubbed the plush sleeve against her newly restored complexion.

"Don't keep touching your face," Annie reminded her.

"Don't touch your face. Don't chew your nails. Don't eat sweets. Boy, are you a bunch of killjoys." Maggie feigned despair.

"Well, cheer up, kiddo. We're having steak with the works for dinner!" Annie announced.

"Yippee!" Maggie was overjoyed. "I could use a dose of good, red meat."

"I think we could all use a dose after this morning." Myra sighed.

Annie's cell phone chimed. It was Kathryn, letting her know she had arrived and should be at the hotel in twenty minutes. "Kathryn will be here shortly." She looked over at Maggie and Izzie, lounging in their comfy spa attire. "You may want to change into something worthy of a Zoom call later. Charles, Fergus, and Avery will be on the call."

"Good thinkin'." Maggie got up. "Come on, Izzie. Let's go get more respectable."

"Bummer. I was enjoying the plush." Izzie chuckled.

"You can plush all you want later. We have dinner coming, and we have to bring everyone up to speed. Go. Vamoose!" Annie clapped her hands.

"Be back in a flash," Maggie said.

"Just don't go flashing anyone in the hallway," Myra called out.

Twenty minutes later, Kathryn rang from her room, which was also down the hall. "I have arrived. Ready for duty!"

"Excellent. Come on down to the suite," Annie said.

The three women whooped it up in the hallway, high-fiving and fist-bumping. "Here we go!" Izzie said as she knocked on the suite door.

Annie greeted Kathryn with a big bear hug. There was no other kind when it came to Kathryn. Even Myra, who was slightly thinner than Annie, managed to wrap her arms around the biggest mem-bcr of the crew. A lot of chatter followed until Annie took the reins. "Okay, Sisters! As you know, we are here to investigate two missing women. One a teen, and the other in her early twenties. I am happy to report that the first girl, Vanessa Rowan, has been found and is with her parents. But before we get down to business, we should have dinner, and then we can get busy."

Everyone applauded. "But," Annie cautioned, "we have not notified anyone, including Milton."

There was a knock at the door, announcing room service had arrived. The server rolled the cart against the dining room table. "You can leave it there. Thank you." Myra signed the check and gave the man a cash tip.

Everyone took a seat at the dining room table while Myra handed out the piles of steak and potatoes. The side dishes went on the table for everyone to help themselves.

There was a lot of chatter, and then Myra hushed the group to say Grace. Maggie finished the prayer with her usual irreverent, "Let's eat!"

During dinner, they discussed the latest news, or lack thereof, in their lives. "I feel like my life is boring," Izzie said. "Don't get me wrong. I love my work, but by the time I'm finished with a project, I am ready to take a nap. Like, for a few days." She went on. "Abner has been traveling a lot, so it's me and Rufus. A girl can take just so many walks with a big oaf like him."

"I thought you said Abner was traveling," Kathryn teased. Everyone burst out laughing.

Izzie rolled her eyes. "I'm going to have to put one of them on a diet."

When they finished their meal, they piled the dishes back on the cart and wheeled it out into the hallway. Annie called room service and asked them to send someone to pick it up. "We don't want anyone disturbing us once we get started."

When the table was clear, the women opened their laptops, grabbed pads and pens. Annie went through the story of Vanessa's ordeal and how she'd come to find the girl at the hospital. "She and her parents should be arriving in Lake Tahoe shortly. We are keeping everything under wraps until we can make the connection between Vanessa's abduction and what we believe could be an illegal pill distribution network."

Myra chimed in. "Unfortunately, there is a very strong reason to believe Spangler Enterprises is involved, but we don't know to what extent. You may have already heard that a woman disappeared from the Cascade Inn in Eugene yesterday. Izzie, that's where you come in."

Izzie nodded.

"Tomorrow morning, you and Kathryn will go to the hospital and visit Milton. It will be your *interview*." Myra used air quotes. "Izzie, you will be taking the role of Regional Facilities Manager for the Cascade Inns. Kathryn, you will be on-call driver."

"Obviously, we want both of you to keep your

eyes and ears peeled for anything that may look out of the ordinary," Annie said.

"Is there anything in particular?" Izzie asked.

"We were able to get some information from Vanessa about the man who abducted her. Bart something. Charles and Fergus are looking into him." Annie continued. "When we were visiting Milton earlier, the two men showed up but were hustled away by Oliver, Mill's younger son."

"Oliver also has very expensive tastes," Myra added. "Not that there's anything wrong with that, but according to Charles, Oliver has spent a huge chunk of money on luxury items. With cash."

Murmurs swept the room.

"These pills that Vanessa got a glimpse of, could she tell what they were?" Izzie asked.

"Unfortunately, no. Mr. Bart-something knocked her out. When she regained consciousness, she was in a basement," Myra replied.

"So far, we think we should proceed like this: Maggie, you go back and interview everyone again. Then go and interview the George family. It's their daughter Lori who disappeared from work."

"Got it." Maggie typed something into the search engine.

"I suggest you start at the Salem Cascade Inn. We don't want to jump at the Eugene location too soon. It might spook whoever is doing whatever."

"But we also don't want them to have enough time to clear out if they think someone is on to them," Maggie said.

"Good point," Myra responded. "Annie, what do you suggest?"

"I agree with Maggie. I think we should strike while the iron's hot. Besides, they're not going to know we're about to show up until we do."

"But what about Oliver? He's going to have to know, and if he's involved in any way, he'll have the place swept."

Annie snapped her fingers. "I'll get Fergus to tap into their security system." She looked at Myra. "What do you think Mill will say?"

"I am sure he'll cooperate. But we need to keep as many people out of this as possible."

"It's got to be an easy hack for Fergus and Charles. I can make a go of it if you want," Izzie offered.

"We need you to concentrate on the structure of the building," Myra said. "Or maybe Mill will be able to tell us how to access the system without going through his IT department."

"I'm sure Charles and Fergus can find a work-around. I'll put it on my list." Annie wrote on a lined pad of paper.

Paper was a requirement during their missions. No matter how secure a techno-system is, paper is a lot easier to destroy than an electronic trail. Once the material is set loose on the information super-highway, it can be detoured by a good, slick hacker. Even with the advanced technology the Sisters had at their disposal, Charles and Fergus were updating passwords, QR codes, erasing data, and rerouting connections on a daily basis. It was something they'd learned when Fergus was at Scotland Yard and Charles was with MI6. There is a reason for the use of the word *craft* in spy-craft. Like any kind of skill, it required constant attention if it was to be maintained and further developed. Some people painted. Some did woodworking, while others built model ships inside bottles. Fergus and Charles shared a craft in counterintelligence.

Until the Sisters were able to uncover who was doing what, to whom, and why, secrecy and discretion were of the utmost importance. They had to be particularly careful since they were working remotely. Most missions required two, sometimes three Sisters to be dispatched to various locations, while the rest worked from the war room, far below Myra and Charles's Pinewood farm. This time, there were four of them, all in the same place, thousands of miles from their headquarters and the other Sisters.

During their missions, the Sisters would communicate using burner phones. A new one every day. Annie picked up a briefcase and placed it on the table. Inside were over a dozen phones. Each of the women would use one per day. The dates were etched into the back, and the phones were programmed with everyone's phone number, each assigned to a speed-dial letter, based on their first initial, with the exception of Myra. She had both M and R in order to

distinguish hers from Maggie's. Once Sasha and
Eileen arrived, they would also get pre-programmed
phones to enable them to communicate with the
Sisters. They had their own cellular system with
their boss Avery, who had his line connected with
Charles and Fergus.

Annie's personal phone buzzed. It was a text from
Mark Rowan:

**Arrived safely. The place is beautiful. Cannot
thank you enough. Mark, Julie, V.**

Annie responded with a simple: **Stay safe.**

She looked up at the group. "The Rowans are settled in."

"Yay!" Maggie clapped.

Everyone's laptop began to broadcast the tune of
"We Are Family," signaling Charles and Fergus were
coming on screen. The women were chair-dancing
to the music, singing the famous lyrics, high-fiving,
and fist-bumping. Charles and Fergus sat back with
their arms folded, watching the moving and grooving, and grinning from ear to ear.

"Well done!" Charles clapped.

"Bloody brilliant!" Fergus added.

Neither of the men ever tired of the women's
gusto and excitement.

"Hello, love." Charles looked directly at Myra.
"And the rest of you lovelies."

Everyone sent their greetings across the screens.

Fergus chimed in with "'elo, mates!"

Izzie noted the time. "You guys are up late."

"Truth be told, I'm a bit knackered, but we've got to carry on, eh?"

"Indeed. Let's get to it," Myra said.

Annie repeated the highlights of Vanessa's reunion with her family, her condition, and whereabouts.

Charles began to give them information about Dickie Morton. "Dickie, Richard Morton. Age fifty. Divorced. Two adult children live in Idaho. High school graduate. VOTEC education in automobile engines. Now he is transportation supervisor for S.E.I. Directly reports to Oliver. We've been working on his financials. Seems Mr. Morton has a very nice cabin near Silver Falls State Park. He paid over a hundred grand for it at the beginning of this year. Cash."

"And you said Oliver bought his apartment, car, and several watches with cash, as well," Myra confirmed.

"Yes." Charles was informing everyone of what he and Fergus had discovered during the day. "All cash transactions."

"What about insurance on his acquisitions?" Izzie asked.

"Just the condo and the car."

"Why wouldn't someone want to insure watches worth nearly twenty grand each?" Kathryn asked.

"Paper and electronic transaction trails."

"Do you think the stuff was hot?"

"Oliver is a player. He wants people to know how much he paid. We phoned the high-end jewelry store in the area. Lovely woman. Said Mr. Oliver Spangler was one of their best customers. Always paid cash."

"Well, there's a trail," Maggie said.

"True, but they are local businesspeople. Insurance companies are a different breed. Everything is logged, catalogued, and logged again. We were lucky the nice woman on the phone was so generous with information."

"Oh, Charles, I am willing to bet that you schmoozed her with your accent. You probably laid it on as thick as a slab of bacon," Myra teased.

"I do my best to accommodate your wishes, love." Charles grinned. "I simply mentioned that I had drinks with Oliver and was admiring his watch. He told me where he bought it, and Bob's your uncle."

"What about this Bart person?" Annie asked. She was still fuming at the thought that he'd punched that girl in the face, never mind the entire abduction thing.

"Ah. Bart Nichols. Age forty. Got a bit of a blot on his record. Hot-wired a car, but because of his age, he wasn't charged with a felony. Was in youth detention for a year. Entered a program for rehabilitating teens, then got a job at Geiser Lumbermill. Not the brightest bulb in the chandelier. Seems he's mostly Dickie Morton's gopher. He's also Dickie's cousin."

"So, can we assume they are working together?" Myra asked.

"Well, love, you know I never like to assume anything; however, Bart reports directly to Dickie, so there is a fine chance they are involved in a rum do."

"Something unscrupulous." Myra nodded.

"We'll do more digging, but we should consider the three men are involved in something untoward," Fergus added.

Annie ran down the list she and Myra had compiled:

1. Sasha will tail Bart.
2. Eileen will tail Dickie.
3. Myra will spend time with Benjamin's wife, Danielle, see if she can get the daughter-in-law's point of view. Watch how Benjamin behaves at home.
4. Annie enlists Oliver's fast-car expertise to keep an eye on his movements and get a handle on his routines.
5. Kathryn clocks in at the main office, stealthily checks dispatch records. She stays in the apartment on the top floor of the office building so she can be on-call.
6. Izzie visits the five Cascade Inns as facilities manager.
7. Maggie interviews families, starting with the George family.
8. Mill tells Benjamin to also meet with the George family and assure them the company is doing its own investigating.

"What about Benjamin?" Fergus asked. "How much does he know about your involvement?"

"Just that we're old friends," Myra said, almost blushing.

"And Milton?" Charles pushed his face closer to the camera.

"He's onboard with our intervention. He took our advice concerning Kathryn and Isabelle. He mentioned concerning invoices, but I don't think he has any idea about the drugs."

"That will be a rude awakening for him, I suspect," Charles said.

"I am sure it will be. But he needs to know the truth," Myra replied.

"Everyone up to speed?" Annie asked.

"Yes!"

"Yep!"

"You bet!"

"Good all. We'll continue to sort the financials and see if we can find out who is funding what, and who has the most to gain, and lose," Charles said, as he turned a camera on the statue of Lady Liberty, who stood proudly in their War Room.

"Let's do it!" Annie whooped.

"Aye-aye!" they said in unison, and saluted the symbol they lived to serve.

CHAPTER SEVENTEEN

The Family Meeting and Introductions

Myra, Kathryn, Izzie, and Annie arrived at the hospital an hour before Mill's sons were due. Patricia usually came during lunch. When they got to Mill's room, Annie and Myra were happy to see him sitting in a recliner near the window.

"You're looking rather chipper today." Myra smiled as she bent over to kiss him on the cheek.

"I'm feeling rather chipper, too," Milton replied, as he turned his other cheek to get a peck from Annie.

"Kat and Isabelle are outside waiting for their interview," Annie said.

"How do you want to play this?" he asked.

"Oliver already knows about Kat coming on. Tell your sons you want to add more support staff; you contacted an agency last evening, and they sent someone over. Enter, Izzie."

"I'll bring them in one at a time."

"No need. I convinced the doc that unless I could have four people in my room, I was going to check myself out of this place. The food is ghastly."

"You're on a special diet, Milton," Myra chided him.

"Yes, but you'd think with all the modernization of things, they could come up with better-tasting food."

"So the doctor agreed you could have more than two visitors at a time?"

"I promised it would just be this once. Said I had important business to conduct, and that if he didn't let me do it today, it would greatly increase my stress levels."

"Now you're catching on." Annie chuckled.

"So, let's meet the new members of my staff." Milton nodded toward the door.

Annie went into the hallway and brought Izzie and Kathryn into the room. "This is Isabelle Fleming and Kat Lamont."

Each took turns shaking Milton's hand. "Nice to meet you, Mr. Spangler."

"Well, it's very nice to have some extra help while I am recuperating."

"We are very happy to oblige," Kathryn replied.

Milton looked at Myra. "Tell me how this is going to work."

Myra handed Milton two separate résumés containing the women's fictitious last names. "As we discussed, you'll explain your intention to hire additional staff. It's a temporary situation, until you're back on your feet."

Milton read the women's qualifications. "Very impressive."

"We don't want you to get any pushback from Oliver or Benjamin, or whoever might be doing things behind your back," Annie said.

"Excellent. Clearly, no one can dispute your areas of experience and expertise." Milton perused their résumés.

Izzie grinned. She knew how to build something from bottom to top. Managing five trucker inns could be challenging.

She also knew she had backup if necessary.

"Ah, Kathryn. Long-hauler for a long time, I see."

"Yes, sir. I studied engineering but found the open road is what I prefer."

Milton nodded. "My sons should be arriving shortly. I'll introduce you and then let them show you to the main office. I appreciate you stepping in on such short notice."

"Anything for a friend," Myra said.

Annie put her arm around Myra. "We are always at the ready."

"Wonderful." Milton gestured for the women to sit. "Please. Would you like coffee? Although I wouldn't recommend it. They have me on decaf, which is horrible. I can't imagine their regular coffee is any better."

Izzie smiled. "No, but thank you."

"Ditto, here," Kathryn answered.

Myra looked at Annie. "We better scoot. We don't want anyone to get the idea we're colluding."

Annie howled and then put her hand over her mouth. "When aren't we colluding?"

"Come on, you." Myra linked her arm through Annie's and dragged her toward the door.

"Good luck!" Annie said as they exited Milton's room.

Milton's suite consisted of two rooms and a private bath. There was a sitting area with a sofa that opened to a bed, two upholstered chairs, another recliner, and a coffee table. "Why don't you two wait in there until the boys arrive?" He nodded toward the sitting room.

Kathryn and Izzie took his cue and moved to the next room.

Just as Annie and Myra began to walk down the hall, Annie spotted Oliver getting out of the elevator. "Dang. Quick. Jump on." She pushed a gurney toward Myra. "Hurry!"

Myra climbed on and pulled the sheet over her head. Annie turned and pushed the stretcher down the opposite corridor.

Myra mumbled under the sheet. "I'm beginning to think you like doing this." She pulled the material from her face. "We could have sneaked into the stairwell."

"What fun would that be?" Annie picked up the pace. When she was sure they were no longer in Oliver's sightline, she pushed the gurney against the wall and helped Myra off. An orderly jogged toward them.

"Excuse me, ladies. This is not a toy. Nor is this a playground. Kindly behave like adults, or I will have to call security."

Annie cringed. "Sorry. I couldn't resist."

Myra shook her head. "Yes, apologies. My sister can't help herself at times. You can only imagine what kind of trouble she caused when we were children."

"Well, you didn't have to jump on, now, did you?" Annie pretended to argue.

"No. No, I didn't. I figured if I let you get your kicks early enough in the day, you'd stay out of trouble for the rest of it."

"Why do you have to be such a party pooper?" Annie placed her hands on her hips.

"Someone has to be the grown-up in this family."

"Just because you're older doesn't mean you're the boss of me."

The orderly couldn't take the quarreling anymore. "Please, ladies." He turned and walked away.

Myra and Annie both bit their lips. "Works every time," Annie said under her breath.

Myra concurred. "Men can't stand to be around bickering women." They linked arms again and decided to take the stairs.

Oliver was the first to arrive. "Morning, Dad. You're looking much better today." He leaned over and gave his father a kiss on the cheek. Milton knew it was rare for Oliver to show any affection, but after all, he was in the hospital, and he could have died. Milton wondered to himself, *Is that what it takes for my son to exhibit any kind of love? A near-death experience. Who raised this kid, anyway? Right. Patricia.*

"Benjamin is on his way. Had to pick up Eva's soccer equipment. Should be here in less than ten minutes." Oliver cleared his throat. "So what's this all about, Pop?"

"Let's wait until your brother arrives. That way, I'll only have to explain it once." He smiled. "Gotta keep up my strength. They may send me home tomorrow."

Oliver looked surprised. "Really? Do you think it's a good idea?"

"The doctors seemed to think so. They said there was no blockage, no damage. Kind of an anomaly. But good thing you boys were around."

Oliver looked nervous. "Do they have any idea what caused it?"

Milton shook his head and pursed his lips. "Perhaps something I ate caused an arrythmia? I have no idea. The good news is that after a few weeks' rest, I'll be back as good as new."

"That's great news, Dad." Oliver seemed genuinely pleased.

Benjamin walked in. "News? What news?" He walked over and gave his father a kiss on the top of his head. That was *not* unusual for Benjamin. Benjamin had a warmth that Milton surmised came from his own mother, Josephine's, side of the family.

"Yes. The doctors are letting me go home tomorrow," Milton repeated.

"That is great news. What's the prognosis and recovery protocol?"

"Listen to you sounding like a doctor," Milton joked.

"I watched a lot of *House*," Benjamin joked back.

"Very fine actor," Milton said.

"I had no idea he was British until he was being interviewed on a talk show," Benjamin added.

"And he's also a comedian and a fine musician," Milton added.

"Lots of talent there." Oliver looked annoyed that the purpose of this so-called meeting was being sidetracked by a British actor that none of them had any connection to. "So, Dad, shall we get on with it?"

"Easy there, son. I'm trying to take things at a slower pace." He handed each son one of the résumés. "I've decided to take on some temporary help until I can get back in full swing."

"You said you hired a woman to work the on-call shift." Oliver was looking at Izzie's résumé for the facilities job.

"I did. Both candidates are in the salon." Milton cleared his throat. "Kathryn? Izzie? Come on over and meet my sons."

The color drained from Oliver's face. Things were moving much too quickly. Two new hires? Overnight? With everyone now in the room, Oliver could not protest or try to slow down his father's new initiative. He snapped to it quickly. "You must be Kathryn." Oliver was taking a small risk, but her strong handshake and towering height made it a good guess.

"Nice to meet you, Mr. Spangler."

"That's my father. You can call me Oliver." A weak attempt at humor.

"Alright, Oliver."

"Benjamin." He introduced himself. "Nice to meet you, Kathryn." He turned to Izzie. "And you must be Izzie."

Izzie smiled. "Yes. Pleased to meet you both." She shook their hands.

"Let's go into the sitting area. It'll be more comfortable." Milton pushed the button on his recliner and stood. Benjamin jumped to his father's side and took him by the arm. "Thanks, son. They've been making me walk several times a day, so I'm pretty steady on my feet now."

"Let's not take any chances." Benjamin held his father's elbow.

"If you insist." Milton let his son walk him to the recliner, where Milton sat up straight. "I'm really quite a terrible patient," he said to Izzie and Kathryn. "But I really do feel quite well now." He was wearing a pair of blue silk dot pajamas with a silk navy-blue robe. He actually looked quite well, too. Once Milton was settled, everyone took a seat.

"As I explained to Benjamin and Oliver, while I am recuperating, I wanted to be sure my sons have adequate support. Kat, I believe you will be staying in the apartment at the main office."

Oliver turned pale again. The place was rarely used, and he had commandeered it for his own enterprise headquarters. "Dad, I have a few things in there."

"Will they be in Kathryn's way?" Milton asked.

Kat interrupted. "I really don't need a lot of room. I'm used to sleeping in my rig."

"No. No. I'll clear everything out. I don't want to disturb you if I need to get to any of it," Oliver was quick to respond. "I'll ask Dickie to move everything into the storage space down the hall from my office." He stood and walked into the other room and blasted off a text to Dickie:

Clear out upstairs apartment. Pronto.

Dickie quickly responded: **Furniture too?**

Oliver thought he was going to have a stroke.

No! Just our stuff. Put in hallway storage.

From Dickie: **Boxes. Right?**

Yes! Now!

Got it, boss. On it.

Oliver wiped the perspiration off the top of his lip, then returned to the others.

"Everything alright?" Benjamin asked. His brother had been acting rather oddly since their father's health scare.

"Yeah. Fine." Oliver placed his phone back into his jacket pocket. "Sorry. Where were we?"

"Kat will be staying in the apartment. Isabelle, do you have a place to stay, or would you prefer one of our rooms at an inn?"

"Since I'll be traveling back and forth, having a room would be convenient. I packed enough for a week, and I assume I'll be wearing a company uniform?"

"We don't require management to wear uniforms, but we have company blazers we would like you to wear when you are at work. I suppose it's a uniform of sorts," Milton said.

"That's perfect."

Milton continued. "The facilities on the premises are at your disposal. Laundry, kitchen. Whatever you need."

Kathryn noticed a slight flinch from Oliver. She made a mental note.

Oliver spoke up. "Chain of command, Dad?"

"Ah, yes. Benjamin, do you have any suggestions?" Milton asked. Technically, both jobs fell under the supervision of Oliver.

"Since Dickie is transportation manager, perhaps Kat should report to him," Benjamin offered.

"Maybe she should just report directly to me," Oliver replied. He wanted to keep a sharp eye on this new hire, and Dickie wasn't up to the job. He had screwed up too much lately.

Both he and Bart. What a nightmare.

"Now, Isabelle. I'd like you to report to Benjamin, if you're okay with that?" Milton looked at him.

"Of course," Benjamin agreed.

"But the Inns are under me." Oliver was almost whining.

"I know, son, but there is already enough for you to do. Izzie can send her dailies to both of you."

"Alright," Oliver acquiesced.

"Then it's agreed. Benjamin, Oliver, have Isabelle and Kat follow you to the main office, and you can get them settled in."

"Perfect," Izzie said. "Thank you for the opportunity."

"I should be the one thanking you for agreeing to come onboard with such short notice."

"I always wanted to visit the Pacific Northwest. This is the perfect opportunity," Izzie said warmly.

"Right now, you are smack-dab in the middle of Willamette Valley. The real beauty is on either side. The Cascades fill the eastern horizon, and the Oregon Coast Range is to the west. Beautiful on the coast. We have a summer house in Bandon. Don't spend enough time out there, but maybe after this episode, I'll make it a point to stay there more often. If either of you want to use the house over the weekend, it would be my pleasure."

"That's very generous of you, Mr. Spangler," Isabelle replied.

Milton replied, "Somebody might as well use it. Benjamin and his family went out every weekend before the kids became teenagers."

"You're right, Dad. We all should spend more time out there together."

"It's almost a four-hour drive from here." Oliver was half apologizing, half explaining why he rarely went there, even during holiday celebrations.

"You're the one with the fast car," Milton teased. "It would take you three." He chuckled. "Well, enough of this family talk. Let's get all of you down to business."

"The coast is quite beautiful," Kathryn added. "I know these roads like the back of my hand. It will be a very short learning curve."

"Wonderful." Milton was smiling. "They're letting me out of this jail tomorrow. I'd like for all of us to meet at my house at the end of the week. A quick briefing."

"Dad, are you sure you're supposed to be working?" Oliver asked.

"I told the doctor that sitting idly would add to my stress levels. As long as I know things are being handled, then I'll be able to relax."

"You know you can count on us, Pop," Oliver offered.

"And us," Kathryn said, looking at Izzie. Then she remembered they weren't supposed to know each other. "Sorry. I just figured . . ."

"No worries. We're all here to assist the Spangler family." Izzie was quick to cover Kathryn's gaffe.

"Splendid. I'll let you all be on your way. Figure on meeting Friday afternoon. I'll ask Ruby to fix tea. One of the boys will give you the time and address."

Everyone shook hands and said their adieus. Benjamin gave his dad another peck on the top of his head. "I will be so glad when you're done fussing over me." Milton waved him off with a chuckle.

"That'll never happen," Benjamin replied.

The four made small talk on their way to the lobby. Benjamin and Oliver went to the valet and gave him their tickets.

"We'll pull our cars around," Izzie said, and gave Kathryn a wink. The Sisters were always careful around their marks, but it had been a while, and everyone was trying to get up to speed in a hurry. No pun intended.

The trip to the main office took about twenty minutes. It was several miles from the downtown area of the capital of Oregon. Things had been moving so quickly, Izzie hadn't noticed the spectacular mountain ranges earlier, with Mount Hood and its snow-capped peaks looming in the distance. *Impressive.* Izzie could only imagine how it would look up close. She had been in and out of Portland a few times, but never spent more than a day or two. Not enough time to see anything worthwhile. Maybe after this gig, she and the Sisters could have a weekend retreat somewhere. She snapped out of her musings. They were turning into the S.E.I. complex.

Izzie admired the two-story office building that looked more like a chalet than a commercial shop. It was meticulously landscaped with rocks and trees. Something she would have designed herself, had she been given the opportunity. The wood-plank sign spelled out SPANGLER ENTERPRISES INCORPORATED. Smaller letters listed the divisions: Cascade Inns, Interstate Trucking, Geiser Creek Lumber and Millwork. A wide, paved roadway led to the mill-works toward the back of the property, where there was a large parking area for trucks. Several other roadways led in various directions. There was no question it was a multi-million-dollar company.

Izzie and Kathryn parked in the "visitor" section, while Benjamin and Oliver parked in their named spots: Benjamin Spangler, Oliver Spangler. No titles, just their names, an equal distance from the front door.

They gathered at the front entrance. "Kathryn, there is also a private entrance to the apartment. I'll show it to you later," Benjamin said.

Oliver quickly sent a text to Dickie: **Did you do it?**

Dickie replied: **Almost done. Ten more minutes**.

Oliver figured he could keep everyone busy touring the main floor and introducing the new people. His mood brightened. He held the door open for everyone else. "After you." He swept his arm toward the door. Benjamin gave him a strange look. "What? I'm trying to be polite."

Benjamin smirked. There was something going on with his brother, but he dreaded finding out.

Benjamin let Oliver take the lead. "Right this way."

The reception area was paneled in a light oak with a black slate floor. It had twelve-foot ceilings, with several indoor ponytail palms along the walls. It had a feeling of openness.

A young man in his twenties was sitting behind a wood and stone counter. Behind him was the company logo with back lighting. The letters appeared to be floating. Simple and tasteful.

Isabelle totally approved.

"Good morning, sirs." He gave them a wide smile and stood.

"Hello, Robert. These are our two new hires. They will be staying on until Dad gets back."

"How is Mr. Spangler doing?" the young man asked earnestly.

"He's doing well. Should be going home tomorrow. Thanks for asking," Oliver quickly answered.

"I am very happy to hear it, sir. We were quite dismayed when we heard the news." The young man had a very articulate way of speaking. *Probably private school*.

"This is Kat." He gestured in her direction. Then turned. "And this is Isabelle Fleming. Kat is going to be our on-call driver, and Isabelle will be overseeing the Cascade properties."

"Welcome. It's a pleasure to meet you. If there is anything I can do, please do not hesitate to ask."

"Robert is like an anchor here. Keeps us in line." Oliver was being effusive.

"I keep track of how many times they visit the kitchen." Robert grinned.

"I thought we were keeping that between the two of us," Oliver joked. *It's so fake*. Everyone was getting slightly uncomfortable with Oliver's ebullient behavior. And so was he. He was beginning to perspire. He shouldn't have snorted on his way there. He excused himself. "Pardon me. Benjamin, can you take Kat and Isabelle around? I'm feeling a bit off." He didn't wait for an answer. He turned quickly and headed to the men's room down the slate-tiled hallway.

"Is he going to be alright?" Kat asked.

"He has blood-sugar issues," Benjamin said. And it was true, or so he thought. "Come, follow me."

Kat and Isabelle waved to Robert. "Nice to meet you!"

"Welcome aboard," Robert called out.

Kat was trying to place the young man's accent. "Michigan?"

"Very good!" Benjamin replied.

"After all the years of being on the road, I have come across dozens upon dozens of accents. I can't even count how many Southern accents there are," Kat replied.

Benjamin walked the women through an area with several cubicles. There were about a dozen people working on their computers or talking on their phone headsets. Benjamin whispered over their heads. "New people. Kat and Isabelle." Those who weren't on the phone said "hello," or "welcome," while the others waved.

Isabelle noted that everyone had a pleasant expression on their face. The air smelled fresh, and the place was well-lit without bright, blinding overhead fixtures. It was a physically comfortable environment, and judging by Robert's attitude, it was an emotionally comfortable environment.

A huffing and puffing Dickie scampered toward

them. "Hello. Sorry. I was dealing with some stuff. You must be Kat and Isabelle? I'm Dickie Morton."

"Hi. I'm Isabelle." She held out her hand. He wiped his on his trousers before he shook it.

"Kat." She took her turn. *So people do get sweaty around here.*

"Where's Oliver?" Dickie asked.

"He got a little flushed. Sugar thing," Benjamin replied. "He should be here momentarily."

"I understand you will be reporting to me," Dickie said pleasantly to Kat. No one would guess his intestines were in a knot. He had enough trouble already. Now he had a new person he had to train and keep an eye on. *Man, he wished his palms would stop sweating.*

"You okay, Dickie?" Benjamin couldn't help noticing the discomfort his employee was experiencing.

"Yeah. Got a little winded coming down the hall. I should work out more often, but you know how it goes. Always something else comes up and gets in the way." He was starting to breathe normally. "Follow me. I'll show you to your desk. It's right around the corner." They entered a large room with whiteboards on each wall. A cluster of desks sat in the middle. Each desk had a swivel chair, so anyone could see any of the boards if they shifted in that direction. Three men and a woman were seated and typing information into a central database.

"This is what we call 'The Pit.' Kind of a company joke." Then he turned to his employees. "Listen up! This is Kat. She's our swing-shift, on-call driver. When you get a minute, introduce yourselves." Benjamin jerked his head toward a desk on one of the side walls in front of a frosted sheet of glass. "This is your home away from home." He pulled out the comfortable swivel chair. "I mean, it's your home away from your home away from home."

Kat sat and spun around. "Nice. I'd say this is almost as comfortable as my rig." She chuckled.

Dickie spotted Oliver walking in their direction. "There's Oliver."

"Sorry about that. Blood sugar." That was his story, and he was sticking to it.

"You alright?" Benjamin asked.

Oliver furrowed his brow. "Of course. Just needed a little orange juice. Everybody getting the gist of the place?"

"Yes. It's a beautiful office space," Isabelle remarked.

"Thanks. Believe it or not, my daughter Addie is going to Pratt next semester. This was the layout she submitted with her application."

"Wow. You must be very proud," Isabelle said, knowing how talented the young woman must be in order to get accepted to a renowned school of design.

"Yes, we are. But we're going to miss her. She'll be on the other side of the country."

Oliver was anxious to get this welcome wagon over and done with. "Let's show Kat the apartment.

The stairs are right outside. Then we can bring Isabelle over to the Cascade section."

"Lead the way," Benjamin instructed.

Dickie didn't know what he was supposed to do. Kat was going to report to him, but this seemed to be Oliver's show. He looked at his boss. Oliver gave him a wide-eyed look and tilted his head in the direction of the stairs.

"Follow me," Dickie instructed the group. A door led from the corner of the room to a flight of stairs. There were two doors at the top of the landing. One led to an outside entrance, the other to a fifteen-hundred-square-foot apartment.

"Wow. This is where I'll be living?" Kat was stunned. "This is nicer than any place I've ever stayed." Of course she was lying, but they didn't have to know that. Travel accommodations with Annie or Myra were usually upscale. Not necessarily over-the-top, but rarely was there reason to complain about lack of service or a comfortable bed.

"It's two bedrooms. We use it for out-of-town clients."

"Will I be in the way?" Kat asked.

"No. We're not expecting anyone. We cancelled all the in-person meetings until we knew Dad's condition and when he'd be up for them." Benjamin was in charge of most of the business, but when it came to their long-time, big-bucks clients, Milton was always at the ready.

"Will there be anyone else staying here?" Kat was wondering because she was about to propose the idea that Isabelle use the suite as her home base, too. It would make it a lot easier for everyone to stay in close contact with one another.

"No. It's all yours," Benjamin said.

"Hey"—she turned to Isabelle—"do you really want to be living out of a suitcase? Like every day?"

"What do you mean?" Isabelle knew exactly what she meant, but she had to play along to keep the ruse going. Everyone assumed they had just met earlier that day.

"Like, why don't you leave the bulk of your stuff here, and then you'll only have to take what you need when you visit the inns. From what I gather, Salem is about halfway between them."

"You don't mind sharing?" Isabelle continued with the act.

"Nope. Might be nice to have some female company for a change." There were over 200,000 female truck drivers, but they only made up less than seven percent of the industry. "I don't get to spend much time with other women." She paused and smiled. "You don't chew tobacco, do you?" Kat teased.

"Ha! No. Do you?" Isabelle looked at her in horror.

"Nope. Can't stand the smell of it, either, and boy, do I get to smell a lot of it on the road. This is going to be a nice change of pace for me."

"You are exactly the target audience for the Cascade Inns." Oliver glowed.

"Maybe she can take a ride with me when I go

down to Eugene? That is, if she's not tagged to work," Isabelle offered.

Eugene? Oliver and Dickie both began to sweat. That was not a good idea. Portland was safer. They hadn't built the powder mill there yet. The plan was to have three manufacturing facilities. The compression machines were costly at five thousand dollars each, and Oliver knew he wouldn't be able to hide those charges. The next two operations would be strictly powder. Depending on who the client was, they would deliver it in tightly packed bricks, or one-inch-square glycine bags, with a one hundred bag minimum. They were going to be in the business of drug dealing, but they didn't want it to include the end-users. The street urchins. The dopers. Ernesto continued to be a "consultant" for a cut of the profits, and Oliver was intent on making profits.

Oliver jumped in. "We'll have to look at the schedule. Maybe when Isabelle goes to Portland. Each of the inns are about an hour away."

The women shrugged. They'd play along. By now, they could tell something was amiss, and Dickie and Oliver were in cahoots, unless they both suffered from blood sugar issues—both were jittery and had droplets on their upper lip.

"So you really don't mind having a roommate?" Isabelle was giving it the old *are you sure?* quiz.

"Seriously. We can watch TV and braid each other's hair." Kat laughed out loud.

The three men were speechless. Was Kat coming on to Isabelle? Or was she joking? If they said something, it could be taken the wrong way. Better to keep their mouths shut.

"My gear is still at the hotel. I'll pick it up later so I can go downstairs and get acquainted with the staff," Kat said, regaining her air of professionalism.

"Mine, too," Isabelle added. "Maybe we can grab a bite to eat before we come back here. Where are you staying?"

"At the Roadside Inn. A couple of miles from here. What about you?"

"A B and B. About a mile away."

"Cool. I'm sure someone can recommend a place to grab dinner, and then we can settle in," Kat said.

Dickie's eyes darted around the room, making sure he hadn't left anything incriminating behind.

"I'll bring you both a set of keys," Dickie offered. He wanted to give the place one more sweep before he turned it over to the two women.

"Thanks."

All five of them climbed down to the main floor. Kat walked toward The Pit. "Hey. So tell me, why is this called 'The Pit'? It looks pretty nice to me."

"You didn't see this place before the renovations," one of her new coworkers responded. "You had to actually step down into the area to get to the desks. As the company got bigger, we needed more space, so Mr. Spangler decided to make the floor level. Now we have a little more elbow room to move about."

"I see."

"I'm Sandy, by the way. That's Charlie, Reggie, and Keith."

"Hi." Kat gave a little wave. "How long have you all been working here?"

Sandy gave her the rundown. Everyone had been at the company at least ten years.

"Must be a good place to work." Kat was subtly fishing.

"Mr. Milton, he's the best. Nice man. Kind."

"You call him Mr. Milton?" Kat asked.

"He said he didn't want to be called Mr. Spangler. There were three Spanglers. He said we should call him Milton, but I just can't. So, out of respect, I call them Mr. Milton, Mr. Benjamin, and Mr. Oliver."

"What about Dickie?" Kat asked.

Sandy leaned in. "I have my own title for him, one that's part of his name!" She guffawed.

Interesting, Kat thought.

"But please don't tell him that!" Sandy put her hand over her mouth, thinking she'd said too much too soon.

"No problem. I know a lot of them." Kat gave her a wink.

"So, you'll be staying upstairs?" Sandy asked. "I thought someone was already up there. Been a lot of foot traffic. They must have left."

"Yes. I'll be upstairs, and Isabelle will be staying there when she's not traveling to the inns."

"For how long?"

"Not sure. For a couple of weeks, probably."

"Isabelle is the woman who will be overseeing the facilities for now, right?"

"Yes."

"How do you two know each other?" Sandy asked innocently.

"We just met."

"And you're going to be roomies?" Sandy wasn't being nosy. Just curious.

"I spend a lot of time sleeping in the cab of my truck. There's an awful lot of space upstairs, and I figured she could use a home base."

"That's mighty kind of you," Sandy said.

"Heck, why not? Us gals have to stick together." Kat leaned in just a bit, garnering Sandy's confidence.

In turn, Sandy whispered, "We could use a full-time person, to be perfectly honest. Someone is always calling out sick."

"Maybe. We'll see how it goes." Kat thought for a minute. "How often do you think I'll be out?"

"Depends. Long-haulers are pretty reliable, so maybe once or twice a month. It's the short runs that can be a problem. We have a really high turnover rate." She thought for a moment. "I'd say two, three times a week. It's quiet today, but you'll be busy."

"I hope so. One thing I can't stand is just sitting around."

"We can always find something for you to do. You know how to use a computer?"

"Sure."

"Good. Maybe you can help with some of the dispatch logs."

"I'll give it a shot," Kat offered.

"Great. How are you at spreadsheets?"

"I have to turn them in after every run."

"Welcome aboard, Kat! I think I'm going to like having you around." Sandy held up her hand for a high five.

Kat smiled to herself. Sandy might be a good ally in the future.

Oliver excused himself to tend to other business while Benjamin showed Isabelle the Cascade Inn section of the offices. "Everyone, this is Isabelle Fleming. She's coming onboard to oversee the facilities. She'll be traveling back and forth, making sure everything is running smoothly. Dad wanted all of us to have some backup support until he's well enough to return to work. With the inns spread out along the interstate, we thought having a traveling manager would take some of the burden off of Oliver, and of course, me." He chuckled. "Make Isabelle feel at home. Speaking of which, she will be using the apartment upstairs as her home base. She'll be sharing it with Kat Lamont, who is our new swing-shift, on-call driver."

"Welcome, Isabelle." Isabelle guessed the woman who'd greeted her was sixty. She was well-dressed and had a current, smart hairstyle. "I'm Jessica. I'm in charge of linens, paper goods, and amenities. That's Norman. He's responsible for all perishable goods, such as food, and beverages. And I'm sure you've already met Oliver. He handles personnel, staffing, and the rest."

"Nice to meet you both," Isabelle replied. "Jessica, when you have a few free minutes, I'd like you to give me an overview of how things are managed. Daily routines, etc."

"Sure thing. How about we chat over lunch?" Jessica suggested. "We have a couple of food trucks that pull in every day. Sometimes it's pizza, sometimes Mexican. I think we have falafel today. Or if you're into less exotic food, we have a cafeteria with freshly made sandwiches, soups, and a few hot items."

"Whatever you prefer. I'm not fussy," Isabelle responded.

Jessica checked her watch. "About a half hour?"

"Sounds good to me." Isabelle looked at Benjamin. "What else do I need to do? Know?"

"I'll show you your workspace and the rest of the offices, and then you can come back here and have lunch with Jess," Benjamin replied.

"Sounds good." Isabelle followed Benjamin to a cubicle on the other side of Jessica's.

"Not glamorous, but workable," he said.

"Thanks. It's perfect. Nice view of the woods."

"We are very conscious about trees, considering the business we're in." Benjamin walked her down the hall. "We are required to plant twenty trees for every one we fell, but we plant up to fifty per tree."

"That's very earth-friendly of you." Isabelle was a big proponent of green areas, as well as protecting the planet from ruination. Sometimes she felt overwhelmed and outvoted when it came to the design of her commercial projects, but she would always manage to find a way to save a tree or two, and plant a few more than required. She decided she liked Benjamin. He had integrity.

After a quick glimpse of the executive offices, Benjamin walked Isabelle back to the Cascade Inn area. "I'm sure Jess will be able to get you settled in. If you need anything, just holler." Benjamin smiled and went back to the executive suites.

"He seems like a very nice man," Isabelle said to Jessica.

"He is." She hesitated.

Isabelle cocked her head. "But?"

"Oh, nothing."

Isabelle knew it was something, but she'd let Jessica tell her in her own sweet time. They had just met each other, but Isabelle thought there was a lot Jessica would like to reveal. Just a feeling, but over the years, the Sisters had relied a lot on their intuition, as well as their uncanny ability to often read each other's minds. *Inexplicable* was the word they used to characterize it.

"You up for Mexican?" Jessica asked, as she pulled her sweater off the back of her chair.

"Love it!"

"The guy who runs the food truck is from Mexico. It's the real deal."

"So glad to hear it. Fake Mexican can be awful."

"Norman, do you want us to bring anything back for you?" Jessica asked.

"Nah. I'll grab a sandwich from the cafeteria.

Juan's food is delicious, but my stomach tends to disagree."

"Thanks for that tidbit of information." Jessica chuckled. "Come on, Iz. You don't mind if I call you 'Iz,' do you?"

"No, not really." *What else could she say? I prefer Isabelle and sound like a snob? Nope.*

"Most of us have nicknames, but some of us don't know what they are!" Jessica cackled. "You know what I mean."

"I sure do. I used to have a boss named Bruce Bristow. He was like a robot, so we called him Bristoid. Not to his face!" Isabelle laughed. It wasn't true. She'd never known a Bruce Bristow, but she was working her way into Jessica's confidence.

"I like the way you think." Jessica held the door that led to the parking lot.

If she only knew what I really thought, Isabelle mused. There was already a line in front of Grande Garcia's truck. "What do you recommend?" she asked, while Jessica greeted her coworkers.

"I love his empanadas, especially the beef."

The aroma from the food truck wafted through the air. "Smells delicious," Isabelle noted.

"If you like tacos, he makes one with shredded chicken and guac."

"Stop. You're making me hungry!" Isabelle joked. Sorta. Actually, it was the scent of the food that was making her mouth water.

Jessica kept introducing Isabelle to everyone they came in contact with.

"I am never going to remember everyone's name," she whispered under her breath.

"Don't worry about it. They're either Joe, Jim, Mack, Bucky, or Jake. I've been here for twenty years and still haven't figured it out. They call each other 'dude' or 'bud,' so it's hard keeping up." Jessica was finally at the front of the line. "Buenos Dias, Juan!"

"Buenos Dias, my favorite customer!" A very large man with a mustache grinned.

"Oh, I know you say that to everyone." Jessica was almost blushing. Isabelle noticed there was no wedding band on Jessica's left hand. That's when she realized she was wearing hers. She needed a story just in case someone asked, and based on the few short minutes she'd spent with Jessica, Isabelle was sure Jess would notice, *and* ask. *He travels a lot for business. True enough.*

"Who is your new friend?" Juan asked.

"This is Isabelle. She's going to be overseeing the facilities while Mr. Spangler is recuperating."

"Bueno. Welcome!" Juan gave her a wide smile. "I have prepared something new today. Tinga tostados. Muy bueno!"

"I'll take two," Jessica said.

"Me, too!"

"And a side of guac," Jessica said. "For both of us." Isabelle reached into her purse to get her wallet.

"Oh, no, you don't. This is on me. A welcome to S.E.I. lunch."

"That's very sweet of you," Isabelle said. "Thank you." Isabelle remembered a conversation she'd had with Myra a few years before. *When someone pays you a compliment or does you a favor, be gracious. Say thank you. No justifications. No explanations. Don't diminish their observation or kindness. Just a simple thank you. They'll appreciate it as much as you appreciate the gesture.*

Juan handed them a box filled with their food, plus two bottles of Mexican soda. "Today, lunch is my pleasure. A welcome to Salem." The women looked at each other. "You too, Jessica."

"Thank you so much," Isabelle cooed.

Jessica was dumbfounded. "Wow. I should stick with you, kiddo. Maybe we can score a few free beers at the bowling alley," Jessica joked.

Isabelle laughed. "I'm not much of a bowler. More like a gutterer, if that's a word."

"Who cares? Free beer!" Jessica hooted. "Come on. There's a nice patio in the back."

The two women strolled through the well-land-scaped area that led to a patio outside the cafeteria. "This is quite lovely for a lumbermill," Isabelle commented.

"Mr. Milton has done a grand job with this place. I remember it from when I was a little girl. My father worked here."

"And then you started twenty years ago?" Isabelle was trying to follow the timeline.

"Yep. I was a stay-at-home mom until the kids went off to school. Then my old man—not my dad, the guy I used to be married to—left me for some chippy at a strip club."

Isabelle almost spit out her food. Jessica had no filter. "You're kidding."

"I kid you not, kiddo. And get this, she wasn't that chipper, either. She had a face that could stop a truck. And she was the same age as me. I was thirty-seven. I think she was looking for a sugar daddy. But was she in for a surprise. He may have shoved a lot of bills into her garter belt, but when we got divorced, he had to pay alimony *and* child support."

"Karma. Isn't it a beautiful thing?" Isabelle took another bite of her spicy lunch.

"Sure is. She dumped him like a hot potato a year later. Boo-hoo."

"Where is he now?"

"Somewhere up north. The checks are issued by the state, because they take it out of his pay. So as long as he has a job, I get two grand a month."

"What about the kids?"

"One is twenty-five, and the other twenty-six. So that money train ended. And I am not planning on getting married any time soon. I'm putting that alimony money away for my retirement."

"Smart move," Isabelle replied. She was beginning to like Jessica. Down-to-earth. No bull. She knew it wouldn't take long before she could uncork some information about Dickie. Maybe even Oliver.

They finished their lunch and went back inside through the cafeteria entrance. Isabelle was also impressed by how well-designed it was. The space had more of a café vibe than an industrial complex food court. "This is nice," she commented, as they made their way around the tables.

"Yep. Mr. Milton and his sons really take good care of their employees."

"I got that impression as soon as I walked in the door. There seems to be a nice sense of camaraderie here."

"For sure. If anybody is in need of anything, home-wise or family-wise, most people pitch in. One of the fellas' kids needed treatment at the Mayo Clinic. Mr. Milton paid for their hotel and airfare, and we took up a collection for the family so they could have some help at home."

"Does everybody call him Mr. Milton?"

"Yeah. Something Sandy started. She's been here longer than me."

"Seems like a wonderful group of people." Isabelle was quite sincere. Everyone seemed likable. Except for Oliver. And Dickie. As far as Isabelle was concerned, Dickie was a hot mess. Both of them needed to be tailed, from what she could gather. She was getting strange vibes about each of them when their names came up.

"I really couldn't have asked for a better place. Especially after the divorce. Imagine how humiliated I was. But ya know somethin'? Nobody looked at me like I was pathetic. They showed respect. Not pity."

Isabelle wanted to hear more about the overall feel of the company, but she thought it would be best if she familiarized herself with each of the inns.

"Jessica, thanks for making me feel at home. I really appreciate it."

"Do as good as you can is what I say. You can't

expect kindness if you're not willing to show it."
Jessica smiled and sat down at her desk.

"Do I need a special password for the computer?"
Isabelle asked.

"Depends on what you're looking for."

"First, just a general idea of how the system works.
I take it you log in all the invoices and bills of lading
for the supplies?"

"Correct."

"Would I be able to see those files?"

"Sure. No big secret there. Toilet paper, tissues,
cleaning supplies. Not classified documents." She
chuckled.

"Maybe you could give me a quick tutorial?" Isabelle asked.

"Sure thing. Just give me a few minutes."

Isabelle sat in front of a computer screen that had
the company logo as the wallpaper. She clicked it.
Up came the main website with company information, personnel, and back story. The usual things to
be found on a company website.

Jessica rolled herself over to Isabelle's desk. "See
that S.E.I. icon on the bottom? Click there." An entirely different menu appeared. "That's our database."

Isabelle wondered if it was secure enough. Given
her newly acquired hacking skills, she could test the
system after hours.

"At the top are all the individual tabs for each division. Click on Cascade. Okay, there you see each
individual location. Click on Eugene. There you'll
see all the inventory, staff, schedules, and the rest."

"Pretty streamlined." Isabelle nodded.

"Everything on these tabs populates to another program where Mr. Milton can view things in a number of ways. Like, if he wants to know the total number of rolls of toilet paper used each month, and so on. Sorry if I use toilet paper as an example, but it seems like that's what I spend most of my time chasing. Can you believe people actually steal rolls of it?"

"I guess if you're a trucker, you might be worried about not making it to the next rest area," Isabelle joked.

Jessica cackled. "Good point."

"So, Mr. Milton is the only one with access to that part of the database?"

"All three Spangler men," Jessica replied.

"Got it," Isabelle said. "I think I can figure this out now. I'm going to go down to Eugene either tomorrow or the next day, so I'll start with that database. Manager and assistant manager?" Isabelle asked.

"Doreen Finamore is the manager. Nice woman."

Another nice person. The company was beginning to sound too good to be true.

"Assistant manager?" Isabelle asked.

"He left. I think it had something to do with that Lori George girl."

Jackpot! "What do you mean?" Isabelle asked.

"We had a young woman. Student. She worked part-time. Showed up day before yesterday, punched in, but then disappeared."

"Disappeared? How strange." Isabelle reacted as if she had no idea.

"Yeah. Mr. Oliver wasn't too happy about it. Her folks went on TV last night. Said she would never ditch her job. Or school. Or her family. She lived at home while she was working on her degree in the hospitality business."

"No sign of her?" Isabelle furrowed her brow.

"Not a stitch. Such a shame. She's the second person gone missing between here and Eugene in the past two weeks."

"Wow. That's scary," Isabelle replied.

"Sure is. Nobody is sayin' anything. Not the sheriff, the news people. Nobody. Her folks want to bring in the Bureau of Indian Affairs, but local law enforcement said they should wait a day or two. They say she isn't a missing person until she's been gone for more than twenty-four hours."

"Actually, that's not true. Only on TV and in the movies. If anyone believes foul play is involved, they are urged to file a police report immediately."

"Huh." Jessica looked confused.

"I know someone who works for the U.S. Marshal's office," Isabelle said. "He specializes in missing kids. Or he used to." Isabelle was referring to Myra's friend Ellie, who had an art center in Asheville, North Carolina. One of her tenants was engaged to the marshal.

"Wow. That's a pretty tough job, wouldn't ya say?"

"I can only imagine. I don't know him very well, but we had a discussion once during a fund-raising event."

"Fund-raiser?" Jessica asked. "We call it a shin-dig."

Isabelle laughed. "Same thing. So, tell me, why did the assistant manager leave?"

"Not sure, but first thing yesterday morning, Oliver told me to fill out the paperwork for his severance and send it to the accounting office."

Isabelle made a mental note to bring up the missing persons myth when she met with the Sisters later. Also, the disappearance of the assistant manager. She wondered how deep the veneer of niceness went.

"Do you think the assistant manager had anything to do with the missing woman?"

"Maybe he just wasn't paying attention." Jessica shrugged. "You know how it goes, sometimes. There are people who can work on their own without having someone looking over their shoulder, and then there are others who take advantage."

Isabelle thought back to her own employment situation, when one of her coworkers had framed her. "And there are those who take it even further."

Jessica gave her a quizzical look.

"Nothing. Just remembering when I worked at another company and one of my colleagues took advantage of a situation. In a big way. But that's the past, and I'm actually better for it."

"Isn't that the way things go? Seriously. When I found out my lousy husband was cheating on me, I thought my world was going to fall apart. And here

I am twenty years later, happier than I ever was. Funny thing about life."

"Yep. You never know where the road is going to lead." Isabelle turned back to her computer. "I've taken up way too much of your time, Jess."

"Don't be silly. Nice change of pace having a new face around."

"Thanks." Isabelle smiled and began to click away at the Eugene Cascade Inn's spreadsheets. When no one was looking, she plugged in a flash drive and downloaded all of the Cascade files. She planned to send the data to Fergus. See if there was some kind of pattern. Meanwhile, she brushed up on the Eugene file in particular. First and foremost, she had to find the blueprints.

CHAPTER EIGHTEEN

Later That Evening

The five o'clock whistle blew, signaling for the day shift to end. Isabelle thought it was quaint. She hadn't heard one in a very long time. She took her jacket from the back of her chair and said good night to Jessica and George. "Thanks again for making me feel welcome."

"Sure thing. Have a good night. See you in the A.M."

George nodded. The man might have said six words all day.

Isabelle walked over to the transportation area and met up with Kat. "I guess we should grab some dinner and then bring our stuff here."

Kat nodded. "Oliver gave me a set of keys for the outside door."

"Not the inside?"

"Nope. That gets locked at five."

"What if you need to work?"

"There's a computer upstairs in the alcove. That's where I'd log in."

"Right. I remember seeing it now."

The two walked through the cubicles, saying good night to their new colleagues. When they approached the parking lot, Kat mentioned there was a small office in the mill itself. That was for any overnight work that had to be done.

"Is there always someone on site?"

"If there isn't a load in or load out, it's supervised by two security guards. The mill doesn't always run twenty-four-seven. And the other two divisions don't require use of the mill."

"You did your homework today." Isabelle patted her on the back.

"And you?" Kat grinned.

Isabelle waited until there was no one in sight. "There seems to be an anti-Dickie, and don't-like-Oliver consensus."

"Yeah. I got the same chilly reaction."

"I wonder, has it always been that way?" Isabelle pondered.

"We'll have to do a little more digging."

"I have to say, Jessica was rather forthcoming. I mean, she didn't seem to be censoring anything she said, although I didn't get too specific." Isabelle pulled the flash drive from her pocket. "But I did manage to download some information about the Eugene location, including the blueprints."

"As Charles would say, 'Brilliant!'"

They got in their respective automobiles and drove back to The Grand Hotel. They had a lot to cover and got the meeting started right away.

"We Are Family" began to play on everyone's laptop. Greetings and salutations were followed by a salute to Lady Liberty.

"First thing," Charles began. "We found a lab in Portland that can do all the tests we need. Poisonous substances and fingerprint DNA. I'll text you the details and contact person."

"Excellent. It's about an hour from here. I can run the evidence up in the morning," Annie offered. She looked at the group. "I *am* the fastest driver." No one disagreed. "I'm going to need a sample of Milton's fingerprints."

Myra handed Annie a newspaper. "Way ahead of you. I took it from his hospital room this morning." She paused. "There may be several different people's fingerprints on the paper, but there should be only two, or three tops, on the glass."

"Who's next?" Annie asked.

Kathryn raised her hand. "Transportation area seems tight and well-organized. The only thing that was curious was a slight attitude about Dickie and Oliver. More so about Dickie."

Isabelle went next. "There's a very chatty woman in the Cascade Inn division. Been with the company for twenty years. Likes her job. Adores the Spanglers, but, like Kathryn, I got a strange vibe when it came to Oliver. Kathryn and I were speculating on how long this uneasiness about the two men has been going on. I'll try to get more info from Jessica tomorrow. Meanwhile, I was able to swipe the files, at least the ones I had access to. The Spanglers are the only ones who can access the entire database."

Fergus chuckled. "For the moment." Everyone else reacted the same.

"I have the blueprints," Isabelle added. "I am going to try to get down to Eugene tomorrow or the day after. I'd like to get more info from Jessica. What do you think?" she asked the group.

"The family said they were going to bring in the Bureau of Indian Affairs, but that could squash whatever we're trying to accomplish. We really don't want the Feds sniffing around," Charles added.

"I spoke to Mrs. George today. I told her I would cover her daughter's missing-person story. Make sure it stayed top of mind. Maybe we can stall their going to the Bureau."

"What about Ellie's friend? The U.S. Marshal? Doesn't he work with missing children?" Isabelle asked.

"He did, but from what Ellie told me, he's been promoted to Witness Protection. Management position, I believe," Myra added. "I don't know if he could be of any help."

"He may have a new job, but he still has years of experience," Charles said.

"Good point. But again, I doubt he could help unless it's off the books," Myra said.

"Let's keep him in mind. We may have to call on him for some advice," Charles said. "We need to find that girl."

"So, I take it that I should go to Eugene tomorrow." Isabelle jotted down a few notes.

"Yes," Annie replied.

Myra was next. "Sasha and Eileen are due here first thing tomorrow. Sasha will tail Bart, and Eileen will tail Dickie. I am going to have lunch with Danielle."

"And when I get back from Portland, Oliver is going to take me to a few car dealerships."

Fergus blinked several times into the camera.

"What?" Annie asked. "I'm undercover."

"Hardly," Fergus said.

"You know what I mean. I phoned him earlier and said I was looking into buying a new sports car for my birthday, and would he accompany me."

"Didn't he think it odd that you would go car shopping in Oregon?" Maggie, the inquisitive reporter asked.

"No. Because I told him I wanted to drive it back home. Take to the open road." She shook her head and grimaced. "Give me a little credit for coming up with a good story."

Myra laughed. "You always have a good story." She looked at Maggie. "What time are you meeting with the George family?"

"Eleven. They both took time off work to try to unravel this mystery."

"I think Benjamin should accompany you there. Show them the huge effort the family and the media are taking, regardless of local law enforcement." Myra made a note to contact Benjamin as soon as they were finished.

"Speaking of which, I know the deputy sheriff told the George family and the employees at Spangler that the family had to wait twenty-four hours."

"We know that's rubbish," Charles huffed.

"Yes, I disabused Jessica of that notion."

"So why do you suppose the local officials are holding back?" Kat asked.

"Good question," Annie answered. "There are too many intersecting situations here, and we know that powerful families can have far-reaching influence on anyone, including the law. Maybe not everyone, but it only takes one or two for a cover-up."

Everyone nodded in agreement.

Annie continued. "Kathryn and Izzie will be sharing the apartment at the main office."

"Did anyone think that odd?" Fergus asked.

Kat chuckled. "I said we could braid each other's hair."

Fergus and Charles rolled their eyes. "Whatever it takes."

Everyone echoed in unison: "Whatever it takes!"

"Let's run this down again." Annie went through the list:

1. Maggie interviews George family.
   Benjamin goes with her.
2. Izzie goes to Eugene.
3. Kat sniffs around office.
4. I go to Portland lab and then meet up with Oliver.
5. Sasha and Eileen scope out Bart and Dickie.

6. Fergus and Charles keep digging for more financials, also whatever certificates or permits may not be compliant.

Everyone was vigorously jotting notes and typing. "Milton is going to be released from the hospital tomorrow," Annie added. "They are hiring a nurse who will come twice a day to take his vitals. He'll be on a heart monitor, as well."

"Glad to hear he's going home. Seems like such a nice man," Isabelle said.

Annie glanced over at Myra. Myra gave her a dagger stare in return. Annie giggled. Charles did not look pleased.

"Right. We shall reconvene tomorrow evening. Say, seven?" Charles asked.

"You got it!"

"Sure thing!"

And a few more voices chimed in.

Fergus ended the call with his usual, "Mind as you go."

"Steady on," Charles said. Then he looked at Myra. "And you and I shall have a little chat later, love." His camera went black, and all that was left was the statue of Lady Liberty, waiting for her salutation.

When the meeting was over, Annie ordered dinner for everyone. Chicken, salmon, pasta, salad. The works.

"I'll drop my things off at the apartment tomorrow and check in with Jessica. See if I can glean a little more insight before I head to Eugene," Isabelle said.

"You going to spend the night there?" Kathryn asked.

"It will depend on what I find out. I may want to get the full picture. Day and night activity."

"I think that's a good idea," Myra said.

"Do you think it's safe for Isabelle to go down there alone? I mean, we have no idea what she might be walking into." Again, Maggie with the inquisitive and calculating mind.

"Maybe there will be a last-minute short-run?" Kathryn suggested.

"How do we pull that off?" Isabelle queried.

"I will simply place an order that needs to be delivered the same day," Annie said. "I shall do it first thing."

"Okay, but where is it going to be delivered?" Kathryn asked.

Annie typed something into her computer. She scrolled down a bit. "Bingo. There is a house being built for a veteran near Eugene. I am sure they can use some extra materials."

"How did you find that?" Kathryn asked.

"I remembered a story about a disabled veteran who was evicted because of Eminent Domain. A big developer came in and had the land condemned, leaving the man without a place to live. A local church donated a piece of property and got some group funding."

"Wow. That would make a great story," Maggie said.

"It was. And you did," Annie reminded her.

"Oh my gosh, you're right. It was part of a bigger story about organizations helping displaced veterans who weren't getting help from the V.A."

"You sure helped give them a black eye," Annie said.

"Well, they deserved it. Remember when my Aunt Sophie applied for spousal support after my Uncle Richard passed away? The V.A. dragged it on for a year and a half. We filled out almost thirty pages of paperwork and certificates, they confirmed receipt, but then every month, they said they were missing page whatever."

"Did they call you to tell you?" Kathryn asked.

"No. I kept calling every month to ask for updates, and that's when they would tell me they needed something else. This went on for months. No joke. I finally wrote to her congressman and got a phone call that same day from his aide. She asked me to fax her a couple of the pages, and within six weeks, we had a year and a half's worth of spousal support." Maggie took a breath. "It was retroactive." She wiggled her eyebrows.

"That's when Maggie came to me and asked if she could do a story about the V.A. and interview some of the men and women who fought for our country and were now being ignored."

"You should have gotten a Pulitzer for that piece," Myra said.

Maggie almost gagged from laughing. "It was a good piece, but it wasn't earth-shattering. Others have exposed worse conditions. That's what the Goldsmith Prize is for: exposing poor government. Besides, I had an ax to grind."

"Well, good on you for covering it," Isabelle said. "But you really didn't remember?"

"It was several years ago. Before this." She made a circle with her finger, pointing to everyone. "Lots of stuff has happened since."

"And more to come," Annie said at a knock on the door.

"Food!" Maggie yelped.

"Maybe that's why she didn't remember. She's ravenous," Kathryn teased.

"She's always ravenous," Isabelle chimed in.

"Ah, but look." Maggie held up her hands. "See? I'm not chewing on my nails anymore."

"Ew. Gross." Isabelle grimaced.

"Well, I didn't eat them! Give me credit for trying to eliminate some of my perceived bad habits."

"Perceived? That is to laugh!" And everyone did. Once again, Maggie, the junk-food junkie, sometimes nail-biting firecracker, was the brunt of the joke.

CHAPTER NINETEEN

On the Move

Early the following morning, Isabelle and Kat brought their personal items to the apartment at the Spangler complex. They entered via the exterior door, since they were the first to arrive. Someone had to unlock the interior access door, which Isabelle assumed would be Jessica, George, or Oliver.

"What if I want to start work early?" Isabelle mused.

"Ask Oliver for a key. Tell him you're an early riser."

"Do you think he'll go for it?" Isabelle asked.

"Worth a try," Kat responded.

They climbed the flight of stairs that led to the spacious guest apartment. They both stopped short as they entered. "Do you smell that?" Isabelle asked.

"Aftershave?" Kat answered.

"Cologne. I smelled it yesterday. Oliver. Eros by Versace. But it's much stronger now."

"So someone came up here overnight?" Kat speculated.

"Or early this morning. Smells kind of fresh. Something is definitely up between those two."

"Dickie and Oliver?"

"Yes. Did you notice how nervous Dickie was when we were up here? His eyes kept darting all over the place."

"Let's take a look around."

"You don't suppose whoever came in is still here?" Isabelle cautioned.

Kat looked at her. "Don't worry, sweet cheeks. I'll protect you." She grinned.

Isabelle walked over to the wall with the French doors that concealed the built-in desk. She leaned over and noticed a smidgen of white powder. "Take a look at this." She motioned to Kat.

Kat dabbed a finger on the remnants of powder and then on the tip of her tongue. It was bitter. She looked at Isabelle. "Maybe cocaine."

"But didn't Vanessa say she saw pills?" Isabelle recounted Vanessa's story.

"Yes, but that doesn't mean old Dickie boy and Oliver aren't into other types of recreational drugs."

"Oh, boy. This is getting very complicated."

"You got that right, sista."

"Should we clean it up?" Isabelle asked.

"If he comes back and sees someone cleaned the desk, he might freak. Let's pretend we didn't find it for now," Kat replied.

The seven o'clock whistle blew, and the place began to bustle. The parking lot filled with cars, and trucks were making their way to the millwork area.

"Let's go downstairs. See who's here first," Kat suggested.

As they made their way to the lower level, Isabelle told Kat she was going to spend the night in Eugene. She needed time to study the floor plans and explore the inn room by room.

"You gonna be alright on your own?" Kat asked. "I don't think I can pull off an overnighter when it's only an hour away."

"We'll see how the day progresses," Isabelle said, as she tried the interior door to the office. It was unlocked. Jessica was already at her desk. She had reading glasses dangling from a chain around her neck and a mug on her desk that said, IF YOU CAN READ THIS, YOU'RE TOO CLOSE.

"Good morning, Jessica. Funny mug."

"Are you talking about my face?" Jessica chuckled.

Isabelle appreciated this woman's sense of humor. "You're quite the card."

"That's how I keep myself entertained." Jessica snickered. "You plannin' on goin' to Eugene today?"

"Yes. I'll probably spend the night."

"I'll let them know." Jessica sent off a quick email to the manager of the Eugene location. She looked up. "Dickie said to let you know that Bart is going to accompany you."

Isabelle tried not to sneer. "Is he going to be spending the night, too?"

"Nope. No more rooms. He can show you around and skedaddle back here."

Isabelle was relieved. She wanted just enough time with Bart to get her take on him, but she didn't want someone watching every move she made. Isabelle's burner vibrated, and she turned to walk toward her desk. "Okay, thanks, Jessica." She didn't want to read the text in front of anyone else. When she was situated properly, she glanced down at her phone on her lap. It was Annie:

Sasha arriving from Seattle in hour. Stall until you get the go from me.

Isabelle looked around and sent a reply: **Got it.**

Now she had to figure out how to delay her departure. Dickie. She'd have a casual chat with Dickie. *Tell me about your job. How long have you been here? Anything you can share about the inns? Which is your favorite?* That would also give her an opportunity to get a better read on him. Isabelle was good at reading body language. She called over to Jessica, "Do you know if Dickie is available?"

"He's usually getting his coffee about now. You can check the cafeteria. Is there anything I can help you with?"

"No. I just had a few questions. Thanks." Isabelle got up and walked to the cafeteria. Dickie was at a booth near the window. Bart was with him. *This could get tricky.* She quickly sent a text to Kat.

Need to get Bart away from Dickie.

Kat responded in seconds: **On it**

Isabelle approached the two men. "Good morning. Do you mind if I join you?"

Dickie smiled. "Not at all. Please. Bart, move over for the lady." Instead, Bart got out of the booth and let Isabelle slide in. He was too nervous to be trapped.

In less than a minute, an announcement came over the loudspeaker: "Phone call for Bart Nichols."

"Excuse me." He walked to the house phone. "Yeah?" Pause. "Sure. I'll be there shortly." He went back to the table. "Our new driver has a coupla questions. Gonna meet her in the yard." He turned and left the cafeteria through the side door.

Isabelle figured between the two of them, they could postpone Isabelle's departure for an hour. At least. Bart seemed the type who wanted to talk a lot, but Dickie was always dominating the conversation.

Isabelle and Dickie talked about Milton Spangler and his tenure. "Yep. Been here almost twenty-five years. Started when I got out of vocational school. Great place to work."

Isabelle thought he seemed sincere. Why would he be involved in something that could ruin his and everyone else's careers? Must be something huge, and by the look and sound of it, drugs were involved. Just how much was what they had to find out. Her phone vibrated. She didn't want to check it in front of Dickie, so she began to wind down their conversation. "I suppose I should be moving along. I know Bart probably has a lot on his schedule besides babysitting me. It's been a pleasure spending a little time with you. I'll report in later."

"I believe you're supposed to report to Benjamin."

"That's right." She tried to interpret his tone. Nothing abrasive or arrogant. "I'll keep you in the loop so you can keep Oliver in the loop."

"Lots of looping." Dickie chuckled.

"I just don't want anyone to think I'm not doing my job or keeping anyone out of the loop." Isabelle smiled.

Dickie gave her words a second's thought. Better for him to know what was going on at the same time as everyone else. "I'd appreciate it. Thanks. This way, I can be ready to handle things if need be. Not that I expect anything to happen, but with Mr. Spangler still recovering, I know Benjamin and Oliver have their hands full." *Oliver, Bart, and I do, that's for sure,* he thought to himself.

"Thanks again. I'll see you tomorrow." Isabelle walked toward the ladies' room before going back to her desk. She checked her phone when she got into one of the stalls.

Ok. Go.

That meant Sasha was in the parking lot. Charles had sent Sasha a photo of Bart and his dossier. He always drove the same green pickup truck with the Oregon plates: 203 SEI.

All the company vehicles had the SEI suffix. The plates on the lumbermill trucks started with the number one; the trucking company started with the number two; and the Cascade Inns started with the number three. Dickie's plates were 201 SEI; and Oliver's were 200 SEI. Easy to keep track of, and easy for the local authorities to spot (and ignore) if they were so inclined.

Bart and Kat were on their way in from the lot. "Impressive fleet," Kat said.

Bart was all puffed up. It was his responsibility to be certain the vehicles were in pristine condition, inside and out.

"I'm ready when you are," he addressed Isabelle. "We're giving you the van, if that's okay. Unless you want to drive a pickup. Just need a copy of your driver's license."

Isabelle froze. That was one thing they hadn't had time to take care of. "I'll drive my own car, if that's alright. Mr. Spangler is paying for the rental, so I might as well use it."

"Okay. But if you want to turn it in for a company vehicle, that's fine with me."

"Thanks. I'll keep that in mind." Isabelle made a mental note to let Myra know she had almost gotten into a bind. Charles or Fergus could get them fake credentials quickly, and she was only an hour away if she needed to get back to Salem in a hurry.

Isabelle followed Bart outside and got into her rental. She waited for Bart to pull around so she could follow him. Several yards down the road, an innocuous-looking vehicle waited for them to pass. A few beats later, Sasha pulled onto the road and began to tail them. Myra sent a text to Isabelle, giving her a description of Sasha's vehicle. It looked like any other car on the road, except for the driver with the Olympia baseball cap.

* * *

Dickie sat across from Oliver's desk. Oliver had no words for him. He had no words for anybody. He had nothing. Oliver rested his elbows on his desk and shoved the palms of his hands against his browbone. "So you're telling me that neither one of you could get any information out of that woman in Blaine?"

"No, sir. She claims she isn't working for anyone but us. Percy went to her first. He was wearing a ski mask. Scared the you-know-what out of her, but she didn't change her story one bit. Then I went in to see if she might come around. I was wearing a rubber screaming skeleton mask. Thought that might terrify her enough to spill her guts. But same thing. Either she's telling the truth, or she is one heck of a good liar."

"I just find it a bit of a coincidence that a new hire should happen to stumble upon our facility. What do you think, Dickie? Some kind of happenstance? Or maybe there's someone on the inside selling our secret to someone." He peered at Dickie.

"What? Me? You can't be serious, Oliver. We all have too much to lose by blabbing, and a lot to gain by remaining silent. Why would I do something like that?" Dickie was truly stunned that his cohort, boss, and sometime friend, would think he'd betray him. "Sorry, Oliver, but you are barking up the wrong tree."

"Maybe Bart?" Oliver stared at him.

"Bart? He's not smart enough to betray anyone."

"Well, he was stupid enough to pick up a hitchhiker when he was supposed to be making a delivery. And I want to know who left the bleeping door open in Eugene!" Oliver shot out of his chair. "You said it wasn't the assistant manager? How can you be sure?"

"Because we caught him with his girlfriend in one of the rooms while all this went down. That's why we let him go. Dereliction of duty. He was supposed to lock the main laundry room door, and only open it if someone needed to get in."

"Did he know why he was supposed to keep the door locked?"

"To keep people from stealing towels, and to keep people away from cleaning chemicals." Dickie recited the company line.

"And you're sure he knows nothing about what was going on?"

"Like I said, he was having a horizontal party, and according to the janitor, it was a regular thing."

"And the janitor didn't think to say anything?"

"He didn't want to rat him out, I guess. He didn't think it was a big deal."

"Well, it is a big deal. I think to be on the safe side, you need to move the woman from Blaine to your cabin."

Dickie did a double take. "My cabin?"

"Yes, your cabin. The one you bought with the extra money you've been making."

"Yeah. Yeah."

"With that new Isabelle person making her way upstate, we can't take any more chances. We can't risk someone finding out what we are up to."

"Understood." Dickie got up from his chair so he could be eye-to-eye with Oliver. "You want me to do this today?"

"The sooner, the better."

"I've got a few things scheduled for tomorrow, but I can drive up there later in the afternoon."

"Okay, but don't push it any longer. We don't want our new facilities manager snooping around while that woman is still there."

"Understood." Dickie paused. "Who is going to keep an eye on her? I can install a padlock on the basement door of the cabin, but someone is going to have to feed her."

"You got a bathroom down there?"

"Yes."

"Windows?"

"No. Just a vent window in the storage area."

"Go to the grocery store and buy a cooler, ice, and cold cuts. Get enough food for three or four days. She can make her own sandwiches."

"Geez, I hope she's not gluten-intolerant." Dickie tried to pull off a joke, but it landed on the floor. Oliver simply stared at him.

"Now get out and get this done."

"But what do we do after three or four days?" Dickie wanted to know.

"I haven't figured that out yet. With the runaway girl and these new people, there's just a tad more going on than I can manage right now. The main thing is we keep her alive until I can figure out the next move."

"Maybe put her on a truck and send her to Mexico?" Dickie wasn't far from where Oliver's own thoughts were going.

"That will require some assistance. Like I said, I can't wrap my head around it today. So, if you don't mind, get busy."

Oliver turned his back on Dickie. He had to think. Think hard.

Annie gingerly packed the tumbler and the piece of carpet in a plastic bag. It was just about seven o'clock. The lab in Portland opened at eight. She would be there right on time. "Where are you meeting Danielle for lunch?" she asked Myra as she was about to leave.

"She invited me to her house. Since Milton is going home this afternoon, she wanted to be closer to his house in case anyone needed anything."

"I should be back in time to drop you off before I meet up with Oliver."

"The two of you are going car shopping, eh?" Myra grinned. "I'm surprised he's not going to Milton's."

"Oliver said he thought his father would be surrounded by people, and he didn't want to overwhelm him any further." She smirked.

"He does have a point."

"True. But I'm trying to find more reasons not to like him." Annie laughed.

"I don't think you'll have to try too hard." Myra smiled. "When do you think you'll be back?"

"Probably eleven-ish."

"Good. I told Danielle I'd get to her house around noon."

"And Oliver and I are meeting for lunch around one. Plenty of time to drop you off and get back here. We're going to some fancy-schmancy restaurant downtown."

"I'm sure you are." Myra raised an eyebrow.

"Okay. Gotta bolt. See you in a few."

"Annie?"

"Yes, Myra?"

"Try not to get a speeding ticket."

"Moi? Surely you jest. Ta-ta!" With that, Annie swept through the room and out the door. She sped through the parking lot as if it were on fire. Typical Annie.

As soon as she got on the interstate, she cranked up the radio and belted out the tune of "Levitating" along with Dua Lipa. It was the only time Annie could sing without being ridiculed or asked to "Please stop!" *Tone-deaf! Ha!* Funny the kind of looks you get from people when you're wailing on the road. Most people smile and nod. Others look at you like you are completely bonkers. Annie didn't care. She was enjoying the open road with the windows down, and cruising at eighty miles per hour. She was only ten miles over the speed limit, and she wasn't the only one. In less than an hour, she was pulling into the large medical facility. There was a security guard at the entrance to the parking lot. Charles had said he was going to get her clearance, and like clockwork, he had.

"Good morning." Annie smiled brightly. "Annie De Silva."

"Ah, yes, countess. Please pull into the visitor spot near the main door. Someone will come out and accompany you inside."

"Thank you." She did as the guard instructed, and another guard was waiting at the door.

"Countess, right this way." He opened the large doors and asked her to walk through the metal detectors. "Sorry. Regulations."

Interesting. Annie looked around. It was a high-security lab used by law enforcement and the military.

"This way, please." She followed the uniformed man down a long hallway. The temperature in the building was chilly.

She shivered a little. "Is it always this cold in here?"

"Yes, ma'am."

Annie figured it was a precaution to maintain the integrity of the materials being tested. They didn't want even the smallest speck of evidence to be destroyed by a fluctuation in temperature. It was safer to keep all the rooms below sixty-five degrees.

He showed her into a room with a long counter protected by plexiglass. "Someone will be right with you." He stood at the doorway.

"Thank you." She smiled. She felt as if she were in a maximum-security prison. If this was one of the places where major criminal evidence was tested, then it made a lot of sense. Notorious criminals would stop at nothing to get their cases thrown out of court.

About a minute later, a professorial-looking man wearing a white coat, latex gloves, a disposable face mask, and eye shield appeared. "Good morning. You must be Anna De Silva?"

"Yes. Thank you for seeing me."

"I understand you have two items you would like tested?"

"That is correct."

"What can we do for you?" he asked.

Annie took the carefully wrapped tumbler out of her tote bag first. "This needs to be dusted for prints, and also whatever DNA you can manage to get without degrading the prints."

"Do you have something you want them matched to?"

Annie pulled out the newspaper. "Any and all prints on this page. Equally important, I need you to check for any toxic substances in the remaining droplets." Annie slipped the tumbler under the plexiglass screen, followed by the paper. The man used tongs to place the items into separate plastic bags. He typed a few things into a computer and printed the work order.

"Anything else I can do for you?" he asked.

Annie smiled. "Yes. We also need to see if there is anything toxic in this fabric." She slid the bag with the piece of rug under the partition. "It might match whatever you find in the glass."

He repeated the same routine and placed the rug in one of his official bags, typed, printed, and attached the work order to the objects and placed all three into a bin.

"How soon do you need this?" he asked.

"The usual." She smiled. "As soon as possible."

The corners of his eyes crinkled above his mask, suggesting he, too, was smiling. "It's going to take at least three days for the entire panel that Mr. Snowden ordered." Charles and Fergus were always flying under the radar, so they enlisted Avery Snowden's agency for such things. "Shall we send the results to Mr. Snowden, or do you have another preference? He said the results could be shared with you and Mrs. Rutledge."

"If it's not too much trouble, could you copy both me and Mrs. Rutledge on the results?" Annie handed the gentleman her embossed business card:

Countess Anna Ryland De Silva
Mobile: 800-555-2754
Email: rhinestonecowboyboots@ards.com

The gentleman chuckled. She kicked back one of her legs to show off the glittery footwear.

"I'll get my people on this right away."

"What do I owe you?"

"There will be a printed invoice waiting for you at one of the windows. You'll see it on the way out."

"Thank you so much," Annie replied with a dazzling smile.

"My pleasure. Enjoy the rest of the day." He nodded.

The guard accompanied Annie down the hall and

stopped in front of another plexiglass window with an opening at the bottom.

"Countess?" the woman asked.

"Yes, that's me," Annie said with a congenial expression.

The woman slid the invoice toward Annie. The total was $5,000. Annie didn't blink an eye. She pulled out her credit card and settled the bill. "Thanks very much. Have a nice day."

Annie followed the guard to the main entrance, where he saw her to her car. She hit the fob to unlock it, and the guard opened the door for her. "Thanks very much. You are quite the gentleman."

"My pleasure, ma'am." He nodded and stepped aside.

Annie was relieved this part of the mission was underway. She carefully left the parking lot, waved to the entry guard, and raced back to Salem. On her way, she phoned Myra. "All systems go, here."

"Great. Eileen is at S.E.I. and will be tailing Dickie when he leaves. She's already put a tracker on his vehicle just in case."

"I really appreciate Milton's license plate system." Annie chuckled. "Do you know the status of Bart and Isabelle yet?"

"They should be arriving in Eugene shortly, if they haven't already."

"Excellent," Annie replied. "I'll see you within the hour. I know. I know. Don't get a speeding ticket. Yes, Mother."

"Oh, shut it," Myra joked, and ended the call.

* * *

Isabelle checked her rearview mirror. Sasha was two cars behind. Bart turned on his directional signal and exited the interstate. Isabelle frowned when she saw Sasha go past the exit. Then she remembered Sasha had a GPS tracker on Bart's vehicle. Isabelle figured Sasha would circle back. Ten minutes later, Isabelle spotted Sasha ahead of her. *How in the world did she do that?* Since Sasha already knew the destination, she was making sure Bart wasn't on to her. But from what Isabelle had been told, Bart wouldn't know if the Goodyear Blimp was hovering over his head. Sasha pulled into the parking lot across the street from the Cascade Inn, where there was a small diner-type restaurant and a liquor store. Isabelle noted the inn's location was perfect for someone who wanted a hot meal, a soft bed, a private shower, and maybe a six-pack after a long day.

Isabelle could tell the inn had once been a two-story motel, but with the modernization of the windows, siding, and roofing, it could pass for a new structure. It appeared the main office area had been added later and the parking lot had been repaved. It wasn't fancy by any stretch of the imagination, but it looked welcoming for road-weary travelers.

Bart parked his truck at the far end of the lot, and Isabelle pulled her car next to his. He gave her a thumbs-up and grinned. He surely didn't seem like a brute, but you could never tell a book by its cover. He seemed like a bit of a goofball, not a man who would punch a teenage girl. She popped the trunk and took out her overnight bag.

"Follow me," Bart said in a cheerful voice. As anxious as he was about this whole, big mess, he was relieved he wasn't standing in front of Oliver or Dickie. They were steaming mad. He knew he'd messed up with the girl, but the other one wasn't his fault. Not this time. Dickie wanted Bart to help find the missing teen, but he also wanted him to follow Isabelle. He couldn't be in two places at once. Didn't Dickie realize that? Bart hoped the teen would show up, and then they could try to get back to business as usual. But then there was the other girl. Woman. Bart dreaded what Dickie might do. Dickie wasn't a violent man; at least, he'd never showed that side of himself when they were growing up. In fact, Dickie had helped Bart get this job. Bart let out a big sigh. Boy oh boy. What a heap of trouble they were in.

He tried to shrug off his anxiety. For now, he had to show Isabelle around the place and make sure she didn't go near the laundry room. He didn't know if he was supposed to spend the night to keep an eye on her, so he called Dickie.

"Hey, boss. We're in Eugene. What do you want me to do?"

"Show her around. But not everything." Dickie was at his wit's end.

"Well, duh, Dickie. I know *that* much." Bart didn't like the way Dickie had been picking on him over the last couple of weeks. Yes, he'd made a mistake. Okay, so he'd made a few. Not securing the bars on the window was probably the first one. "Do you want me to stay here tonight?"

Dickie lowered his voice. "No. I want you to get back here and help me look for that teenager."

"Got it. I should be back in a couple of hours."

"Good." Dickie slammed the phone down on his desk. The two men who'd captured the housekeeper were now on the lookout for the teenager, so the pill-mill was at a standstill, especially with that Isabelle woman hanging around. His phone rang. It was Oliver.

"Are you still in the office?" Oliver asked. He was standing on the sidewalk outside the restaurant, waiting for Annie.

"Yes. I'm going to go to the grocery store in a bit."

"What time are you planning on going to Blaine tomorrow?" Oliver smiled at the people passing by. *Could they see the steam coming out of his ears?*

"I figure around noon."

"Let me know when you've completed the assignment." Another nod and smile to a couple walking their dog.

"Will do."

Annie finished her mission, picked up Myra, and drove her to Benjamin and Danielle's house. "They should have the lab results in three days."

"Great. I take it your trip was uneventful." Myra peered at her.

"Now I know how Maggie feels when everyone gangs up on her." Annie smirked.

"You'll get over it. What I meant was, you didn't run into any obstacles?"

"No. Avery phoned ahead. Good thing. That place was a fortress. Could rival Pinewood, but not quite." She chuckled.

They pulled into the stone-paved circular driveway of Benjamin Spangler's home. "Beautiful place," Annie remarked.

"Do you want to come in and say hello?"

"Not right now. I don't want to be late for Oliver and our sports car adventure." Annie raised an eyebrow.

"Please try not to buy anything," Myra said as she exited the car.

"Party pooper." Annie tooted the horn.

Danielle opened the front door and waved as Annie pulled away. "Myra. How are you today?"

"I'm just fine, my dear. And you?"

"Better. I am so relieved Mill is going home today. I don't think Benjamin has slept in the past three days."

"I can only imagine." Myra gave Danielle a kiss on the cheek and followed her into the foyer. "Such a lovely home," Myra remarked.

"Thanks. It's been a great place to raise the kids. Most of their friends preferred hanging out here, so we could keep a close eye on everyone." She paused. "Such a shame about that missing girl."

"I suppose there's no news." Myra hid her knowledge very well.

"A very strange thing happened, but we don't know if it's connected. A woman found a young girl in the woods several miles from here. She and her husband brought her to the hospital, but she took off before a doctor could take a look at her."

"That is very odd. Do they think she ran away from the hospital because she didn't want her parents to find her?"

"The couple said the girl barely said a word. She was cut up and bruised. They managed to get her to the hospital, the same one where Milton was, but she took off. So odd. Her parents must be worried sick."

"I am sure they are." Over the years, Myra had become a very good actress, able to conceal vital information and her emotions.

"Come. Let's go sit on the deck. I wasn't sure what you liked, so I ordered a charcuterie and salad."

"Sounds wonderful. The food at the hotel is quite good, but it's nice to have a change of taste." She smiled at her pun.

"Funny," Danielle said. "How long do you plan on staying?"

"I'm not really sure. Annie is out with Oliver looking at sports cars."

"Sounds like that will be right up Oliver's alley." Danielle popped open a bottle of champagne. "Mimosa? Bellini? Plain?"

"Plain, please. She's threatening to drive a new sports car cross-country."

"I really appreciate you both coming out here. Patricia is a complete disaster."

"It's understandable. I don't know what I would do if Charles had a heart attack." Myra took the champagne glass from Danielle's hand. "Thank you."

Danielle looked around, not that there was anyone else there. "Patricia wouldn't know what to do if she had to cancel her hair appointment." She paused. "I really shouldn't say anything about my mother-in-law. Sorry."

"It's okay. In-laws can be tricky." Myra waited for Danielle to offer more gossip. Or facts. Whichever.

"So, how are your children? I haven't seen them in ages."

"They're all doing well. Logan is away at school, and Addie will be going to Pratt. I don't know if I'll be able to handle the distance."

"It will be an adjustment for everyone." Myra clinked Danielle's glass with hers. "Here's to bright futures. For everyone."

"I'll drink to that. Benjamin looks a fright. I was worried he'd get sick during this ordeal. I mean, his father, the missing teen, and now the young woman in Eugene. It's been quite a heap of trouble."

"I understand Benjamin is planning on visiting the young woman's family this morning. He's going with Maggie Spritzer, Annie's top journalist."

"Yes. I thought I'd hear from him by now. I'd say no news is good news, but not for the Rowans or the Georges. It breaks my heart thinking about what they're going through."

"We have to keep the faith, my dear." Myra began to fidget with her pearls. "Maybe Maggie's interviews will shed some light and give the public additional information. I heard the young woman's family was going to call the Bureau of Indian Affairs."

"I don't blame them. The local police were very slow to move on the case. But if the Bureau gets involved, that could cause a lot of headaches for Benjamin and the family. Who knows what they'll do? They might blame us for her disappearance."

"That would be dreadful." Myra decided to call her friend Ellie. If she could talk to the marshal, she might be able to get some advice from him.

"Let's talk about happier things, shall we?" Danielle downed her glass of champagne and poured another. "I know I probably should slow down, but the past few days have been a nightmare."

"What about Oliver? He surely must have been helping Benjamin."

Danielle almost spit out her drink. "Oliver? Helpful? He only helps himself. And if you ask me, I think he's been helping himself to the petty cash drawer." She placed her fingers on her lips. "Oh, my. I've said too much. See, this is what happens after one glass of champagne." Myra was hoping Danielle might finish her second so she would blather on. "Don't get me wrong. Oliver has always been good to the kids. But lately, well, I just don't know."

"What do you mean?" Myra placed her hand on top of Danielle's. She could tell there was something eating at the younger woman.

"He's been very edgy. Flying off the handle sometimes."

Myra listened intently as Danielle went on about all the high-ticket items Oliver had purchased. "I don't know what he's invested in, but I know what his salary is and, well, it's none of my business, really."

"But it is Benjamin and Milton's business," Myra reminded her.

"I suppose you're right, but aside from marketing, I have had very little to do with the operation of the company, and Benjamin tries very hard to keep business dealings separate from family. When he's home, he's totally focused on us, the house, his parents." She took another sip of her champagne. "But these past few days . . ." Her voice trailed off.

Myra wanted to change the subject. Danielle was becoming a little sloshed. She looked at the beautiful spread of food in front of them. "This looks lovely, and I'm a bit peckish. Shall we try some of these delectable delights?"

"Oh, of course. My apologies. I'm a terrible hostess."

"Not at all," Myra encouraged her.

"It's just that I don't usually have anyone to talk to, except for at charity events. Of course, there's Benjamin, but I really don't want to get between him and Oliver." She shook off her mood. "Sorry. I didn't mean to burden you with family gossip."

"No burden. And I totally understand. It's not always easy to keep business and personal life separate." Myra noticed Danielle's eyes were watering up. "Are you alright?"

Danielle dabbed her eyes. "Yes. Thank you. I'm glad you and I decided to have lunch. Just the two of us."

"Sometimes it's good to have an impartial ear. Helps keep things in perspective."

"I couldn't agree with you more."

CHAPTER TWENTY

Interviews and More

Maggie and Benjamin arrived at the George family residence at the same time. "Good morning. I'm Maggie."

"Nice to meet you, Maggie. I hear you're a crackerjack reporter." Benjamin held out his hand.

"Well, I do like to eat Cracker Jacks," Maggie joked. "Nice to meet you. I'm sorry we didn't have the opportunity the last time I was here."

"Two weeks ago, wasn't it?"

"Yes. That's when your dad offered the reward. My boss, Annie, is best friends with Myra, and she wanted me to help cover the story. Is there any other news?" Maggie had to play it cool.

"Unfortunately, no."

"Well, we have to keep wishing, and hoping, and praying," Maggie said. "By the way, I heard someone say that a young girl was brought to the hospital

but then disappeared. Do you think that may have
been the same teen?"

"I have no idea, but if it was, then at least we
know she's still alive. As of yesterday, anyway."

Benjamin rang the doorbell. A woman with a
long black braid answered. "Hello."

"Mrs. George? I'm Benjamin Spangler. This is
Maggie Spritzer."

"Yes. Please come in." The woman stood to the
side to let them in. "My husband, John, is out on the
porch. Follow me, please."

The house was filled with Native American arti-
facts, including blankets and pottery. "Is this all
your craftsmanship?" Maggie asked.

"Yes, most of it. Even though we've assimilated,
we also want to keep our legacy and ancestry alive.
We come from the Kalapuya people. My husband's
father, Jacob, moved here years ago. He wanted his
son and the next generations to be educated through
the public school system. I met John at a cultural
event. When we got married, I moved here, too."

"It's beautiful." Maggie spoke softly. It was as if
they were in an art exhibition. They walked through
the modest home, and Maggie spotted a line of photos on the dining room credenza. "Is that Lori?" she
asked.

"Yes. My beautiful daughter." The woman was
resolute. Not an inkling of emotion. She showed
them through the kitchen and then out to a screened-
in porch. A man sat staring out into the grass. Gar-

dens of vegetables and herbs lined one side of the yard. "Would you care for some tea?" Mrs. George asked.

"That would be lovely." Maggie was not a tea drinker, but she didn't want to insult her hostess.

"Yes, thank you," Benjamin added.

"It's herbal," Mrs. George replied.

"I am sure it will be delicious." Maggie smiled, her freckled cheeks giving her a childlike glow.

"John, this is Maggie from the newspaper, and Benjamin Spangler."

Benjamin held his breath. He didn't know what to expect from a father whose daughter was missing; missing from her place of employment; missing from his company.

The man stood and held out his hand. First to Maggie. "Thank you for coming." Then he turned to Benjamin. "Please, take a seat."

"I hope you don't mind if I ask you a bunch of questions." Maggie pulled a pad and pen from her bag.

"That is why you are here, is it not?" the man replied, but without any facial expression. Then he turned to Benjamin. "And what is it that you have come here for?"

Benjamin cleared his throat. "Mr. George, I am a father of three. I cannot possibly imagine what you are going through. But I am here to tell you that we have hired an outside firm to investigate this situation." Benjamin knew there was someone investigating—he just wasn't sure who it was, except that Myra and Annie must have something to do with it.

"The police have been no help. They want us to wait another day before we can file a report."

"And that is not a law or a rule, which is why we're both here." Maggie pointed her pen to Benjamin and then to herself. "I want to bring your daughter's disappearance to the public's attention, and Benjamin wants to assist in the search."

"We considered contacting the Bureau of Indian Affairs," John George said.

"Yes, we are aware of this," Benjamin responded. "But before you do, I am asking that you give us a few days to gather whatever information we can. I can give you my personal assurance we will do everything in our power and means to find her."

Maggie jotted down a few notes. "Mr. George, I am sure you know getting the government involved can create more red tape for you. The authorities never want to make a decision or take a stand."

He nodded. "I cannot disagree, but we are very frustrated with the way the deputy sheriff has handled this. I should say *not* handled this."

"I completely understand, and that is why we are here." Benjamin looked into the man's eyes. "Please, Mr. George, give us a few days."

Mrs. George returned with a tray, a teapot, and several cups. She set them down on the small café table where the others were sitting.

"These people are here to help us," John said to his wife. She managed a little smile and nodded. She poured tea in the cups and handed one to each of them. They waited for her to take the first sip. She waited for them to.

Maggie lifted her cup. "Here's to Lorraine and her quick and healthy return home." Finally, everyone drank their tea.

When they were finished, Maggie asked a litany of questions about Lori. Her habits. Her friends. Her schedule.

Mrs. George was much more talkative at that point and offered to show Maggie Lori's bedroom. Benjamin reassured John George that they would get to the bottom of his daughter's disappearance and gave him one of his business cards, which contained his private cell number and home phone number. "Feel free to contact me at any time." He got up from his chair as Maggie and Mrs. George reappeared.

"I'm going to write an article about Lori, her heritage, her interests, her goals. We want to make her a person instead of just a missing stranger. Plus, the article may spark someone's memory about something they may have seen or heard that day."

"Should we continue to go on television?" Mr. George asked.

"Give it a day. Sometimes when people keep hearing the same story over and over, they become immune to it and tune it out. We want to keep this top of mind, but we also want to be sure people will pay attention when we have something to say." Maggie was giving the Georges her best advice. She handed them her business card. "Call me if anything else occurs to you."

"Likewise," Benjamin said. "Thank you for your time."

"Thank you, as well." The Georges stood in the driveway and watched their new champions walk toward their vehicles.

Maggie told Benjamin she was going to go back and interview all the people she'd talked to after Vanessa's disappearance. Benjamin was going to the hospital to take his father home. Patricia would be waiting for them. Myra was going to stop at Milton and Patricia's later that afternoon. Meanwhile, Annie was being wined and dined by Oliver.

Maggie headed to the gas station to interview the original witness. She was planning on asking him to recall what had happened that day. He had already changed his story once. When she arrived at the gas station, the attendant approached her with a suspicious eye. "You again?" He was gruff.

"Sorry to bother you, but some new information was discovered yesterday. I was hoping you could run things down for me again."

"What kind of new information?" He had a wary look on his face.

"Apparently, a couple found a girl in the woods, but when they took her to the hospital, she ran away."

"So's what's that got do with me?" The man was not pleased to see her.

"I thought you could just go over what you saw one more time."

"Look, I told you and the cops I never seen her get into a Spangler truck. It was a busy day, and I was in a hurry."

"Did you see her at all?"

"Yeah, but like I said the last time you was here, I was in a hurry. She was there one minute and gone the next. She musta gotten into somebody else's car or somethin'."

Or somethin' for sure, she thought to herself. *The guy is too tense. Why wouldn't he want to cooperate?* "Again, I apologize." She decided to switch to the latest news. "You probably heard that another young woman has gone missing?"

"Don't know nothin' about it." He tapped the toe of his boot on the ground. "If you don't mind, I got work to do."

Maggie was relentless. That was a big part of why she was so good at her job. "The paper and media company I work for are doing a story about runaways."

"Yeah, well, good luck with that. We get a bunch of 'em around here."

"That's exactly why I'm writing the story."

He began to turn to walk away and gave her a stink-eye stare. "Like I said, I wasn't sure, 'cause I was busy. And if you don't let me get back to my job, I ain't gonna have one."

Now he isn't sure. I wonder how much they paid him to keep quiet. But more importantly, who? "Thanks for your time." Maggie didn't need to know any more. The guy was guilty of something.

She wanted to interview the people who'd found Vanessa in the woods, but they refused to "get involved." Maggie had a feeling things were closing in on someone. Again, who? And how many people were involved in the cover-up?

Her next plan was to go to Eugene and interview the other employees at the inn, but that would be the following day.

Oliver was effusive. Bombastic. He loved to talk about all of his possessions and adventures. He may have thought he was impressing Annie, but she could not care less. She almost felt sorry for him. Almost. It was as if he were trying to prove something. She knew that when people had everything handed to them, they had little or no sense of who they really were. When things were constantly superficial, how could anyone understand substance? "Tell me, Oliver. Why hasn't some wonderful woman snatched you up yet?"

"I'm elusive." He chuckled. "Seriously, I haven't met 'the one.'" Air quotes.

Annie tried not to roll her eyes. "Describe what 'the one' would be like for you?"

Oliver twirled his Negroni cocktail. "Intelligent. Witty." He paused.

"And attractive," Annie said plainly. "Why not? With all the treatments and injectables available, there is no reason why a woman shouldn't be attractive." She couldn't believe she was saying this, but she wanted to gain Oliver's confidence, and the only way was to speak the same superficial language as he.

Oliver looked down at the table. "You're not wrong." Then he looked up at her. "You're a very attractive woman. Intelligent. Witty."

"And old enough to be your mother." Annie gave him a sly grin. She had no issues with men dating older women, but this would be a stretch, even for her. She had never cheated on Fergus, but she had been a wild woman at one time.

Oliver laughed out loud. "Would you be offended if I was actually hitting on you?"

"Not at all. But I do have a point." She raised her glass of champagne. "Thank you, anyway."

Now that Oliver was squirming in his seat, he decided to change the subject. "So what kind of car do you want to test-drive today?"

"Lamborghini?" She raised her eyebrows.

"That's uncanny. I have my eye on one, myself."

"Well, if you'd rather change it up, I can do a Ferrari, Maserati, or Aston Martin."

"You really are my kind of woman." Oliver grinned. "Why don't we try a couple of them?"

"Sounds grand!" Annie chuckled. The conversation moved on from favorite places to movies, and the usual small talk banter.

As they were leaving the restaurant, Oliver excused himself and went to the men's room. When he returned, he lightly squeezed his nostrils together and sniffed. Then he explained they would have to drive to Portland. That was where the biggest sports car dealership was. "Well, that will give me a chance to drive your Porsche." The valet brought Oliver's car around, and Annie dashed to the driver's door.

"As you wish." Oliver made an ostentatious bow.

This was the second time that day Annie would be whizzing along I5 from Salem to Portland. But this time, it was going to be much more fun.

When they arrived at the dealership, Oliver was greeted by two men who were as impeccably dressed as he was. They could be on the cover of *GQ* magazine or *Esquire*. Annie noticed all of them were well-manicured, too. The men obviously knew Oliver and were happy to see him. Again. "Can't stay away from that beauty?" One of the men nodded toward a shiny red Lamborghini Huracán.

"Ooohhh . . . it is a beauty," Annie exclaimed. She sashayed her way across the showroom.

Oliver leaned in toward the two men as they watched. "She's Countess Anna De Silva."

"Ooohhh . . . she's a beauty, too," one of the men commented. "Is she in the market for a shiny new car?"

"She made some noise about driving something cross-country," Oliver said with authority. "She wants to test-drive a few different makes and models."

"Absolutely! I am sure we can accommodate her."

One of the men crossed the room and addressed her. "I'm Eric. What did you have in mind?"

"Sorry. I get very excited around fast cars. I'm Annie."

He opened the driver's door. "Please get a feel for this beautiful piece of art."

Annie slid in and melted into the soft leather. "It's scrumptious," she said. "May I take it for a test-drive?"

"But of course." He opened the door so she could unfold herself from the coupe. "Come with me." He took her to a computer terminal, where he typed a few strokes and waited to see what was available. "We have a silver one that's accessible."

"Fab! Let's do it. Oliver? Ready?"

"Give me one sec." He took off for the men's room again, and once again, he pinched his nose and sniffed as he exited.

It was obvious to Annie that Oliver was doing cocaine. She had never done it herself but had been around many people who had. Did. It was at almost every party she'd attended in the late 1980s. *He needs a lesson in discretion.*

It wasn't company policy to allow two non-employees to drive a $300,000 car out on the street, but the salesmen would make an exception in this instance. If anything happened, Annie could cover the cost. They weren't too sure about Oliver. He had been hemming and hawing for over a month about the car he wanted. He kept promising a deposit, but it hadn't arrived yet.

A man in a service uniform pulled the car around to the side entrance. Annie jumped into the driver's seat, and Oliver slid into the passenger side. "Be back in a bit!" Annie waved and pulled away slowly enough not to give the two salesmen palpitations.

Oliver directed her to a country road where she could tear it up. And tear it up she did. He glanced over at the speedometer. 120 mph. Fast enough. He was both awed and terrified. He'd never met anyone like this woman before. He could actually go for someone like Annie. She was rich enough for his standards. Age? Just a number.

Annie knew Oliver was looking at her as if she were his latest prey. She played along. The man had no idea whom he was dealing with.

After twenty minutes of zooming around the outskirts of Portland, they returned to the dealership. Oliver was quick to return to the men's room.

One of the well-groomed sales associates asked her how she liked the ride.

"Spectacular! What's next?" She smiled from ear to ear. "I've had my eye on a McLaren 720S. Do you happen to have one of those lying about?"

"No, I apologize, but we can order one for you."

"Oh, darn. I'll be leaving town in a few days, and I was hoping I could drive something home."

"How about the Ferrari Roma? That is an exquisite automobile. Handles corners like no other."

"Sounds intriguing." Annie was wondering why Oliver was taking so much time in the men's room.

Oliver loosened his collar as he tried to comprehend what he was hearing. "The reporter was back at the gas station?" He tried not to shout. "What did she want?" He was listening. "I thought you bought him a new toy to keep his mouth shut."

"I did, boss. But he called and said he didn't like the way she was asking questions."

"I don't care what he likes. He got his token of our appreciation. Tell him to cool his jets."

"But what if he threatens to go to the cops?"

"How many times can one person change their story, Dickie?"

"I dunno. A couple?"

"Right. And he's done just that. Besides, Deputy Nelson isn't going to do anything."

"Okay. If you say so, but he sounded really nervous."

"Tell him to take a pill."

"Speaking of pills. Ernesto called."

Dickie thought his heart was going to stop. "Ernesto? What did he want?"

"He said you owe his people a kilo."

"So, get busy!" Oliver was pacing.

"But boss, we had to shut down both operations. We don't have any place to get it done."

Oliver knew he was in way over his head. His operation had practically shut down, and he had to deliver. "Okay, listen to me. Get that girl to your cabin, and get Blaine set up ASAP."

"Do you want me to call Ernesto?" Dickie asked.

"I'll handle it. How long do you think it will take to put a kilo together?"

"It's gonna take a few days to set up, and then a couple more after that. Probably a week."

"Get it done in three days." Oliver ended the call. He looked at his reflection. He was beet red. He pulled his brown bottle from his jacket pocket, but his hands were too sweaty to hold it, and it slipped into a toilet. He stared down at the floating bottle. Did he dare put his hand into the bowl to rescue three hundred dollars' worth of cocaine? He yanked several paper towels from the dispenser, wrapped them around his fingers, and dipped them into the unflushed water. He tossed the bottle into the sink, discarded the wet towels, and began to scrub his hands. His breathing became erratic. He grabbed the sides of the sink to steady himself when one of the salesmen walked in.

"Oliver. Everything alright?"

Oliver tossed a remaining towel over the brown bottle. "Yes, just had to take an annoying phone call."

The salesman folded his arms and leaned against the opposite wall. "This Annie friend of yours. She's a piece of work. In a good way."

Great. Casual conversation. Just what I need. "Yes, she is quite engaging." *Can you please get out of here?* "Did she ask for another test-drive?"

"Yes, the Ferrari Roma."

"Good. Do you have one on the lot?"

"We do."

"Excellent." *This guy is never going to leave.* "Did you set it up for her?"

"They're getting it ready."

"Excellent. Now if you'll excuse me." Oliver

nodded toward a stall as if to say he wanted some privacy.

The salesman blinked. "Oh. Of course. Sorry. Meet you outside."

As soon as the salesman was out the door, Oliver scooped up the bottle and dashed into the stall. He wiped it dry with another towel, opened the bottle, and sprinkled some powder on the back of his hand. This situation required more than the usual bump. Then came the second nostril. His world may have been spinning out of control, but at least he was spinning with it.

This was the worst situation Oliver had ever been in. When he was younger, it was his big brother Benjamin who always came to his rescue. Then his grandfather, Senator Wakeman, and over the past two years, he'd been able to buy his way in and out of situations. Now, if he couldn't deliver, he wouldn't get paid. If he didn't get paid, he couldn't keep up with the hush money he was spreading around. If he couldn't keep up the hush money, then tongues could wag against him. He looked down at his Tom Ford blazer. And he surely wouldn't be able to keep up his lifestyle. He might never be able to show his face again in this glorious, luxury sports car showroom.

He thought his head was going to explode. For real. The coke hit his sinuses like an ice pick. He steadied himself against the stall door. *Get it together. Get it together.* He straightened up and went back to the sink. Grabbed a few more towels, rinsed them in cold water, and placed them on his forehead. This time, if anyone asked, he could say he must have food poisoning. Or something. *My cocaine high is freaking me out!* was not an option. After a few slow, deep breaths, he took another look at himself in the mirror. He took another towel and dried the hair along his temples. He slapped on a smile and returned to the awaiting speed devil. *Bad choice of words*. He chuckled.

"Ah, there you are!" Annie linked her arm through his. "We have a new ride to experiment with."

"Experiment?" The salesman looked alarmed.

"Kidding." She gave a cutesy shrug. She noticed Oliver's body temperature seemed a bit high. *And so does he*, she added.

The sleek Ferrari Roma was built for the open road. Not for leisurely driving. It was compact. Tight. And so was the interior, although it boasted a "roomier" feel than comparable models. Once again, Annie gently moved the vehicle to the street and then onto the open road.

"He was right. This really hugs the corners." Annie whipped the car around a hairpin turn. Oliver clutched the handle piece above the door with his right hand, and the console with his other. It was like the worst ride at an amusement park. At least *they* had some safety measures in place.

Annie looked over at her companion. He did not look well. "Oliver, are you alright?" She slowed down to eighty miles per hour.

"I got myself into a bit of a pickle." He didn't know how far to take this, but it was worth a try.

"What kind? Dill? Gherkin?" Annie knew it was no time for jokes, but she had a funny feeling this pickling was of his own doing.

"More like a pickle barrel." Oliver was choosing his words carefully, making up the story as he went along. "It's embarrassing."

"Oliver, I can guarantee you that everyone on this planet has done something embarrassing in their lifetime. Although some may never notice that what they did should have caused embarrassment, but never mind. Continue, please."

"That beautiful Lamborghini?"

"Ah, yes, the beauty."

"I gave them a deposit in order to have it customized. And now I have to come up with the rest of the money. I invested in some fake-coin stock and now I can't cover the cost of the car." He thought that story might appeal to a woman who had similar vehicle interests. "I haven't told anyone about this. It's too embarrassing." He dropped his chin to his chest.

Was he pouring it on thick, Annie wondered, *or was he genuinely disgraced?*

"What kind of money are you talking about?" Annie asked.

"Two hundred. Grand." Oliver spit the figure out.

Annie nodded. "How soon do you need it?"

"By the end of the week; otherwise, I forfeit my deposit. A hundred grand."

It was true he wanted money for the car, but if he hoped to live long enough to drive it, he had to either come up with the kilo or the money. Ernesto had fronted part of the cost of building the pill-mills. Oliver had been able to skim money from one company to the next, but the cost of the pill compression machine was something he couldn't easily hide. Ernesto had given him the cash for it. Now Ernesto wanted Oliver to repay the debt. The problem was he couldn't do one without the other. He hoped Dickie was on the stick and could get the machine running in Blaine as soon as the woman was moved. Moved. Then what?

"Let me think about this." Annie stared straight ahead as she pushed the car's top speed. *Is this a way to trap him?* she considered. *Or could any action I take make me culpable?* It was a topic for the group. She couldn't make that decision on her own. She and Oliver cruised around for another quarter of an hour, then returned the precious gem to the dealership. They thanked the sales associates, took their cards, and promised to be in touch.

They walked to Oliver's car. "Want me to drive?" Annie offered. "Because even if you don't, I'm going to."

The hour drive back to Salem seemed like an eternity. Very few words were spoken. The happy mood had flattened. Oliver was also out of cocaine.

They arrived at The Grand Hotel just before five o'clock. "I'm heading over to your folks to meet up with Myra. You planning on stopping by?"

His father. Home from the hospital. With all the

chaos, it had slipped his mind. "Yes. I told Mother I'd call her when we got back."

"Good. I'll see you later." It was a half-question.

"Probably." He waited for Annie to say something more about the money.

"Wonderful. Thanks for a very fun day!" She tossed her silk scarf over her shoulder and blew him a kiss. *Let him think he's getting what he wants.* Then she disappeared through the large doors of the hotel.

He knew he could pay her back. Not right away, but eventually. This could be the stroke of luck he needed.

When Maggie got back in her car, she sent a message to Charles, asking him to check out the financials of the gas station attendant and the deputy sheriff. She noticed a brand-new ATV at the side of the building. It could have belonged to anyone, but somehow, she suspected it was the attendant's.

Before she headed back to Salem, she reached into her tote and dug for a bag of chips, but after groping and not hearing the crackling of a snack bag, she felt a round object and pulled it out. An apple! Annie!

Once she got back to the hotel, Maggie wrote a nice piece about Lorraine George. She presented a three-dimensional human being. A person. *She could be your neighbor. Your friend.*

Next, she phoned the local television station.

When she gave them her credentials, they put her through to the producer immediately. "Maggie Spritzer! To what do I owe the honor?"

"Hey, Steve! Thanks for taking my call."

"For you? Anytime," he responded cheerfully.

"I'm in town doing a follow-up story about Vanessa Rowan and the growing number of runaways and missing persons. I interviewed the George family this morning."

"Nice people. Seemed frustrated."

"Yes. Anyway, if I give you some copy and a photo collage, do you think you could slip it into tonight's broadcast at eleven?"

"Of course."

"Great. Do you want me to email it to you?"

"That's fine." He paused. "How long are you going to be in town?"

"I'm not sure."

"If you're free one night and would like to have dinner, give me a call."

Maggie pulled the phone away from her ear and stared at it for a second. "Uh, yeah. Sure. That would be nice. Thanks. Okay, gotta go. Sending info now. I'll be watching!" Then she ended the call. She couldn't remember the last time someone had asked her on a date. Sure, she and Ted had a "thing" for a while, but it was easier just being friends. Now, she thought, *Was it a date?* Depending on how things went, and what the Sisters needed, maybe she could extend her stay a day or so longer. But that plan was still open-ended for the time being.

She sent a group text to everyone, updating them on the evening news and the gas station attendant. Everyone planned to check in around eight o'clock.

Annie arrived at Milton and Patricia's around five-thirty. Patricia answered the door. "Hello, Annie." She still had a deer-in-the-headlights expression on her face. "Everyone is on the patio." She turned and walked through the foyer, down a wide hallway that led to a great room with floor-to-ceiling windows. The main floor featured accordion window coverings that folded back to make an opening that stretched across the entire rear of the room. The adjacent dining room was fitted the same way.

Beyond the windows was a tiered slate patio that also stretched from one end of the house to the other. It offered a breathtaking unobstructed view of the hillsides and valley. A stone path meandered through the landscaping to lead the eye outward. The pool and outdoor barbecue area were on the side of the house, surrounded by *Ligustrum sinense*, otherwise known as Chinese privet. Patricia explained that it had been a great setup when the kids were younger and came over to visit. They could knock themselves out behind the bushes while the adults lounged on the patio and watched the sky change from hues of blue to pink and lavender. It was Milton's sanctuary.

* * *

Myra was already on the patio with Danielle. Benjamin was on his way, and Oliver was expected shortly. Helen and Gary had gone back to Bandon once they heard Milton was in better condition. Milton was sitting in a double-wide Mamagreen Boulevard heritage denim chaise, with a dark slate base.

"You are looking just peachy to me!" Annie smiled as she gave him a kiss on the cheek.

He took her hand. "You as well, my dear. I trust you didn't scare the pants off my son this afternoon?"

"I don't think so." *But something did.* She grinned and gave Myra one of their mutual covert glances.

"And did you purchase any new trinkets?" Myra teased. Annie might have beaucoup bucks, but she wasn't the type who would squander her money on a car she could rarely drive. After she drove the thing home, no one would ever get in the car with her. Not unless they were unconscious. Besides, it would be a shame to waste such beauty. It belonged on the open road.

"No, darling. But it was fun."

"I am sure Fergus will be relieved. We're all relieved, if you must know the truth."

"Speaking of being relieved, I bet you are feeling that way to be home?" Annie addressed Milton.

"State of mind has a lot to do with how one copes with recuperation. This view puts me in the perfect state of mind."

"We are so glad to hear it, Milton." Annie turned

to Myra. "I think we should let you chill out and maintain that state of mind. What do you say, pal?"

"I agree. Milton, I cannot tell you how happy I am to see you up and in your own environment."

"Well, they really couldn't convince me there was any reason to keep me. My heart is fine. Blood work is fine. And all the other bodily fluids they've taken are fine. The heart attack was an anomaly. Nonetheless, they suggested I continue to rest for at least two weeks. I go back to the doc in a week, and he will start giving me exercises to work into my daily routine."

The doorbell rang, and Patricia excused herself to answer it. It was Dickie.

"Mrs. Spangler. I brought what you asked. But I have to tell you this has put me in a very uncomfortable position."

"I understand, Dickie, and I surely appreciate it." Patricia looked over her shoulder. Everyone was still on the patio, and she practically shut the door in Dickie's face just as Benjamin and Oliver's cars pulled into the driveway.

"Dickie, what brings you here?" Oliver asked quizzically.

"Your mother forgot something at the office and asked me to drop it by." He couldn't look at either of them.

"Did you see Dad?" Benjamin asked.

"No. Your folks have company, and I didn't want to intrude." He left out the part that he wasn't invited in. "Gotta run. Have a good evening." He could feel

Oliver's eyes burning a hole through the back of his head. He had to get that woman out of Blaine.

As Myra and Annie were leaving, they exchanged pleasantries with Oliver and Benjamin. Oliver placed his hand on Annie's elbow. "That was fun today."

Annie knew he was fishing for some kind of answer. "Yes. Thank you. Very much so. See you tomorrow."

CHAPTER TWENTY-ONE

Eugene
That Same Day

Bart politely introduced Isabelle to the staff. "We're short an assistant manager right now. He usually worked the night shift. But these fine people are covering until we get a replacement. Of course, they're getting overtime." He chuckled.

"Nice to meet all of you." Isabelle nodded. "I'm just here on a temporary basis until Mr. Spangler is ready to get back to work. My purpose is to make sure everyone has what they need and that things keep moving along smoothly. From what I've gathered, with the exception of the assistant manager, this is a well-run operation."

There were a few head bobs and a few side glances. She wondered how many of the employees knew about the former assistant manager's indiscretion. Probably everyone. There were only ten on staff, and the place wasn't massive. "I'll be spending the night, so if anyone wants to discuss anything with me, I am available until tomorrow afternoon."

Murmurs of thanks and acknowledgment buzzed through the group. "Well, let's not give Isabelle a bad impression. I'm sure you all have work to do." Bart chuckled. The group dispersed, and Bart continued to show Isabelle the facility, hoping she wouldn't want to see the laundry area. But alas, she asked when they finished their rounds.

"Bart, where are the laundry facilities?"

"We had a problem with a few of the machines. Backed up and flooded the area. We had someone come in to clean it up, but we're sending out the linens to a commercial place for the time being."

"How long will it take before it's operational? Sending to an outside service must be costly. I'll have to check to see if insurance will cover it." She pulled out a small notepad and jotted something down.

Bart was nervous. There wasn't a leak, but they *were* sending the laundry out until he could pack up the powder machine and get it out of there. He knew he had to wait until Isabelle was asleep. He could lie and say he wanted to check on the status of the room, but she might want to tag along. No, it was better if he pretended to leave and then snuck back later that night. He was supposed to be keeping an eye on her, anyway, but he'd have to sleep in his truck.

In the meantime, Annie phoned Geiser Creek and ordered lumber to be delivered to Eugene, today!

She used one of her business names, so as not to draw any attention to herself. If Sasha was tailing Bart, and Eileen was on Dickie, Annie and Myra wanted to be sure Isabelle had some backup. As soon as Dickie heard there was an immediate delivery required, he notified Kat. "Get your gear. You've got a run to Eugene. Some V.A. project, and they need a few more pieces. Box truck oughta do it."

"Since it's late in the day, how about I spend the night at the inn in Eugene? It'll give me a chance to experience the place—a real bed, shower, and a rug under my feet." Kathryn was attempting to sell Dickie on the idea. "I could spread the word. Good, free publicity."

"Let me check to see if there's an extra room." He phoned the inn and asked, then turned to Kat. "You're in luck. We just got a cancellation. Otherwise, you'd have to shack up with your roomie."

Kat feigned a confused expression. "Oh, Isabelle. Right. Is that where she is?"

"Yes." He had to get moving if he wanted to get the woman out of Blaine and back to his cabin. It was six hours to Blaine, and then another six hours back. He knew Oliver was freaking out, so Dickie cancelled the meeting for the following day and decided to drive to Blaine that evening. It was better to do the transfer at night, anyway.

It was around dinnertime when Bart told Isabelle that Kat had been given a run to Eugene and would probably arrive shortly.

"I guess I'll take you ladies to dinner, if that's alright." Bart was behaving like a person with some authority. She accepted graciously. As they crossed the road, she noticed Sasha slumped down in the passenger seat of her car, pretending to doze.

At the restaurant, Bart was greeted by a middle-aged woman wearing a robin's-egg blue uniform. "Hello, Bart. Back in town again so soon?"

Bart tried not to seem rattled. He'd forgotten that he'd had lunch at that same place just a few days ago when he'd locked up the laundry room. "Yeah. Just can't keep away from your cooking, Marie."

"Don't believe a word he says." Marie chuckled.

Isabelle didn't need any convincing of that. "Hi, Marie. I'm Isabelle. I'm the temporary facilities manager for the Cascade Inns."

"Temporary? That's too bad. You've got a much prettier face than this lug." She jerked her thumb at Bart and chortled.

Isabelle smiled and followed her to a four-top table in the front corner near the windows. Kat was pulling into the parking lot across the street, and Isabelle sent her a text. When she got out of the truck, she waved and made a motion of washing her hands and splashing water on her face. Bart nodded, and Isabelle gave her a thumbs-up. Isabelle watched Kat go into the main office. Several minutes later, she exited without her Geiser Creek jumpsuit and bounded toward the restaurant.

"Hey guys!" She made her way to the table. "I love the idea of uniforms. I don't know why I never thought of buying a bunch of jumpsuits for when I drive. Always wear jeans and a flannel shirt, but I kinda like the one-piece zip-up thing." She pulled out a chair before Bart had the opportunity to make the gentlemanly gesture. Kat was a huge presence, even for him.

Small talk ensued as they ordered Marie's meatloaf with gravy, mashed potatoes, and carrots. More small talk, food, then it was time for Bart to make a move. At least pretend.

He took the check from Marie and handed her cash. "And can you make me a roast beef with cheddar on rye?"

"Didn't you have enough to eat? You practically licked the plate and ate four biscuits." Marie pretended to scold him.

"One for the road."

"It's only an hour drive, Bart. You got a hole in one of your legs?" Marie asked.

Isabelle and Kat suppressed a laugh. That was the joke they made about Maggie.

Marie added the sandwich to the bill and handed it to him.

"Need that receipt, please," he reminded her. As the three left the restaurant, Bart turned to them. "I'll be heading back. Let me know if you need anything."

"Thanks for all your help. And dinner." Isabelle held out her hand.

"Ditto," Kat said with a firm grip.

The two women followed Bart across the street. They went inside, and Bart got in his truck and left the parking lot. Sasha immediately went into action.

She was several car lengths behind him when he made a right turn into a neighborhood. Sasha thought it was strange that he didn't go straight onto the interstate. Two blocks down, he made another right turn, and then another. He was at the intersection two blocks from the inn. He crossed the main road, turned his truck around, and positioned himself so he could see the parking lot of the inn.

That's odd. Sasha sent a text to Charles: **Appears target is waiting for a target.**

Charles answered: **Explain, pls**.

Sasha tapped out the message: **Target went around the corner and is now situated within sight of inn.**

Charles replied: **Interesting. Stay with him.**

At the same time, Bart called Dickie to let him know he'd taken the women to dinner and he was now parked a few hundred yards away from Isabelle's car. "She can't go nowhere without me noticing." Bart was somewhat enjoying playing secret agent man.

"Well, don't lose her," Dickie replied. "I'm on my way to Blaine."

"I thought you were gonna do that tomorrow."

"Oliver is having a nervous breakdown, so I gotta get her out of there."

"Where you takin' her?" Bart asked.

"My cabin." Dickie was not in the mood for idle chatter. "Listen, let me go do what I gotta do, and you do what you gotta do."

"Right, boss. I won't let her out of my sight." He didn't realize Dickie had already ended the call.

Sasha had a feeling Bart was either tailing Kathryn or Isabelle. She figured she'd find out soon enough. She slouched down and pulled the bill of her cap over her eyes. She was going to get a little shut-eye. The GPS she'd planted on Bart's truck also had a signaling device to alert her when the vehicle was set in motion. By the way Bart was positioned, Sasha didn't think he was going anywhere, by truck or by foot. If he was secretly keeping an eye on the inn, then he couldn't afford to be recognized.

Kat and Isabelle went to the main office to get keys to their rooms. There was only one double bed per room, so it would be uncomfortable for them to stay together.

From where he sat, Bart watched Isabelle walk up the flight of stairs to her room; Kat was on the floor below. He tried not to have fantasies about the two women together. He didn't consider himself a pervert. Didn't all men have that fantasy? Especially if they were included in the fun? Most of his pals had mentioned it on one or two occasions when they saw two attractive women together without male companionship. In high school, when you saw two girls together, you hoped one would go for you, and the other for your friend. Now that he was over thirty, two women at a time was much more intriguing. He had to stop his thoughts from wandering. Females were what had gotten him into trouble in the first place. Not that he'd had any plans whatsoever for that teenager. He just liked being a hero to a cute young thing. So much for that idea.

Isabelle phoned Kat on her burner. "I just got a text from Charles. Sasha is tailing Bart, but he drove around the neighborhood, and is parked a block or so from here. According to Sasha, it looks like he may be tailing one of us."

Kat laughed. "That's a riot! I wonder which one."

"My guess would be me. Everyone seemed a bit jumpy about my coming down here."

"Considering someone disappeared from this inn, yeah, that sounds about right."

"Bart told me the laundry room was locked because there had been a flood, and it's in the process of being cleaned up."

"And you don't believe him?"

"Would you?" Isabelle asked.

"Good point. So what are you going to do?"

"I'm going to look at the blueprints and then take a stroll to the laundry room."

"You plan on breaking in?" Kat asked.

"If necessary. You game?"

"Aren't I always?" Kat replied. "So if he's got eyes on the front of the inn, how do we leave our rooms without being seen?"

"You're on the first floor. Is there a rear window?"

"Hang on, let me check." Kat went into the small

bathroom. "Just a vent window in the bathroom. I doubt I could fit through it."

"Well, then, I'm going to go to the main office and take a closer look around. Pretend I need a bottle of water."

"Alright. I'll wait a few minutes and meet you there. I'll go to the truck and scoot around the front so he won't see me go inside."

"Okay. See you in a few." Isabelle hung up and went to the front office.

"Hi. You're Bethany, right?" Isabelle greeted the substitute night manager.

"Yes. Hi. What can I do for you?"

"Nothing, really. Just wanted to take a look around again. It was a lot to absorb today." She tapped her notepad with a pen. She didn't want to ask any questions about Lori, since she wasn't sure whom she could trust.

"Gotcha." Bethany bobbed her head.

"Oh, Bart mentioned the laundry room is closed."

"Yeah, a leak or something."

"So when it's fully functional, how does housekeeping get everything up and down the stairs?"

"A dumbwaiter." She craned her neck. "Down the hall next to the staircase."

"Clever."

Isabelle went down a short hall that led to a small storage space for the office supplies, water, and snacks. At the end of the hall was a fire exit, a door that led down to the basement, and another door that covered the dumbwaiter. There was a hydraulic lift that could hold up to two hundred pounds. It was large enough for a single laundry cart. Or a single person, if they were petite. *Maybe that's how they got her out of here.*

Isabelle needed no further convincing that Lori George had not left of her own volition. She felt it in her gut. Which was confirmed by everyone's bizarre behavior at the mere mention of Eugene. She had to get down to the basement level. Change of plans.

She sent Kat a text to tell her to distract the manager. Ask her to go outside and gaze at the constellations. Anything to get her out of the building for a few minutes.

Kat sent back a message that she would get her phone and pull up the app for Night Sky. Wherever you aimed your camera, the name of the constellation would pop up at the bottom of the screen. It was the one gadget Kat really appreciated, especially when she was in Montana. She figured she could get some pretty good stargazing in here in the Pacific Northwest.

Kat walked into the main office. "Hey there. I was wondering if you could help me out. I have this app on my phone that tells me what the constellations are. You have any favorites I should try to catch?" Kat made a gesture for Bethany to follow her.

Bethany looked around. "I guess it's alright. I'll leave the door open in case the phone rings."

They walked a few feet from the main entrance to the side of the building. Close enough to hear any incoming calls, but dark enough to get a decent view of the sky. Bethany was curious about the sky map, and Kat was more than happy to explain and show her how to use it. Before becoming a long-hauler, Kat had been a nuclear engineer. A graduate of MIT. All things cosmic and subatomic were of interest to her.

Isabelle pushed the button that opened the door to the dumbwaiter. She peeked inside to see if there were any other buttons to push to lower the rig, then spotted the emergency lever. She looked closely. It was separate from the alarm. She took a chance, folded herself in, and pushed the button with a *D*. The motor whirred quietly, and the lift descended to the basement floor. Except for the light coming from the shaft, the room was dark. She turned on the flashlight part of her phone and scanned the room. No signs of flooding, but maybe the cleanup company had done an impeccable job. She looked at the blueprints and counted off feet the old-fashioned way by using her own. She had done it over a hundred times and had a pretty good idea her foot was nine inches if she wasn't wearing shoes. According to the blueprint, the room should be twenty-five feet deep, but she counted only twelve. Half the size? She measured again. When she reached the other side of the room for the second time, she placed her hands against the wall. It was a sliding panel. She saw there were latches at the top and bottom, keeping the panel secure. Isabelle placed her phone on the floor with the light shining upward. *Click.* Got the first latch.

Click. Got the second one. She took a deep breath. Moving the panel could set off all sorts of alarms, but she had to go for it. She slid the door slowly. No alarms, but there was another door in front of her with a digital padlock. That was going to require some help, and she wasn't equipped with the tools she needed. She took a close-up photo of the lock and sent it to Charles and Fergus. Maybe they could come up with a solution, except time was of the essence. Bethany would be looking for her. Charles answered immediately.

Try: 6-4-3-5-7

Isabelle had no idea where Charles got that number, but she gave it a go.

No

Try: 4-6-3-5-7

Still no.

Try: 7-5-3-6-4

A slight buzz sounded, and the door unlocked.

How did you do that?

Charles replied: **Greasy fingerprints. It had to be a combination of those**.

Glad you got it on the third try. Don't go anywhere.

She scanned the small room with the light from her phone. And there it was: a long steel table with a machine at one end, covered in white dust. A cart containing boxes of one-and-a-half-inch-square glycine envelopes was against the wall. She pulled out one of the small bags and tried to scrape a few flecks of dust inside. It wasn't much, but it was something.

She took a few photos, backed out of the room, and pulled the door shut. The lock engaged automatically. She moved the panel back into place, fastened the latches, and folded herself back into the dumbwaiter. She pressed the red *U* button and hoped no one had noticed she had been missing for almost fifteen minutes. As the cart moved upward, she sent the photos off to Charles.

When the dumbwaiter reached the main floor, she peered out to see if anyone was around. Empty. Her heart was racing. She had to get back to secure quarters quickly. She climbed out of the dumbwaiter, shut the door, and walked back to the small lobby area. Kat and Bethany were entering at the same time. Isabelle let out a long exhale. A little too close for comfort.

"Kat showed me this really cool app on her phone." Bethany grinned. "It has a telescopic lens, too!"

"We were able to see a few shooting stars," Kat said gleefully.

"Sorry I missed it." Isabelle pretended to pout.

"I'll let you play with my toy tomorrow night when we're back in Salem," Kat joked. She yawned and stretched. "I think I'm going to turn in."

Isabelle noticed a few board games on a shelf. "Do many visitors use these?"

"Sometimes. Once in a while, there'll be two or three truckers who want to relax with some company."

Isabelle nodded. "Come on, Kat, let's give it a go." She pulled one of the boxes off the shelf.

Kat blinked several times. "Scrabble?" Then she realized Isabelle had something important to share. "I haven't played in years, but sure. I think I can muster another hour of consciousness."

"Super," Isabelle said, and turned to Bethany. "What time do you knock off in the morning?"

"Six."

"I may not be up, so if I don't see you, it was nice meeting you. And remember to call me if you need anything."

Isabelle tucked the game under her arm so that if Bart was, in fact, tailing her, he would see that the two women were going to play a board game. Nothing suspicious about that. As soon as they got into the room, Isabelle began to tell Kat about the secret room, the machine. Everything. She showed her the photos and told her how Charles was able to crack the code.

"Holy guacamole!" Kat said. "You took a very big chance."

"I know, but it was an opportunity I couldn't ignore."

"You are something else." Kat gave her a high five. "We'd better tell everyone."

It was almost time for the Sisters to check in with one another. Kat's laptop was still in her room, so she cozied up to Isabelle for the Zoom meeting. As soon as everyone tuned in, people were talking a mile a minute.

Myra took charge. "Sounds like we've had a productive day. Isabelle, you go first."

Isabelle recounted her discovery of the secret room and the machine. "I'm guessing a powder mill." She uploaded the photos.

Kat dabbed her finger in the smidgen of residue. "This seems a little different from what we found on the desk in the apartment."

"In what way?" Myra asked.

"This is much finer. The powder on the desk was a little grainier."

"Hang onto it for now," Charles suggested. "If we bring it to a lab and it's a controlled substance, which I assume it is, you could end up in the nick."

Fergus agreed. "We don't want to go down that road again."

Everyone agreed. There was once a time when the Sisters were under house arrest, but a clever Lizzie Cricket figured out a way to remove the ankle monitors and wrap them around the barn cats.

Maggie was next with her information about the George family interview. "My friend Steve is going to run my story about Lori George on the eleven o'clock news. We want to give her more of a three-dimensional presence. I sent off a collage of photos and some quotes from her parents."

"Did they mention getting the Bureau involved?" Myra asked.

"Yes, but I think they'll hold off for a few days. Though if local law enforcement doesn't step it up, they're not going to have any other choice."

"No ransom demand, correct?" Charles asked.

"No. Nothing. If she was kidnapped, you'd think

someone would come up with demands," Maggie added.

"True." Myra thought for a moment. "I'm going to call my friend Ellie Stillwell. She has an in with a U.S. Marshal. Maybe he can help without bringing in the bureaucrats." She checked her watch. "I should probably call her now. It's eleven o'clock there." Myra stepped away from the live chat and dialed Ellie's number.

"Myra. Is everything alright?" a sleepy voice asked.

"Hi, Ellie. So sorry to call so late, but I'm in Salem, Oregon, and a young woman has gone missing."

"That's terrible." Ellie was wide awake at that point.

"Do you think you could call your friend Marshal Gaines?"

"Yes, but why, if I may ask?" Ellie and Myra had met several years before, when Ellie first opened her art center in Asheville. Ellie was an avid animal lover and held several events to raise money for shelters, which was right up Myra's alley. They had remained good pals since.

"The young woman disappeared from an inn owned by my friend Milton Spangler. She is of Native American heritage; local law enforcement doesn't seem to be doing much, and her family wants to call the Bureau of Indian Affairs. I was hoping you could call the Marshal and see if he had some free time to come out here to assist. Unofficially, of course. And we would pay all his expenses, and for his time."

Ellie fell silent for a moment. "Do you think she's been kidnapped?"

"There haven't been any ransom demands. We think she may have been in the wrong place at the wrong time."

"Chris used to work in the missing children division, so he has a lot of experience in that area. Let me call him and see if he's available. Give me a few minutes, and I'll call you back, or I'll have Chris call you directly. Is that okay?"

"Yes. Thanks so much." Myra was stroking her pearls as she returned to the table, where everyone was speculating who Bart was tailing. "Ellie is going to call Marshal Gaines and get back to me."

"Brilliant. What's next on the list?"

It was Annie's turn. "Seems like our Oliver is in a financial bind. He needs two hundred grand."

"Oi. What for?" Charles asked.

"Says it's for his new car, but I think he's got some kind of drug issue going on."

"Well, that fits with what we found on the desk in the apartment," Kat said.

"It could be tied into the pills and powder," Isabelle added. "He may be running a counterfeit fentanyl operation."

"And that may be why some of the local authorities have been laid-back in trying to find either of the girls," Maggie suggested.

"Charles, did you find anything unusual in the deputy sheriff's financials?" Annie asked.

"There are monthly deposits of two thousand dollars going into his account from an offshore shell company," Fergus said.

"Another culprit to add to this mix." Annie jotted down some notes. "That makes Dickie, Bart, Oliver, and Deputy Nelson."

"What about the gas-station guy?" Maggie asked.

"That was probably a one-off to get him to change his story," Charles said. "There's been no other activity as far as we could tell."

"Alright. We have a lot of work cut out for us." Myra was stroking her pearls again.

"Has anyone heard from Eileen? Eyes on Dickie?" Annie asked.

Fergus chimed in. "They are heading north on I5. Been on the road for a couple of hours."

"Do you suppose they're going to Blaine?" Isabelle asked. "That's where the last U.S. inn is located."

"That's a good guess," Charles replied. "I'll check in with Avery." Charles disappeared from the screen for a couple of minutes.

"What's next?" Myra asked.

Fergus looked down at a sheet of paper on his desk. "Lab results should be in tomorrow."

"Wow. That was fast."

"It helps to know a lad or two." Fergus winked. "Did you ever find out what Milton was going to talk to his sons about?"

"We're going to see Milton tomorrow. Patricia has a few appointments in town, so we offered to bring lunch."

"Splendid," Charles said. "The lab is going to send all the results to me as soon as they're finished."

Myra's phone rang. It was a man's voice. "Hello, Myra? This is Chris Gaines. Ellie asked that I call. What can I do for you?"

Myra explained the situation as best she could. She knew she didn't have a lot of information to share, which was why she was seeking his help or advice.

"I have the next three days off. I could fly out there with Chandler tomorrow. We worked a lot of missing cases together, so when the service was going to retire him, I brought him home with me." Myra was wondering what kind of person Chandler could be, someone who had no place to live after being in the U.S. Marshal's service. Was he reliable? "Chandler is my dog," Chris clarified. "But this has to be totally off the books."

"Oh, we'll pay you cash," Myra offered.

"No, I mean I cannot get paid to do side work. Against regulations. But it doesn't mean I can't help out a friend of a friend."

"How will we compensate you?" Myra asked.

"Make a donation to one of the retired K-9 associations."

"That, we can certainly do." Myra was relieved. She'd thought he might decline the request. "We will also make your travel arrangements. Just tell us which airport you'll fly from and how we can get a ticket for Chandler."

"Charlotte airport, and I'll take care of Chandler. They usually let him fly for free."

"Wonderful. I cannot thank you enough, Marshal."

"Anything for Ellie. And please call me Chris. Remember, I am off duty."

"Whatever you say, Chris." Myra was smiling from ear to ear. "Text me your info. DOB. The usual."

"Will do. See you sometime tomorrow."

"Thanks again." Myra ended the call. She turned to the group. "We have a bonafide U.S. Marshal joining in the search tomorrow. But he's technically off duty. He's bringing his partner, Chandler." Myra grinned. "Retired K-9 in the people-finding business."

Hoots and yelps filled the airwaves. "Bravo, love!" Charles grinned.

"I know a few lads or two, myself," Myra said proudly.

"Phillip sent a text. He and the flight crew are ready, so let's send them to Charlotte. This way, Chris and Chandler don't have to go through all the airport rigamarole," Annie said.

"Great. I'll send Chris the info," Myra said.

"Okay! We're moving and grooving." Annie swayed back and forth.

Maggie looked around the table. "Food? Anybody? Anybody? It's past eight."

Annie pulled out the room service menu and handed it to her. "Did you eat your apple?"

"Yes, I did." She stuck out her tongue in her typical Maggie fashion. "And thank you. No orange fingers." She held up her hands.

Isabelle and Kat touted the down-home food they'd had at Marie's and how "almost normal" Bart seemed to be when he wasn't around Dickie.

They were about to wrap up the meeting when Myra remembered she had taken photos of the *Ligustrum sinense* privet. "I want to send this to Yoko and see if she can get something like it for the farm." She showed the photos to Charles.

"Those are lovely. For around the garden off the atrium?"

"That's what I was thinking," Myra said.

"Have at it." Charles smiled.

The atrium had become one of Myra's favorite rooms in the house. Even though the farm covered dozens of acres, with no neighbors visible, she wanted the atrium to feel a little cozier, more private. It was a sanctuary that Charles had built for her while she was away on one of her "missions." "Adventures." Sometimes they were interchangeable. Myra uploaded the photos to Yoko's cloud account. No need to wake her fellow Sister and landscape consultant over bushes.

Everyone signed off after they saluted Lady Liberty. They ordered dinner and waited up to watch the late evening news. The piece Maggie had written was read almost verbatim by the newscaster. A montage of images of the missing woman faded in and out.

"Bravo, Maggie!" Annie hooted. "That should rattle a few chains, jog a few memories."

"Or scare the pants off someone." Myra smirked.

CHAPTER TWENTY-TWO

The Next Day

It was just after midnight when Dickie finally pulled off the interstate at Blaine. Eileen was not far behind. As suspected, he drove directly to the Cascade Inn and parked in the rear. Eileen pulled out her surveillance gear and walked along the side perimeter of the building. She set up a small motion-activated camera to cover the rear, then climbed a big oak toward the front, where she could view the front and sides. Once she was situated, she logged into the camera to observe when Dickie left the building. With the little advance warning they had, it wasn't possible to set up any equipment ahead of time. They were on a seat-of-their-pants operation.

About thirty minutes later, her phone began to blink, letting her know that the camera had been engaged and was recording activity. From what she could tell, Dickie was removing a box the size of a dishwasher from the building. He was using a hand truck. He looked in every direction, then opened the rear doors of his van. He stood for a moment with his hand on his chin. It appeared he was trying to figure out how to get the box into his truck. He turned the hand truck around and tilted it back. Then he climbed into the van and pulled the box up and inside. When the large box was completely inside, he jumped out, shut the doors, and locked them. He looked around again before getting in. Eileen knew he was going to drive off, so she scrambled down the tree and jogged over to her vehicle. Within a minute, Dickie was driving past her. She checked the GPS signal. He was heading back to the interstate.

Lori was waiting in terror for the worst to come. It might have been two days. She wasn't sure, but she'd been served four meals by a masked man. She heard the bolt on the door slide open. Again, a masked man walked in, but this time he was carrying two zip ties, tape, a hood, and a very big box that had the name of an appliance company on it. She didn't know if she would throw up or pee in her pants. The man didn't say anything except, "Show me your wrists."

Dickie debated whether or not he should tie them behind her back or in front. It was a long trip. He knew she wasn't going anywhere, so he opted for tying them in the front. She'd be a little more comfortable. That was probably the first act of consideration he'd given anyone in a while.

Dickie wasn't naturally evil. Much like his boss, he was in way over his head. Then he tied her ankles and said, "Get on your knees."

Lori was sure the masked man was going to kill her. Instead, he placed the opening of the box over her head. "Now lie down on one side." She obeyed as he turned the box to one side. He shoved her legs in farther, closed the opening, and taped it shut. She was in darkness except for the sliver of light from the corners where the tape didn't cover the flaps all the way. She felt a slight movement as he slid something under the box. She was tilted and then felt as if she were moving on wheels. The wheeling sensation stopped after several yards. She heard doors opening. Then more tilting. She heard him grunt, and then she was horizontal again. She heard doors slam shut and lock. An engine started, and she was in motion again. Maybe he was going to take her somewhere else to kill her. Again, she began to pray.

Eileen hung back a few cars and sent Avery a message:

Heading south on I5.

It was three hours before Dickie pulled off to get gas. Eileen was in need, as well, so she waited for him to pull away before she pulled the pump from the machine. She still had him on GPS, and it wouldn't take long for her to catch up. Less than ten minutes later, she had him in her sights. Another three hours passed, and then he finally got off the exit at Four Corners and headed to OR-214 to Silver Falls State Park. About a mile down the road was a large grocery store, and he pulled into the lot. Less than fifteen minutes later, he exited the store pushing a shopping cart. From what she could see, there was a large cooler and several bags. She had a terrifying thought. *What is he going to do with that cooler?*

About twenty minutes later, he pulled into the driveway of a secluded cabin. Eileen drove about a hundred yards past. The sun was about to come up, and she had to find a blind where she could observe his movements. He backed his truck all the way to the beginning of the driveway, near a shed. Eileen crept along through the foliage and saw him remove the box, but he didn't have a hand truck this time. He had to drag it up two steps and into the back door. Then he went back to the truck and brought the cooler and bags inside. Eileen wanted to run after him, tackle him, and find out what was in the box. But what if it was a dishwasher, and he was simply planning on staying at his cabin for a few days? She bit her lip. She hated being in these situations, but it was what she was paid to do: watch, listen, do not engage.

She alerted Avery.

Subject at cabin with large box. Suspicious.

Avery replied: **Understood. No action**.

That was Eileen's message to do nothing except observe, unless she was actually witnessing foul play.

Inside the house, Dickie was rummaging around. Lori heard the sound of a drill. She was panicking and making muffled sounds of despair. She had been quiet for the duration of her captivity except for when she vehemently refuted working for anyone besides the Spanglers.

"Simmer down," was all she heard after the drilling stopped. Her captor slipped a utility knife down one set of flaps. Then he abruptly left the cabin.

Eileen watched Dickie hurry from the back door to his van. He was carrying a small piece of black fabric. She clicked a photo.

Lori grasped the flap and tried to pull the box open, but she was in an awkward position and was only able to slip her fingers through the opening he'd made. She stopped when she heard him clambering the steps.

"Now where were we?" He pulled the flaps open and helped her up. "Don't try anything funny."

He opened the basement door and cut the ankle ties off. "You're gonna go down those steps." He switched the light on, and she began to descend into the basement. He was close on her heels. He opened another door. "Get in."

Lori thought it might be one of those survivalist shelters and did as she was told. "Now sit down." Again, she obeyed.

Dickie went back to the kitchen and then brought the cooler and the groceries to the basement. "Here you go. Make the best of it." He removed the tape from her mouth. "If you behave, this will all be over soon." He had absolutely no idea how, but he certainly hoped it would. He was confident she wasn't going anywhere, so he cut the ties from her wrists. "See ya," he said, as he left her sitting with tape over her mouth. When he got to the top of the stairs, he made sure the padlock was secured. Even if she screamed and yelled, there was no one around to hear her.

Dickie checked the clock on the stove. Almost seven. He'd been up for twenty-four hours. He needed some shut-eye before he went to work, so he stretched out on his couch.

Eileen crawled along the bushes to see if she could get a better look at what was going on inside. The kitchen light was still on, and the box was sitting in the middle of the room. About an hour later, she saw a shadow and ducked below the sill.

Dickie unfolded all the flaps of the box so it was now flat. He brought it to the shed, just in case he needed it for transporting something later. He went back into the cabin, took a shower, and left for work, with Eileen following not too far behind.

She sent a message for Avery:

Subject stashed FLAT box in shed. On the move.

Avery conveyed the information to the Sisters, while Fergus and Charles were reading the results of the lab tests.

* * *

The beeping of garbage trucks jolted Bart awake. He checked his watch. It was six in the morning. He'd missed his opportunity to get the machine out of the building. *I can't be everywhere at the same time.* He figured the most important thing was to keep an eye on Isabelle. He craned his neck and spotted her car. Let out a sigh of relief. An hour later, he saw Isabelle go into the office, and then she shadowed the remaining housekeeper as she did her rounds.

By noon, Isabelle was anxious to get back to the main office. Kat had already left. Isabelle said her goodbyes and began her trip back to Salem.

Sasha was still on Bart's tail, who was still on Isabelle's. Bart pulled into the company's employee parking lot in Salem, and Sasha moved her car to the end of the visitor lot.

Sitting in a car across from her was Eileen, who had been following Dickie all morning. He was still in his office.

Bart was exhausted. This secret-agent-man existence wasn't half as exciting as he'd thought it would be. He dreaded having to drive back to Eugene later that evening, but he knew Dickie would split his spleen if he didn't get the machine out of there stat. He wearily walked to the transportation shed, where Kathryn was checking out some of the vehicles.

"Nice line-up," she commented, studying the modern Ford Transit Van with a high roof.

"Yeah. Got three of 'em in this year. Makes it a lot easier to haul and move around inside."

Kat nodded. "I appreciate having room to move."

Bart made small talk with her, asking the usual questions about how long she'd been driving, her favorite highway, rest stop, diner. Kat thought he seemed like a decent sort of guy. Too bad he'd hit a girl and kidnapped her.

CHAPTER TWENTY-THREE

The Winners and Losers

"This is quite the rum sort, innit?" Fergus said to Charles. "Three sets of prints, two different individuals' DNA."

"Let me take a look at that," Charles said. "According to this, two sets of prints match for familial DNA. That means two people who handled this glass are related, and the other is not."

"Correct, mate," Fergus said.

"We're going to have to tell Myra she needs to find out who served the drinks that night."

"Right."

"I'll ring her." Charles hit the speed-dial number for Myra.

"Morning, love."

"Hello, Charles. How are you this fine day?"

"Well, it's almost lunchtime for us."

"It is, indeed."

"Speaking of lunch, when you see Milton today, ask him who served the drinks the night of his heart attack."

"Of course, but why?"

"There are three sets of prints. Two have closely related DNA."

"I don't understand." Myra was perplexed.

"Two people who handled the glass are family members. The other is not." Charles spelled it out for her.

"Oh, well, that's interesting. What about the sample from the rug or the glass?"

"They're still working on it. Should have something later today or tomorrow," Charles replied.

"Alright."

"What time is Gaines arriving?" Charles asked.

"Around three," Myra said.

"According to Eileen, there was some suspicious activity last night at Dickie's cabin," Charles said.

"What kind?" Myra asked.

Charles explained the drive from Salem to Blaine to Silver Falls. The big box in and the folded box out. "Could be an actual dishwasher, or it could be contraband."

"This is getting very convoluted," Myra said with dismay. "We have missing people, possible drugs, mysterious DNA, and appliances?"

Charles chuckled. "That about sums it up."

"Oh, dear. Well, we shall see what we can gather today."

"Be safe, love. Tootles." Charles signed off.

Myra informed Annie and the others of Eileen's observations. "Maybe when Chris gets here, we should check out Dickie's cabin?"

"But what are we looking for?" Annie said.

"Drugs? A person?" Myra said. "We have small samples of the powder."

"What about Lori's DNA?" Annie asked.

"Wait! I have something!" Maggie exclaimed. "Her mom gave me this amulet that Lori made. She made a bunch of them to sell at an Indigenous Peoples festival."

"Why did she give it to you?" Myra queried.

"As a symbol of appreciation? A physical thing to connect me to Lori? She hoped my story would bring her safely home? All of the above?" Maggie speculated.

"You didn't get any Cheetos dust on it, did you?" Annie asked jokingly.

Maggie rolled her eyes. "No. Somebody stole the bag from my tote." She held up her fingers. "No orange stuff."

"Well, then, all the dog has to do is sniff it, right?" Myra asked.

"Excellent!" Annie clapped. "Let's put it in a plastic bag so we don't contaminate it further."

"I beg your pardon?" Maggie feigned being insulted.

"After we're done with lunch, I'll pick up Chris and Chandler and take them to the cabin. Maggie, Myra? One of you will have to keep Dickie distracted."

Maggie raised her hand. "I'll tell him I'd like more background on the Spangler business and why Mr. Spangler still has the rewards posted."

"Great idea," Myra said. "Isabelle will be back this afternoon. Then she may want to go up to Blaine."

"It's a six-hour drive," Annie reminded her. "But my jet will be here later today, so Izzie can fly up there."

"How are we going to explain that to Dickie and Oliver? Remember, only Milton knows that Isabelle is with us."

"Good point," Annie said. "Maybe I can work it into the conversation somehow."

"We'll figure it out. We always do." Myra smiled.

Maggie phoned Dickie and asked if he was available that afternoon to do a short interview about the Spangler family business.

"I'd be happy to do it." Dickie was a little more relaxed now that the latest package was sequestered away from any possibility of discovery. "Do you want to meet at the office?"

"That would be perfect. I'll take some photos if that's okay."

"I'm sure it will be fine." Dickie was all puffed up. Someone was actually interested in hearing what he had to say.

It was getting close to noon. Myra and Annie stopped at a gourmet shop and picked up a variety of sandwiches. Patricia had volunteered Ruby to prepare something, but Myra and Annie insisted they would bring lunch.

When they arrived at the Spanglers', Patricia was on her way out. "Hello. Milton is on the patio. I'll be back around three." She zombie-walked to her car.

"Is she alright?" Annie squinted.

"She hasn't been alright since we got here," Myra replied, as she watched Patricia get behind the wheel of her BMW.

"Do you think that's a good idea?" Annie motioned to Patricia starting the engine.

"We have our hands full, dearie. She's a big girl." Myra tended to agree with Annie, but what could they do? Tell Patricia they didn't think she was fit to drive? That could cause a big issue. And they had work to do.

They entered the house and made their way to the kitchen, where Ruby was having a cup of tea. "Hi, Ruby! We brought lunch for Mr. Spangler. Can you help us with some flatware and dishes?" Myra asked.

"Of course." Ruby got up, went to the large cupboard, and took out plates and platters and set them on the counter. "Beverages?"

"Herbal tea?" Myra asked.

"Yes. Peppermint, chamomile, ginger?"

"I'll take peppermint," Annie said.

"Ginger for me, thanks."

Ruby busied herself with the tea making while Myra plated the sandwiches and Annie tossed the salad.

They brought everything out to the patio, where Milton was gazing at the spectacular view.

"Hello, darling!" Annie said as she carried the tray of goodies.

"Ah, two of my favorite people." Milton got up and gave Myra a hug, then Annie, after she set the tray down on the table.

"This looks wonderful. Patricia has had me on pablum and kefir."

"Oh, she does not." Myra *tsk-tsk*ed.

Once everyone was settled at the table, the women began their subtle interrogation.

"Mill, the night of your heart attack, what were you drinking?"

"Brandy, why?"

"Just curious. They still haven't found out what caused it, have they?"

"No. Whatever it was got into my system, and out just in time, I suppose."

Annie was trying to figure out the best way to ask who had poured his drink. "So, it was you and Oliver?"

"Patricia came in with Benjamin to say hello to Oliver," he recalled. "That's when she poured my brandy and Oliver's tequila. She handed the glasses to Oliver, who handed mine to me. Benjamin had a glass of pinot noir, if I remember correctly. Why?"

Myra steadied herself. Her mind was racing, as was Annie's. "Just curious. It's such a mystery."

"Yes, it is," Milton replied.

Myra placed her hand on Milton's. "Mill, what was the real reason you got in touch with me?"

He let out a long sigh. "Lots of unexplained things. I needed an objective point of view. Everyone around here knows everyone, and it would be hard for me to find someone who could get down to the nitty-gritty without raising concern."

"I understand. So tell me. Start from the beginning." Myra spoke softly, with compassion.

"For one, the electric bill for the Salem inn is almost double the others. I suppose there's a reasonable explanation. The cost of concrete and steel for renovations was higher at Salem, Blaine, and Eugene, but there could be an explanation for that, as well. But then I noticed there were three steel doors that were ordered for those three inns. They were fireproof and bulletproof."

"Why would you need bulletproof doors?" Annie's forehead furrowed.

"That's what I wanted to know. I was going to ask Oliver. Then I got a call about our certificates from the Department of Agriculture."

"What about them?" Myra said, as Annie was jotting down notes.

"They occasionally send out inspectors to confirm the logging companies are complying with regulations by planting the required number of trees."

"If I remember, you plant more than required." Myra's jaw was almost about to drop.

"I do. At least that's what I thought was going on. Apparently, someone has been cutting corners."

Myra and Annie looked at each other. "Don't you get certificates?"

"Yes, and they suggested the certificates had been

falsified before they were submitted." Milton looked forlorn. "I suppose whoever doctored them figured the DOA wouldn't scrutinize every piece of paper. It's a bureaucracy."

"Who is in charge of submitting them?" Annie asked, but she had a good idea what the answer was.

Milton sighed again. "Oliver."

"Oh, dear. So that's what you wanted to discuss with him?"

"Yes, all of it."

"Milton, I don't know what to say." Myra shook her head.

"Myra, I think Oliver is in some kind of trouble." He hung his head.

Annie didn't know if she should say something at that point. She glanced at Myra. Myra gave her the secret *not now* look.

"What kind of trouble?" Myra asked.

"I think he may be doing drugs." Milton began to turn pale.

"What makes you say that?" Annie asked, although she shared the same suspicion.

"I've been around enough people who used coke back in the day. But from what I understand, it's back, especially among young men who are upwardly mobile. Plus, he's been acting erratic. Big mood swings."

"Where do you think he's getting it from?" Myra asked.

"I'm sure it wouldn't be very hard. The interstate is a cocaine and heroin highway that stretches from Mexico to Alaska."

"This is a lot to digest," Annie offered. "How can we help?"

"I'm not sure. How do you find out if someone is sucking money up their nose?"

"I have an idea." Annie leaned in. "What if we get Kat to nose around? No pun intended. She could say she's tired. Needs a boost."

"That might work, but I don't think Oliver would be so stupid as to incriminate himself." Milton sighed again.

"What if we get a saliva sample?" Annie offered. "Or get hold of his handkerchief."

"And do what?" Milton asked.

"Get it to a lab," Myra replied.

"I'm not going to ask," Milton said. "I'll leave it up to you."

"I told Oliver I'd be in touch today. I can fake a sneeze, ask for his pocket square, and there you have it."

Milton fanned the words away. "I don't want to know any of the details. As I said, I will leave it up to you."

Annie excused herself and walked into the house. She called Oliver. "Good afternoon, Oliver. I was thinking about what we discussed yesterday."

"Ah. And?" Oliver sounded antsy.

"And can we meet for a cocktail at my hotel later?"

"I am sure that can be arranged. What time did you have in mind?"

She checked her watch. She had to be at the air-port by three-thirty, then the half hour flight to the cabin and another half hour back. "Say six-thirty?" She wanted to give herself some breathing room in case of traffic or some other detour.

"Perfect. I'll call you from the lobby." Oliver sounded elated.

Eileen followed Dickie to the office complex. He parked in his usual spot. Eileen moved her vehicle to the end of the lot. Several cars separated hers and Dickie's. Once Dickie was inside the building, Eileen moved closer to his vehicle. She spotted a black ski mask on the floor of the passenger seat. That must have been the black cloth Dickie had carried from his van to the cabin. She took a quick photo and sent it to Avery.

Avery forwarded the shot to Charles, who notified Annie and Myra.

Ski mask.

Dickie walked into his office looking as if he had been to hell and back. He felt worse than any hangover he'd ever experienced. *So this is what stress and sleep deprivation do to you.* He opened his desk drawer and spotted a bottle of acetaminophen. It was the same bottle that contained several of their manufactured pills. It was also the same bottle he'd had one day when Patricia Spangler complained of a headache in the office. He meant to give her aspirin, but she took the bottle from his hand. There was no way he could stop her. A few days later, she was back in his office asking for two more of "those pills." He hesitated. She gave him a cold stare. He had no choice. If he didn't give them to her, she would blow the whistle on him.

It became a regular thing with Patricia, who started looking for a weekly supply. *How many corners could one man get backed into?* And now they had to halt manufacturing the tablets until all the problems had been resolved. His life was a train wreck in slow motion. He could see the cars flying off the tracks and smashing to pieces. He buried his face in his hands.

Yoko peered at the photos Myra had sent her. The privet was lovely, but she wondered why Myra would want foxglove, as well. Granted, they looked good together, but foxglove was highly toxic. She needed clarification and sent Myra a text explaining that the smaller plants in front of the privet were dangerous.

When the DNA on the glass proved to be a bit of a mystery, Fergus asked for further tests. Milton's DNA did not match the other familial DNA. Fergus snapped his fingers. "Charles, take a gander at this."

Charles grunted. "It would appear that Milton is not related to the other two people who handled the glass. I need to check with Myra. See if she got anywhere with Milton." He checked his watch. It was six o'clock Eastern time. Myra should be on her way back to the hotel. He decided to phone instead of text.

"Hello, love," Charles greeted his wife.

"Oh, Charles, I was just about to call you. I have so much to tell you."

"As do I. But you go first."

Myra explained the course of events the night Milton had his heart attack. People entering, leaving, serving drinks. "Well, Milton suspected there was some monkey business going on with the invoices and payments." She went on to explain the higher bills for three of the inns, and the bulletproof doors. Then she described the issue with the certificates. "Milton thinks Oliver may have a drug problem."

"I have rather stunning news. The lab results we requested regarding the DNA. Milton has no familial DNA markings."

"What do you mean?" Myra was baffled.

"It means that Oliver is not related to Milton," Charles said grimly.

Myra was speechless. "What are you talking about?"

"If two of the DNA samples are related and one is not, the first two subjects have no biological connection to the third."

Myra was clinging to her pearls as if they were attached to a lifeline. "Charles, are you positive?"

"Unless the lab results are wrong, then yes, I am positive."

"So, then, who is Oliver's father?" Myra was beyond flabbergasted.

"We can check the national database. See if anyone comes up as a match," Charles suggested.

"So this means that Patricia had an affair with someone." Myra was thinking out loud.

"Would appear so." Charles could only imagine the shock Myra was experiencing about her friend and the betrayal. "Listen, love, I'll check further. Meanwhile, tell Annie."

Myra spoke slowly and deliberately. "I will. She is on her way to the airport now."

"You alright?" Charles asked sweetly.

"Not really." Tears were running down Myra's cheeks. "Poor Milton."

"I know, love. I'll ring you in a few. We're waiting for the results from the rug sample and the contents of the glass."

"Okay." Myra ended the call, sat, and stared blankly at the wall. She wasn't going to say anything to Milton until the other issues were handled. Her reverie was disrupted by the sing-song melody coming from her laptop. It was Yoko. Myra opened the camera and greeted her friend. "Yoko! Nice to see your face. You got my photos?"

"Yes. That is why I am calling. Did you know there was a row of foxglove running in front of the privet?"

"Foxglove? No. I thought it was part of the hedge."

"No. And it is the deadliest plant in North America," Yoko explained. "It's lovely, but ingesting any of it can cause seizures, even death."

Again, the news stunned Myra. "Why would someone grow something like that in their garden?"

"The foxglove looks like it may have been planted recently. They're young plants."

"I see. Well, we will absolutely have no foxglove on our property."

"And the privet?" Yoko asked. "It's harmless and grows well."

"Yes. Thanks, Yoko. I owe you big time," Myra said.

"I didn't do anything special."

"I think you may have uncovered a major clue. But I'll know more later. Thanks again." Myra signed off. *Foxglove*. She phoned Milton.

"Mill? Sorry to bother you, but I want to duplicate the hedges you have separating the pool area. Can you give me the name of your landscaper? I want to find out what it is."

"We've been using Guaranteed Plants and Landscaping for years. I can give you their number. Hang on." A few seconds later, he ticked off the phone number.

"Thanks, Mill."

"Myra? Sorry if I unloaded a dumpster on you and Annie today. I just didn't know who else to turn to."

"No worries, Mill. That's what friends are for. See you tomorrow. Try to relax."

Annie spotted a handsome man in his early forties standing on the tarmac. Next to him was a German shepherd wearing a K-9 vest. She jumped out of her vehicle and waved. "Chris?"

The man had thick black hair with a touch of gray at the temples and smoky eyes. He had an exotic look and could almost pass as the actor Jay Hernandez on *Magnum P.I.* His long stride carried a toned body. Chandler had no trouble keeping up with him. Annie extended her hand. "Thank you so much for coming all the way out here."

"And miss a chance to fly on a private jet?" He shook Annie's hand. Chandler sat and extended his paw.

Annie bent over. "Nice to meet you, Chandler." He gave a happy yelp in return.

Chris secured Chandler in the back seat and then climbed in the front. "I must warn you. I'm a lead foot." Annie raised her eyebrows.

"Don't scare me," he joked.

On the way to the cabin, Annie brought Chris up to speed on the suspicious delivery. She also mentioned the ski mask Eileen had spotted in Dickie's van. When they arrived, there was no one in sight. They parked on the opposite side of the street. Chris took off Chandler's vest to avoid curiosity in case anyone spotted him. Chris let Chandler sniff the pouch, and then the three walked up the driveway as if they were going to pay Dickie a visit. Chandler got in a downward dog position. "What does that mean?" Annie said.

"He's got nothing."

"According to Eileen, the box went through the back door, so let's start there."

The dog showed a little interest when they reached the back steps but then made his way toward the shed. Chandler gave a slight *woof*. Not overwhelming enthusiasm, but something. Chandler continued to sniff.

"We have to see what's in the shed," Annie said.

"We don't have a warrant," Chris reminded her.

"No, but we have these." She pulled out her lock-picking kit.

"You can't be serious." Chris almost laughed, but his instincts told him the woman was serious. "I can't be any part of this. You do understand?"

"Of course. You can go round to the front of the house so you can honestly say you did not see me do anything illegal."

Chris shook his head. He understood, and he moved quickly to the other side of the house.

Picking a padlock was a piece of cake for Annie. She had become quite adept at breaking and entering. But only when necessary. At that moment, it was necessary. She unlatched the door and slid it open. Chandler pounced on the cardboard. "Good boy!" Annie petted him. She called out to Chris. "We got a hit!" Chris jogged over to the open shed. The flattened box was on the floor, and Chandler was on top of it.

"According to Eileen . . ."

"Who is Eileen again?" Chris asked.

"She works for a P.I. agency we use."

"You find a need for a P.I. often?" He smirked.

"Pretty much." Annie placed her hands on her hips. "Anyway, Eileen spotted Dickie moving the box into the house, and later brought the flattened box back here." She pointed to the cardboard dog bed. "The woman must be in the house." Annie dashed to the back door.

Chris was concerned they were going to find a dead woman. "Are you planning to use your same B-and-E technique? Otherwise, I'll . . ."

"Yeah. Yeah. I know. Step aside."

Even though this woman was doing all things illegal, he was amused by her verve and determination. "I can't watch this. Take Chandler with you. He's good protection." He strode to the side of the building. The back door was an ordinary Schlage lock. The kind that you could find at Home Depot or any hardware store. Within seconds, Annie had it open. She called out: "Hello? Anybody here?"

Lori thought she was hallucinating. When she first heard footsteps above, she thought the man had come back to eliminate her. But then she heard a woman's voice. "Here! I'm down here!" She climbed up the stairs and began pounding on the door. "Help me! Please!"

Chandler began barking loudly. Annie called out to Chris: "In here!" He dashed inside as Annie removed the padlock on the basement door. A tattered and frightened young woman matching the description of Lori George stared back at her. "Oh, my goodness!" Annie wrapped her arms around Lori. "Come. Sit."

Chris pulled out a kitchen chair so she could sit, and then took a glass from the drying rack and filled it with water. The young woman was shaking uncontrollably. He handed the glass to Annie, who helped the girl bring it to her lips. "You're Lori?" Annie asked. The girl nodded. "You're safe now." Lori began to sob. Annie put her arms around her. "It's going to be alright."

"Where's . . . where's . . . the man?" Lori stuttered as she looked around the kitchen with wide eyes.

"He's not here, but we'll get him."

"Oh, please! I don't want to see him again!" Lori continued to sob.

"Oh, sweetie, I didn't mean we were going to get him back here. We're going to get him. And I mean get him good!" She looked up at Chris, who looked on with disbelief. He wasn't in town for an hour, and he was in the middle of a kidnapping recovery. Usually, it took days, weeks, or sometimes never to find the victim.

"This is a record for me." He had a wonderful smile.

"You've never worked with us before." Annie grinned.

"And who exactly are the *us*?" he asked.

"Long story for another time. We've got to get Lori to a doctor." Annie remembered how terrified Vanessa had been at the hospital. She decided to phone the Rowans' GP. She knew he'd be discreet. Plus, Lori was an adult, so there was no parental consent necessary. She scrolled through her phone call history log and found the doctor's number. "Hello. This is Annie De Silva. I brought Vanessa in the other day." A pleasant voice on the other end greeted her. "I have another slight emergency and was wondering if Dr. Foster had a few free minutes?"

The voice on the other end replied, "Are you sure you shouldn't go to the hospital?"

"It's rather sensitive. Please. It's important."

"Just a minute, Mrs. De Silva." The receptionist put Annie on hold. It seemed to take forever before Dr. Foster got on the phone.

They exchanged pleasantries, and then Annie explained she had a friend who needed a quick checkup. It wasn't an emergency, but it was urgent. Dr. Foster agreed.

Chris found a cotton throw on the sofa and wrapped it around Lori. Chandler put his head on her lap. Lori continued to cry, but the sobs were subsiding. "Come on, sweetie. We're going to get you sorted out." Annie walked Lori outside and tossed the car keys to Chris. He dashed toward the parked car and pulled it around the back. The bright light made Lori squint, and she covered her eyes with her forearm. Chandler did not move from her side. Gaines jumped out of the vehicle, secured Chandler, and then buckled Lori into her seat belt. She wrapped her arms around the dog and buried her head in his furry neck.

Annie bolted to the driver's side and hopped in. "I know the way."

Chris stared in amazement. The service could use a few spunky women like Annie. It wouldn't be until later that day that he would discover not only was Annie a superb lockpick, but she also had a reputation for being a fine pole dancer, as well as a very wealthy countess. He'd guessed about the wealth part because of the jet, but the rest came as a huge surprise.

Once Lori stopped crying, Annie reached over the seat and handed her a phone. "Call your folks. Tell them you are okay. You're being taken to a doctor, and you will call back in a couple of hours."

Lori's hands were shaking as she pressed the buttons on the phone. "Mama?"

A stunned woman answered. "Lori? Lori? Where are you?"

"I'm with some friends." Chandler gave a *woof*. "And a dog." She smiled for the first time. "They found me."

"Where were you?" Mrs. George was excited and concerned.

"I'm not really sure, but these people found me, and I'm alright."

Chris motioned for Lori to give him the phone. "Mrs. George? U.S. Marshal Christopher Gaines here. Yes, we have your daughter. She's rumpled, and in shock, but she's going to be alright."

"But where are you?" Mrs. George insisted.

"Outside of Salem. Can you and your husband drive up here?"

"Of course! Where should we go?"

Annie looked over at Chris. "Tell them to meet us at The Grand Hotel. Give them my name, and call my room from the lobby phone. They should not tell anyone about this until we can all be in the same room. If we're not back from Dr. Foster's, someone will be there to meet them."

Chris repeated what Annie had said. "Yes. The Grand Hotel. Annie De Silva." A pause. "Right. I suggest you pack some fresh clothes for her." Another pause. "Be careful on the road." Chris knew the excitement of recovering their daughter could supersede following road safety precautions.

Annie pushed a button. "Phone Myra." The mechanical voice repeated what Annie said. Myra answered after the first ring.

"We've got her. She's okay." Myra was overjoyed to hear the good news.

"Thank God," Myra said. "Where are you now?"

"Taking Lori to Dr. Foster and then to the hotel. Her folks will be meeting us there. They're on their way from Eugene."

"Perfect."

Charles surmised that if Patricia had had an affair, it would most likely have been with someone in government. Those types stuck together.

Fergus accessed the DHS database. After 9/11, members of Congress who served on certain committees were encouraged to give a DNA sample. Just in case. Just in case bodies had to be identified. It was creepy, but important.

It took about an hour before they got a hit. Oliver's DNA matched that of Congressman Garret Lambeau, age seventy-two. A lifer inside the Beltway. "This is juicier than those telenovelas." Fergus chortled.

Charles echoed Myra's earlier words. "Poor Mil-

ton. Now we have to put the rest of the pieces together. Did we get a hit on the contents of the glass?"

Fergus checked his computer. "Just in." He
looked it over. "Digitalis from the foxglove plant."

"Seriously? Isn't that an Agatha Christie ploy?"
Charles raised an eyebrow.

"I believe so. And my bet is on Patricia. Poison is
a woman's weapon," Fergus said.

"But why would she want to kill Milton?" Charles
ruminated.

"That's a very good question," Fergus answered.

"Right. Now we have two pieces of vital information. Oliver's real father is a U.S. Congressman, and
Milton was poisoned with foxglove."

"We've seen worse. At least she didn't succeed."

"True. I'll let Myra know what we found." Just as
he was about to call her, his phone rang. "Hello,
love. I was just about to . . ."

Myra interrupted him. "They found Lori. She's
alive and okay, all but for the trauma."

"What a relief," Charles said. He conveyed the
information to Fergus.

"Brilliant!" Fergus responded.

"Her parents are driving up from Eugene, Annie
and Chris are taking her to the doctor, and then we
are going to meet here, at the hotel."

"Where was she?" Charles asked.

"Dickie Morton's cabin. Thank goodness for
Chandler. And Eileen. And Christopher. And Annie,
who had to use one of her forbidden skills to open a
few locks."

"I have one more piece of information for you, love," Charles said. "We found out what was in the beverage."

"Foxglove!" they said in unison.

"How did you know?" Charles asked.

"The photos I took of the privet. I sent them to Yoko, and she recognized them. She phoned me earlier."

"Fergus believes Patricia mixed the potion that caused Milton's heart attack."

"Really? Not Oliver?"

"He claims it's the weapon of choice for women." Charles grinned at his pal.

"But why?" Myra was stupefied.

"That's a question only she can answer," Charles said.

"Poor Milton," Myra lamented again. "But what about the pills Vanessa saw, and the hidden room Isabelle found? Who is responsible for them?"

"No one specific—it's a group effort. That much I am certain of. It can't just be Oliver. There are too many moving parts."

"True." Myra sighed. "I guess our work is not done yet."

"No, but it appears things are unraveling, and we're picking up the loose ends. You'll get it sorted," Charles assured her.

"Thank you, darling. I'll call later, once things settle down here."

"Right. Tootles." Charles ended the call.

* * *

Annie, Lori, Christopher, and Chandler arrived at the doctor's office in thirty minutes. Annie checked the time. She had an hour before she was supposed to meet Oliver. It had been a very busy day.

Dr. Foster and the nurse were waiting for them in the examination room. "Who do we have here?"

"Hello. My name is Lori George." The girl was truly shaken.

The doctor looked at her closely. "You're the missing woman from Eugene?" Lori nodded. Then the doctor looked at Annie. "Are you in the people-rescue business? Twice in one week!"

Chris gave her a look. Annie flapped her wrist. She would tell him later. "What can I say, doc? I'm a human magnet." She scratched Chandler's neck. "But this guy is the real hero."

"And to whom do I owe the pleasure?" Dr. Foster looked at Chandler, who gave him his paw.

"This is Chandler. Retired U.S. Marshal's Service."

Dr. Foster shook Chandler's paw and then washed his hands. "No offense." He smiled at the big pooch.

Annie looked at Lori. "Do you want me to stay with you?" Lori nodded.

"We'll be outside," Chris said, and took Chandler into the reception area.

Nurse Crowley took Lori's blood pressure. It was a bit low, probably from shock. Dr. Foster checked her other vitals. All seemed normal. He checked her skin to see if she was dehydrated. "Did you drink a lot of water?" he asked. She nodded. "Good. It probably helped you keep your strength. Most people don't realize that when they're dehydrated, the rest of their bodily functions can't work at their optimum levels." Lori nodded again. He checked her for any cuts or bruises. Nothing that required attention. "You're in tip-top shape." He thought for a second. "For a woman who went through what you did. Now I want you to take it easy for the next couple of days. No work, no school. Understood?"

Lori bobbed her head again. "Thank you."

Annie helped her off the table and walked her out to where Chris and Chandler were waiting. "All good?" Chris asked.

"You bet." Annie had her arm around Lori's shoulders. "Right?"

Lori smiled. "Yes. Much better now."

They returned to the vehicle and drove to the hotel. Annie sent the three of them up to the room. She checked her watch. The George family would arrive in about forty-five minutes. Oliver was due in twenty. One more grand scheme to pull off before the end of the day.

Kat and Isabelle were back at the apartment, waiting for further instructions. They were both fidgety. There were too many balls in the air, and they didn't know who was going to catch what.

Isabelle jumped when the phone rang.

"Myra. What is going on?" Isabelle was getting concerned. Neither she nor Kat had heard anything for several hours. It wasn't unusual, but the silence was worrisome. One never knew what Annie and

Myra could get themselves into, or the rest of the Sisters, for that matter. But Annie and Myra were the ringleaders, and it was usually the two of them who led the charge, whether it was into a blazing fire, or tunneling their way out from a locked barn.

Myra gave Isabelle the rundown about Lori, the foxglove, and Oliver. "Her parents should be here shortly. Annie is meeting Oliver in the lobby bar in a few minutes. Mill thinks Oliver has a drug problem. We think he has a distribution problem, as well as his own personal addiction. We just need a little more information before we break all the bad news to Milton. And we still need to figure out how to turn over our evidence without implicating ourselves for breaking and entering."

"I was the one entering," Isabelle said.

"And Annie. She did both."

"Again?"

"Of course. But that's how we found Lori. With the help of Chandler. He gave Annie the clues."

"Don't ya just love dogs?" Of course, it was a rhetorical question. Being an animal lover was a requirement to be part of this unique group of women.

"Can't live without them," Myra said. "I think the two of you should get over here. We need a meeting."

"Roger that!" Isabelle was happy she and Kat wouldn't be left out of the group gathering.

Annie seated herself at a low cocktail table. She ordered a glass of champagne. She spotted Oliver

walking across the tiled floor. She waved. He gave
her a big smile and waved back. He leaned over to
give her a kiss, but she gave him her cheek. "Nice to
see you again." He was effusive.

"Indeed." Annie crossed her legs, showing off her
spectacular boots. "So, Oliver, tell me again about
your situation." She couldn't help but notice a
smidge of white dust at the very edge of his nostril.
This was too good to pass up. She immediately
reached for his pocket square, pulled it sensuously
out of his jacket, and dabbed it on his nose. "There.
Much better," she flirted. His mouth was agape at
the possibility that she was coming on to him.
Annie's flair with sleight of hand allowed her to slip
his handkerchief into her tote while he was focused
on delivering his big fib again. *Money for his car,
blah . . . blah . . . blah . . .*

Annie felt her phone vibrate. She checked to see
who it was. Myra. She had to take the call. "Excuse
me, Oliver. Sorry, I must take this." She put her
hand on his shoulder for reassurance and stepped far
enough away so that he would not to be able to hear
the exchange. "What's up?"

"The George family just arrived."

"Okay. I'm with Oliver."

"Lori seems to have relaxed a little. She took a
long hot shower and is wrapped in a cozy robe."

"Chris told her parents to bring a fresh set of
clothes."

"Good thinking. For a man!" Myra chuckled.
"We have a lot of loose ends to wrap up, and we're

going to need you up here. Can you ditch Oliver? Reschedule?"

"I don't think I have to."

"Oh?" Myra wondered what her wily friend had accomplished in a few short minutes.

"Got his handkerchief. Dabbed his nose with it, so there should be enough DNA on it, plus a smidge of powder."

"You can add magician to your résumé." Myra chuckled again. She was over the moon that they'd found Lori.

"Already did, my friend. You need to catch up." Annie laughed and looked in Oliver's direction. She made a serious face and then ended the call. She rushed over to where he was sitting. "Oliver, I am terribly sorry, but I have something that needs to be handled right now. Can we reschedule? Tomorrow, perhaps?"

Oliver's face went from cheerful, to glum, then back to cheerful. "Oh, of course, Annie. Nothing serious, I hope. Well, I mean it is serious, but I hope it's not life-threatening." He was almost sincere.

"Nothing too awful, but necessary. I'll be in touch." She turned on her rhinestone-studded boot-heel and moved quickly to the elevator bank. The Sisters had to have a video meeting in the suite. She pivoted and went to the front desk, where she reserved a second two-bedroom suite for the George family, so they could relax and have dinner. Once Lori was more settled, she might be able to discuss some of the details of her ordeal. Having a U.S. Marshal on hand would be very helpful, as well. Once she secured the rooms, she went back to the elevator bank. She looked to see if Oliver was still nursing his drink. He was gone. Probably feeling defeated. Too bad.

Annie entered the suite and greeted the George family. Mrs. George was still crying. "I don't know how to thank you."

"We could not be happier, believe me." Annie gave her a hug. Then Mr. George wrapped his arms around both of them, while Chris and Chandler looked on. It was a very happy and satisfying moment for everyone. Annie explained that she'd reserved a room for them and invited them to stay the night. She went on to say that it was important for Lori to tell them everything she could remember. "Order whatever you want from room service." She handed them the key card. "Your suite is right down the hall. If you feel like talking later, just knock on the door."

Words of thanks and appreciation filled the room as the reunited family moved on to their own quarters.

Annie folded her arms and looked at Chris. "Now what do we do about you?"

He narrowed his eyes. "What do you mean?"

"We gals have to have a little sit-down."

"And I am not invited," Chris stated.

"You are correct." Myra gave him a slight smile.

"Why don't you go get some dinner in the restaurant, and then we can recon in an hour or so." It wasn't a question, and Chris knew it.

He scratched his head. "You know, I could lose my job over this."

"How?" Myra asked.

"Why?" Annie chimed in. "You haven't done anything illegal. Plus, you rescued a kidnapped woman. That's hardly reason to terminate your employment. I would think it deserves a promotion."

"Absolutely!" Myra and Maggie agreed.

"Yeah, well, it's a slippery slope. But if my career turns to dog doo-doo—no offense, Chandler—I trust you will help me find gainful employment."

"Gainful employment for Christopher Gaines." Annie smirked.

He looked up at the ceiling. "Good thing I'm accustomed to atypical behavior."

"Yes, if I recall, your fiancée, Luna, is rather gifted," Myra said.

"Among many other things." He snorted. "Mind if Chandler stays with you? I promise he is not outfitted with listening devices."

Annie looked at Myra. "Ha. I hadn't thought about that."

"See you in a few." He gave a two-finger salute. "Chandler, keep an eye on them." The dog gave him a soft *woof*.

Just as Chris was leaving, Isabelle and Kat entered. They introduced themselves. "Chris was just leaving," Annie said.

"Handsome," Kat said admiringly, after Myra shut the door.

"Let's get this party started," Annie said. She opened her laptop and messaged Charles and Fergus. Within a minute, everyone's laptops began playing "We Are Family," and the women were rocking in their chairs.

"We have several items we can check off the list," Annie began. "I'll start with the most recent. Please hold your applause until I'm done." She winked and began: "Missing woman rescued in cabin owned by Dickie Morton, after Eileen observed him delivering large box; Annie and U.S. Marshal discovered missing woman with the help of Chandler; traces of foxglove identified in the rug and the glass, and a row of them are on the Spanglers' property; fingerprint DNA found familial match between Patricia and Oliver; Oliver's DNA matched Congressman Garret Lambeau of West Virginia; Isabelle observed and took photos of secret room in Eugene, found traces of powder; Vanessa recognized Bart as the man with the pills who abducted her." She took a short bow. Then came the hoots, hollers, and high fives.

Maggie was feverishly scribbling everything down. "Wow, oh, wow."

"Next comes the really hard part. Telling Milton his son is not his son, and he's a drug addict. Then there's the drug manufacturing part."

"I think we should show Chris the photos before we do anything more," Isabelle said. "He could order a search warrant, no?"

"We can certainly ask. Besides, you had every right to be there. You can tell him you have reason to believe there is suspicious activity at the inn."

Fergus chimed in. "She's right. You can't be incriminated for entering a part of the building you were supervising."

Isabelle let out a sigh of relief.

"Milton mentioned that the electric bills at Salem and Eugene were higher than the other inns, and there were additional renovation costs for concrete and bulletproof doors. Perhaps Chris can include those items in the search warrants," Myra said.

"We might be able to get Milton's permission, provided he won't be held accountable."

"Very true," Fergus said. "Milton can explain he has suspicion of wrongdoing on his property. That will enable law enforcement to dust and fingerprint the scene."

"Ah. Law enforcement. It would appear the local deputy might have an issue following up, so what do we do about him?"

All eyes went to Kathryn. "No, not Pearl." Pearl was a thorn in Kathryn's side. She was also the group's travel concierge, but not in the typical way. Once the Sisterhood captured the culprits they identified, Pearl would dispose of them. No one was ever murdered, but given the choice, the perpetrators might choose death over the sentences handed down by the Sisters. Myra and Annie were constantly forcing Kathryn to deal with Pearl, in the hope they could mend their differences.

"We will also have to figure out what to do with Bart and Dickie."

"And Oliver," Annie said.

"And Patricia. We believe she was the one who spiked Milton's drink," Myra stated.

"Patricia? Why?" Isabelle asked.

"The foxglove," Fergus offered. "It's a woman's weapon of choice."

"Okay, but why would she want to kill Milton?" Isabelle persisted.

"That's a question she will have to answer," Fergus responded.

"And how do we get her to do that?" Isabelle asked.

"I have an idea. It's an old trope from a lot of British mysteries," Charles offered.

"Continue, please," Myra urged.

"You get all the suspects in the room, and you simply lay out the facts," Charles replied.

"I think we have to get all the evidence collected first, don't you?" Myra asked.

"Yes, which means the marshal has to execute the search warrant, which means we have to get Milton's permission," Charles said.

"We can't call Milton at this hour." Myra checked the time.

"I don't think we can wait, love. Anything could happen, especially if someone thinks we're on to them."

Myra sighed. "I suppose you're right." She picked up her phone and called Milton. Patricia answered.

"Hello, Patricia, I am so sorry to disturb you, but it's important I speak with Milton."

"What is this about?" Patricia asked stiffly.

"Something he asked me to research."

"Can't this wait until morning?" Patricia's voice was terse.

"No, I'm afraid not," Myra pushed.

"Just a moment."

Myra could tell Patricia was not happy about this intrusion. About a minute later, Milton got on the phone. "Myra? Everything alright?"

"No, Milton. Some of your concerns have been confirmed."

"Oh? How so?"

"We need you to give permission to search three of the inns. Permission to a U.S. Marshal."

"How am I supposed to do that?" Milton was befuddled.

"I can have him come to your house, and you can sign a letter of permission." She looked at Fergus. He nodded.

"When do you want to do that?" Milton asked, exhaling deeply.

"In about an hour?"

"Tonight?" He sounded stunned.

"Yes, Milton. I am sorry, but this cannot wait." Myra was stroking her pearls.

"Well, fine, then. Who should I expect to be arriving?"

"U.S. Marshal Gaines, and his K-9, Chandler."

"Alright, Myra. I hope you know what you're doing."

"That's why you called me, remember?" she said kindly.

"Yes. Yes, I do." Milton was tired. Spent.

"Thank you, Milton. We'll speak in the morning."

Myra hung up, wondering how he was going to respond to all the other accusations and revelations.

"I hate to assume anything, but the letter should grant permission for a search of Blaine, Salem, and Eugene. Those seem to be the hot spots right now," Charles suggested, while Fergus typed the official document.

"I'll have this off to you in a jiffy," he said to the group.

"Alright, so let's play this out. Chris brings the letter to Milton. Milton signs it. Chris notifies the DEA, and they dispatch agents to the three locations," Charles said.

"What about Dickie and Bart?" Kat asked. "What are we going to do with them? I mean, what is Pearl going to do with them?"

Everyone looked around the table and into their laptop screens. "Technically, they are both kidnappers," Charles said.

"I suggest Pearl take them to an impoverished community in the hinterlands, where they'll spend the rest of their lives digging ditches to help the villages get clean water," Myra recommended. "They'll never see civilization again."

"And Oliver?" Charles asked.

"I know it's going to break Milton's heart when he finds out Oliver isn't his son." Myra sighed.

"Yes, but we can't let that sway us from this mission," Charles insisted. "The man has put people's lives in danger. Remember, if he is the ringleader in this drug manufacturing, which I have no doubt, he is contributing to the addiction and deaths of thousands."

"You're right, Charles."

"If he's doing cocaine, then fentanyl would cause the exact opposite reaction in him," Maggie said.

"So, let's shoot him up with fentanyl for a few days and make him go through withdrawal," Kat suggested.

"Then Pearl can take him someplace where there are no roads for fancy sports cars," Annie added.

"And Patricia?" Maggie asked.

"I think jail would be a perfect place for her, actually," Myra said. "The humiliation would be torture for her, as well as for Congressman What's-his-name."

"Ah, another Beltway scandal." Maggie chuckled.

"But this one is juicier than most of the others." Annie had a wicked grin on her face.

"Really juicy. How do we get her arrested?"

"The evidence points to her."

"So we've got to get the deputy, Dickie, and Bart out of the way ASAP," Kat said.

"We'll take Oliver to Pinewood and keep him there for several days. Then Pearl can dispose of him," Myra said.

"What about Milton?" Isabelle asked.

"I'll break the news to him about Oliver not being his son. Once that fact settles in, I am sure he'll have no problem when I tell him we've sent him off to a permanent rehab center."

"That could work," Annie said. "I'll invite Oliver to Tahoe. I'm sure he'd go for it. Once we're on the plane, we'll drug him with fentanyl and bring him to Pinewood, where we'll continue to knock him out. We've done that before. Then he'll go into withdrawal. Then buh-bye."

"I like it," Kat said. "But how do we get the police to arrest Patricia?"

"I think Marshal Gaines will be able to make a recommendation."

"That man had no idea what he was getting himself into." Charles laughed, and so did the rest of the group.

Maggie's laptop dinged. The letter of permission came through from Fergus.

Annie checked the time. "Speaking of the marshal, he should be back shortly. We should wrap this up."

"Right-o," Charles said.

"Everyone know what their assignments are?" Annie asked.

Kathryn raised her hand. "How do we get Dickie, Bart, and the deputy?"

"We hack into their phones and send them text messages to meet at the office," Charles suggested. "Simple. When they arrive, there will be a blackout, and Pearl and her people can do what the men did to Vanessa and Lori. And away they go."

"Okay. As soon as Kathryn can get Pearl here, we should be able to pull this off," Annie said.

Kathryn was already sending Pearl a message. Pearl replied.

I have people that can get there in an hour.

Kathryn read it out loud, then added, "Man, that woman has people everywhere."

"And that's why we love her, Kathryn." Myra smirked. "She is always there for us, whenever and wherever we need her."

"She has one heck of a network," Kathryn remarked.

"We know nothing about it, and it shall remain that way, just as she knows nothing about what we do on our end. *Capisce*?" Annie added.

Everyone nodded and agreed. They turned to the image of Lady Liberty and saluted. "Whatever it takes!" was their battle cry, with fist bumps all around.

Charles sent Avery a message that Sasha and Eileen should be on alert. Bart would be on the move, and if Dickie had left the office, he too would be heading back within the hour.

A knock on the hotel room door signaled Chris was back. Myra and Annie were going to share the plan with him. Slowly. They were about to dump a heap of information on his lap. Chandler headed to Isabelle. "You must be sniffing Rufus." She gave him doggie scrunches.

"If I dare ask, what have you come up with in my brief absence?" Chris was dubious, based on what he'd already witnessed.

"Chris, we have a letter that needs to be signed by Milton Spangler to allow you and the DEA to search three of his properties. He has reason to believe someone has been using his facilities to manufacture illegal drugs."

Chris listened carefully as Isabelle recounted her probe of the laundry room and showed him the photos.

"And from what Lori told us on the way to the doctor's office, she was being held in a similar space, but without any equipment. It appeared they may have been in the process of setting up another facility."

"That would make sense, given the location and proximity to the Canadian border and Ketchikan, Alaska." Chris nodded.

"Milton is expecting you to bring this over for him to sign. It will give you and any other government agency permission to inspect the premises."

"If we went the normal route, it could take days. Maybe weeks," Annie added. "And if they suspect anything, they may dismantle their operations to avoid any connection to the two missing women."

"Who are no longer missing," Chris said.

"Yes, but no one knows they've been recovered except their immediate families. As far as law enforcement and the media are concerned, they are still missing."

"Alright. I'll get on it. Let's have the address."

"Er, there are a couple more things."

"I knew it was too good to be true." Chris smiled drolly.

"We have reason to believe Patricia poisoned Milton."

"And you know this how?" He was bracing himself for what he was about to hear.

"A lab found traces of digitalis in the glass he was drinking from. There's foxglove growing on the property."

"And it's a woman's weapon of choice," Maggie added.

Chris let out a slight laugh. "So, how are we going to pursue that?"

"Ah. He's using the term *we*," Annie taunted.

"I'm already in up to my neck. Next item on the agenda, please." Chris pulled out his phone. "I'll call the DEA and have them on standby. I'll need all the locations."

"Perfect. I'll text them to you now," Myra said, and began scrolling through her phone for the information.

Annie cleared her throat. "This is the tricky part."

"There's more?" He raised an eyebrow.

"What we were thinking of doing is to confront Patricia, Oliver, and Milton at the same time. Well, actually, we'd give Milton a heads-up. No need for him to have another heart attack."

Isabelle spoke next. "What about the congressman?"

Chris scrunched up his face. "A congressman?"

"Garret Lambeau," Maggie said. "Oliver's biological father."

"This just keeps getting better and better." Chris

pursed his lips. "The guy is a slippery career politician."

"Ha. Aren't they all?" Annie snickered.

"He was one of the people trying to defund law enforcement," Chris said.

"Well, maybe this will defund his retirement," Maggie said.

"Doubtful. I don't think even murder would get some of those jerks out of government," Chris replied. "So what's your plan?"

Myra laid it out for everyone, except the Pearl portion. Chris did not need to know, nor should he know, about that part of the plan. "Chris, you'll go to Milton's and get the letter signed. Do what you have to do to share it with the DEA."

Chris looked at his phone. The addresses popped up on the screen. He forwarded them to his contact at the Drug Enforcement Administration.

"We have to get Oliver, Patricia, and Milton together before news breaks of the raids."

"Or someone can call Milton and tell him when the DEA agents arrive at his facilities. Then he can call Oliver and insist he come over to the house. Something this serious can't wait until morning. He won't need an excuse to get people out of bed."

"Chris, you can arrest someone for murder, correct?" Maggie asked.

"If I have reason to believe a crime has been committed, yes."

"Great. Then we'll all go over to Milton's," Annie said.

"And you have the evidence?" he asked.

"Fingerprints on Milton's glass, traces of foxglove, and foxglove plants," Myra repeated. "Plus, we expect a confession."

"That should be enough to detain someone," Chris noted.

"What about the rest of us?" Maggie asked.

"You will break the story of Patricia's arrest. Call your pal at the station when we give you the go-ahead," Annie said.

Chris stared at the floor.

"Something wrong?" Myra asked.

"Are you sure you're not part of a special forces organization?" He smirked.

"Yes and no." Annie raised an eyebrow.

"Better I don't know." He looked around the room.

Izzie and Kathryn were standing by to hear from Pearl. The plan was for them to meet up with her people at the office complex and help implement the gas-and-grab. Three unconscious adult men would require some heavy lifting.

"Ready?" Chris asked. Chandler *woof*ed. "I mean everyone?"

"Whatever it takes!" they all shouted.

"I am going to hate myself for this," he muttered under his breath.

"Nah." Annie gave him a friendly push.

Myra phoned Milton. "We're on our way."

"What do you mean *we*?" Milton asked. "You're coming here, too?"

"Milton, we have some serious things to discuss."

"That sounds ominous."

"I'll explain everything when we get there. See you in a few minutes."

When Myra, Annie, Christopher, and Chandler arrived at Milton's, Patricia answered the door with the most unpleasant expression on her face. She said nothing, turned, and walked everyone into the study, then left.

Myra gave Milton a hug. Then it was Annie's turn. They introduced him to Chris. Myra went to the sideboard and opened a fresh bottle of brandy. She knew Milton would need something to steady his nerves, and she wanted to be sure there weren't any additives in his drink. She handed him the glass.

"Please explain before I have another heart attack," Milton asked politely.

"That's one of the reasons we're here," Chris began to explain. "We have evidence that shows you received a mild dose of digitalis poisoning. It was obtained from the glass you had been drinking from, and a small piece of carpet that was tested."

Milton looked down at the rug. "Where?"

Annie moved the chair to uncover her handiwork. "Sorry."

"Both the glass and carpet contain traces of foxglove."

"Foxglove? But where did it come from?" Milton asked.

"Your garden, Mill. In front of the privet I was admiring."

"That was only planted a little over a week ago." Milton shook his head. "I don't understand."

Annie took the reins. "The foxglove was mixed with your brandy. It could have been lethal, but the doctors gave you a lot of fluids that helped flush the toxins out. It was a seizure brought on by poisoning. Not a heart attack, as they had assumed in the beginning."

"So that's why you asked about who gave me the glass?" Milton hung his head.

"Both Patricia's and Oliver's fingerprints were on the glass, in addition to yours, of course," Chris added.

"But why?" Milton was devastated.

"We don't know for sure." Myra looked at Annie and Chris. The next shock was about to be delivered. Myra squatted down in front of Milton and took his hands. "Mill, this next bit of information is going to hurt."

"What could hurt more than finding out your wife or your son tried to kill you?"

"That's the other part of it. Mill, there's no easy way to say this, but Oliver is not your son."

The room was completely silent. Milton began to nod. "This may sound cruel, but I am not surprised. I could never understand how he could be so different from Benjamin. I always blamed it on Patricia's coddling. Now I know why."

Myra watched him carefully. He appeared to be taking the news better than she'd expected. "Did you know she was having an affair?"

"I suspected it. She was taking too many trips back and forth to D.C. Am I wrong to guess it was Garret Lambeau?" he said miserably.

"What makes you say that?" Chris asked.

"She mentioned his name more frequently than any other of her Beltway cronies. And she was always in a delightful mood just before and after her trips." Milton shook his head. "I should have confronted her, but we had things nicely arranged."

Myra stood and put her hand on his shoulder. "Are you alright?"

"Actually, yes. I always felt guilty that I didn't have the same relationship with Oliver as with Benjamin, and I resented it. As far as Patricia, well, we haven't been blissfully happy in years. If ever. We were well-suited but probably never in love, really."

Annie glanced at Myra with a *now what?* shrug.

"Mill, we want you to call Oliver and have him come over tonight. Benjamin, too. I know it's late, but the DEA agents will be on the Blaine, Eugene, and Salem premises within the hour. You're calling a family meeting."

"What am I supposed to say?"

"We'll do most of the talking," Chris assured him.

"We wanted to let you know what was going on and not blindside you later," Myra said.

"Alright. Let's do it." He phoned Oliver first. Then Benjamin. Both asked lots of questions, but Milton told them they'd find out when they got there.

Milton finished his brandy and held the glass up to Myra. "Just a smidge, please?"

Izzie and Kathryn got the message that Pearl's people were near the property. Before anything went down, they had to remove their belongings from the apartment. Fergus hacked into the security system and disabled the motion-detector cameras and the alarms. Once Kathryn and Izzie retrieved their things, they were able to access the interior offices using a key card Kat had swiped from Bart when they were chatting about trucks earlier that day.

Charles and Fergus cloned Oliver's phone number and sent text messages to the deputy, Bart, and Dickie:

Meet me in my office. Pronto. No questions.

Kathryn and Izzie made their way through the dimly lit building, deposited their suitcases in their cars, and met up with Pearl's people on the south side of the building. They were two very brawny-looking men with canisters of incapacitating gas in their backpacks. They also had a couple of hand trucks and furnished Izzie and Kathryn with gas masks. Then they waited.

Oliver arrived at his parents' house within fifteen minutes. Benjamin showed up right after him. Milton decided if he was going to drop a few bomb-shells, he'd rather do it with the backdrop of the mountains and valley. Besides, the fresh air would do him good. Once Patricia and the boys were seated on the patio, he went back into the study and summoned Annie, Myra, Christopher, and Chandler. Expressions of total confusion filled Oliver, Patricia, and Benjamin's faces as he introduced them to the marshal and his trusty dog.

Chris ran the meeting. He checked his phone. "In approximately fifteen minutes, the Drug Enforcement Administration will be descending upon the properties located at Salem, Eugene, and Blair."

Oliver jumped out of his seat and shrieked, "What? You can't do that! Not without a warrant!"

"They have my permission," Milton said sadly.

"But why?" Oliver was outraged.

"We have reason to believe that illegal drugs have been manufactured at those locations."

"That's outrageous." Oliver kept up his fury. "What gives you the right?"

"As your father said, he gave us permission."

"Dad? You did this?" Oliver was stupefied and horrified.

Benjamin looked on with disbelief and spoke softly. "Dad? What's going on?"

"Like the marshal said. Illegal drugs."

Oliver was pacing. He was cornered. But he could still deny everything and blame Dickie.

Marshal Gaines disabused him of that notion. "We know it's you, Oliver."

"But that ridiculous! Why would I do such a thing?"

"Money," Annie added. "Your desperation spelled it out. You were either in debt with some unsavory people, or you had a serious drug or gambling problem. My guess was both. You got into business with the wrong people while you were indulging yourself in copious amounts of cocaine."

"Again, ridiculous." Oliver huffed.

Annie pulled out the handkerchief. "I think this may prove otherwise."

"You can't have that. It's my property!" He tried to grab it from Annie's hand, but Chandler got between them.

"You may want to back away," Christopher suggested, and Oliver took his seat. Chris's phone pinged. The raid was on. He read the message out loud: "They found the false panels and bulletproof doors."

"But how?" Oliver was in a state of disbelief. Then he remembered Isabelle's trip. "That woman! I knew she was up to something!"

Myra and Annie said nothing. Patricia went pale, paler than even before. Her hands were shaking, and she was beginning to sweat. "Are you alright, Mrs. Spangler?" Chris asked.

"I need . . . I need some aspirin." She got up to leave.

"I'll go with you," Annie offered.

"I don't need your help, thank you." Patricia defiantly walked out of the room. Annie, equally defiant, followed her.

Patricia's hands continued to shake as she opened one of the drawers in her walk-in closet. Annie stood outside and watched. "They got you hooked, too?" she said.

Patricia was startled. "What are you talking about?" She clutched the mock aspirin bottle to her chest.

Annie pried it out of her fingers. Patricia made a valiant attempt to recover it, but Annie was in much better shape and yanked the bottle out of her hands, sending Patricia tumbling backwards. Annie reached down and pulled her up. "Come on. There's much more to this sordid story." Patricia tried to resist, but again, Annie outmuscled her.

When they returned to the patio, Oliver was sitting with his head in his hands. Benjamin was still baffled. This was all surreal.

Christopher continued. "Oliver Spangler, I am placing you under arrest for the attempted murder of your father, Milton Spangler."

Patricia cried out: "No! No, it wasn't Oliver! It was me!"

Milton looked at her sadly. "Why, Patricia? Why?"

"I wasn't trying to kill you, Milton. I was just trying to stop the meeting. I knew Oliver was in trouble. I hoped I could buy some time until I could figure it out." Patricia was weeping.

Chris bit his lip. "Mrs. Patricia Spangler, I am arresting you for attempted murder and aggravated assault."

"No! No! No!" She was screaming.

"But before you go, there is one more thing that needs to be shared." Milton was standing tall. "I know about your affair with Garret. I also know he's Oliver's biological father."

Oliver was shrieking. Patricia was wailing. It was

a cacophony of agony, despair, and disbelief. All the facades were in ruins.

Chris placed Patricia in handcuffs and walked her toward the front door. He turned to Myra. "How did you know she'd confess?"

"A mother will do anything to protect her child," Myra said with sad eyes.

Annie tossed the bottle of counterfeit fentanyl she had wrestled from Patricia over to Chris. "Evidence?"

Christopher opened the front door and helped Patricia over the threshold. Cameras and portable lights were immediately in her face. Questions from a reporter were being jackhammered. "Did you cheat on your husband, Mrs. Spangler? Is it true that you poisoned him?" Lights were flashing. People were yammering. It was humiliation in its highest form. She now had a true understanding of the expression "die of embarrassment."

Back on the patio, Milton leaned against the outdoor stone fireplace. It was terrible to think that he actually felt a sense of relief.

Dickie and Bart arrived at the office at the same time. Deputy Nelson was already there, smoking a cigarette. "What's this all about?" he asked the other two men.

"Got no idea." Dickie looked at Bart.

"What? Beats me, boss."

"Let's get this over with." Nelson jerked his head in the direction of the side door. It was the only one in use after business hours. As soon as the three men were halfway down the hall, canisters of incapacitating gas came rolling toward them. They started coughing and grasping at their throats. Seconds later, they were on the floor.

Pearl's operatives quickly moved the three men out the south door and into a waiting van. One of the brawny men pulled out a syringe and injected the listless bodies with a sedative. "Nighty-night," he said to the sleeping lowlifes. He slid the doors shut, locked them, and hopped into the driver's seat, as the other one got into the passenger side. They gave a short salute and drove the three away, never to be seen or heard from again.

Milton turned to Oliver. "It's time for you to go." Oliver sulked his way toward the door. Some of the press still lingered.

"Don't you people have something better to do?" he screamed at them. That, too, would appear on the eleven o'clock news later that evening.

Milton sat at the table with Benjamin, Myra, and Annie. "Are you alright, Dad?" Benjamin took his father's hand.

"Aside from this drama?" Milton smiled. "It's been a heck of a week, wouldn't you say?"

EPILOGUE

The following day, the women packed up and headed back to Virginia with some extra baggage. Once they carried out their plan, Oliver would be swiftly dispatched to a place with unpaved roads, no electricity, and no designer suits. They told Milton he was going away to rehabilitation. They just didn't tell him what kind.

Marshal Gaines got commendations for dismantling a drug ring, and for rescuing a kidnap victim. Chandler also received an award, and a year's supply of dog chews.

Vanessa Rowan mended her relationship with her mother and began a small baking business to help raise money for Danielle's charities. Lori George finished her two-year degree and got a job as a concierge at the Four Seasons in Montreal. She and Vanessa are writing a memoir together.

Patricia was sentenced to ten years in a women's penitentiary for aggravated assault and attempted murder.

Bart, Dickie, and Deputy Nelson were never seen or heard from again.

Benjamin and his father divvied up the S.E.I. responsibilities, and Danielle decided to help with the family business. They were all in it together.

Milton enjoyed spending more time at work. It was what he'd always loved: the scent of freshly cut wood, the camaraderie of his employees, and now, an occasional dinner with Jessica. She was a hoot.

A gripping new page-turner from the legendary
#1 international bestselling author Fern Michaels

FIGHT OR
FLIGHT

**A woman imprisoned by her painful past faces a
crisis that might just set her free to claim the life
she deserves . . .**

From the comfort of her beautiful mountain-top retreat, Katherine Winston creates her bestselling
young adult series, Girls with Unusual Powers. No
one in the nearby small town has any idea of her true
identity. To them, she's just the reclusive woman on
the mountain, and Katherine is grateful to be left
alone.

It wasn't always this way. Though her parents were
as neglectful as they were wealthy, Katherine built
up a busy, full life. Then tragedy struck and she re-
treated, panic-stricken at the idea of engaging with
anyone again. Aside from her two faithful dogs who
provide companionship and security, Katherine mostly
interacts with people anonymously online through
reader fan pages.

Now one of those fans appears to be in danger, and
Katherine desperately wants to help. But that means

moving beyond her isolated world for the first time in years. More and more, Katherine can't shake the feeling that some of her fears may be justified. Someone is watching her, she's sure of it, and they're getting closer all the time. And only by leaving her self-imposed exile can she hope to find the answers she needs, the courage to trust again, and an unexpected new beginning . . .

Visit our website at
KensingtonBooks.com
to sign up for our newsletters, read
more from your favorite authors, see
books by series, view reading group
guides, and more!

Become a Part of Our
Between the Chapters Book Club
Community and Join the Conversation